A NORTH AMERICAN EDUCATION

TRIBAL JUSTICE

CLARK BLAISE

TRIBAL JUSTICE

DOUBLEDAY CANADA LTD.

TORONTO, ONTARIO

DOUBLEDAY & COMPANY, INC.

GARDEN CITY, NEW YORK

Some of the stories in this book were previously published as follows:
THE FABULOUS EDDIE BREWSTER, HOW I BECAME A JEW and NOTES BEYOND
A HISTORY in NEW CANADIAN WRITING 1968, © 1968 by Clarke, Irwin &
Company Limited. THE FABULOUS EDDIE BREWSTER also appeared in *Tam-
arack Review* under the title THE MAYOR.
Other stories appeared in *Shenandoah, American Review,* and *Journal of
Canadian Fiction.*

ISBN: 0-385-01038-9
Library of Congress Catalog Card Number 73–10856
Copyright © 1974 by Clark Blaise
All Rights Reserved
Printed in the United States of America

To Bharati, Bart and Bernard

CONTENTS

TRIBAL JUSTICE

BROWARD DOWDY

We were living in the citrus town of Orlando in 1942, when my father was drafted. It was May, and shortly after his induction, my mother and I left the clapboard bungalow we had been renting that winter and took a short bus ride north to Hartley, an even smaller town where an old high school friend of hers owned a drugstore. She was hired to work in the store, and for a month we lived in their back bedroom while I completed the third grade. Then her friend was drafted, and the store passed on to his wife, a Wisconsin woman, who immediately fired everyone except the assistant pharmacist. Within a couple of days we heard of a trailer for rent, down the highway towards Leesburg. It had been used as a shelter for a watermelon farmer, who sold his fruit along the highway, but now he was moving North, he said, to work in a factory.

A Mrs. Skofield was renting the trailer. She was a fat, one-eyed woman who gave me a bottle of Nehi grape without my asking, then led us down the highway from her tiny gas-station-general-store to the trailer. As we walked she explained that the trailer wasn't exactly hers, but she reckoned she was entitled to what she could get from it, since a no-count farmer had skipped off in the middle of the night, owing her money and leaving the trailer behind. My mother asked if it had water, or electricity, and Mrs. Skofield snorted, "What y'all expect, honey? Weren't no tourist livin' there."

It was blisteringly hot inside. Even the swarm of fruit flies buzzing around the mounds of lavender-crusted oranges were anxious to escape. The furniture was minimal: two upturned crates, a card table, a coverless bed, a wood-burning stove, and an icebox. Behind the trailer, away from the highway and facing the forest of live oak and jack pine, someone had built a porch foundation of planks and cinder block.

"We'll take it if you finish that porch," my mother said.

"Screens is hard to come by," Mrs. Skofield said, "but we got heaps of gunnysack. I'll get my brother to put up some curtains you can roll up and down that'll be better than any screens ever was."

"What about—" my mother started, then looked out the door.

"The brother'll dig y'all a squatty-hole. And you can have five gallon of water a day from the store. We'll sell y'all ice cheap."

"What about people?" I asked. "Is there any kids?"

"Ain't nobody now, hon, but just you wait you a couple weeks and you'll have all the company you want."

"How come?"

"Fambly named Dowdy lives down that there trail," she said, pointing to a narrow cleft in the trees. "They ain't come down yet, but they'll be here. Come down from Georgia."

"They white?" my mother asked.

Mrs. Skofield snorted, then said, "Y'all just spot you a nigger in them woods and my Seph'll fix it. A single white lady can't take no chances."

"My Billy is fightin' Japs," my mother said. "Leastways he will be."

Mrs. Skofield went on to describe the lake that lay behind the trees, and how it was world famous for fishing. We moved in that day, and by evening I had already discovered a quiet inlet where I caught sunfish with just a blade of grass on my hook. And even before the Dowdys came, I knew the woods. My tender feet itched maddeningly with tiny threadlike worms my mother kept removing with carbolic acid, but at last my feet toughened and I was no longer bothered. By July, when our neighbors finally came, I was lean, brown, and lonely, and craving friendship that would free me from my mother's needs.

Then on a muggy day in July the Dowdys' rusting truck loaded with children, rattling pans, and piles of mattresses in striped ticking churned down the sandy ruts I had come to call my trail. I helped them spread their gear on the floors of a pair of tarpaper shanties, and watched their boy my age, Broward, pour new quicklime down last summer's squatty-hole. Within hours, he had shown me new fishing holes, and how to extract bait worms from lily stalks.

A few weeks later, Broward and I were fishing from a half-sunk rowboat in the inlet, merely dabbing the hook and dough-ball in the water to attract a swarm of fish, and snapping it out fast enough to avoid hooking another one. It was hot and lazy, and we didn't talk.

"Brow'd, Brow'd," came a cry from the shanties. It was his mother, whom we could see, sitting on the floor of the kitchen where a door should have been.

"Your mother's calling you, Broward," I said, attempting to head off a showdown.

"I'm fixin' to come," he answered. "She ain't gettin' supper less'n I'm there anyhow. She ain't fixin' to whale me before dinner."

"Brow'd," she shrieked, "you git the hell over here 'fore I tear the skin off'n your back, you hear?" We saw her get off the floor and disappear inside.

"See, I tolt you so," he said, flashing his nervous smile. "Here, got another doughball so's I can bait up?" I took a slice of bread from the cellophane package—the one my mother had sent me up to Skofield's to get—moistened it in the warm muddy water and shaped it into a ball the size of a marble. Broward thanked me as he always did, then formed it around the tiny hook that dangled on the end of the string tied to the long cane-pole. The instant it touched the water, a school of bream rose to meet it; Broward snapped the bait and two tiny fish—one hooked and one caught by the gills—were sent flying to the bank. I jumped ashore and dropped the new acquisitions into the reeking flour sack that half floated by the boat, attached to a flaking oarlock. Then I stretched my legs their full length to get back into the boat, for Broward suspected that under the old deserted landing where I had been standing, swarms of water moccasins made their nest.

"You watch you don't never leave your catch in deep water," he cautioned. "Once I lost me a whole day's catch to turtles that was just snappin' off their heads soon's I throwed them in. I hate them critters," he said, untying the sack. "Ever time you catch you even a li'l one, don't forget to chop off his head." He leaped ashore, and pulled the sack after. "I gotta go now. She's sent my brother down to fetch me."

One of Broward's younger brothers was scampering through the tall swamp grass towards us. It was Bruce, about three, blond and blue-eyed like all the others. And like the rest of the family, his stomach was bloated out like a floating fish's. Bruce wore only a filthy pair of underpants, with large holes cut around his rump and penis. As dirty as the cloth was, it was difficult to distinguish where it left off and Bruce began. Bruce, Broward explained to me, was "shy—real shy. He don't take up with strangers much." He threw his grimy little arms around Broward's equally soiled knees, and whined, "C'mon, Brow'd." Broward set the sack down to disentangle his brother's buried head and hugging arms, then took it up again—the precious, unrationed fish that fed us all that summer—and taking Bruce's hand, trudged back through the grass and mud to their two shanties.

"Why don't y'all eat with us?" he asked. It was the first time, after a month's daily fishing, that he had invited me home even though I passed through the clearing in front of their shanties twice a day.

"I can't Broward," I replied. "You got all those others to feed as it is. Anyhow my mother's expecting me."

"Set real quiet and they won't even see you," he said, and I laughed. "You gotta do what she says, I guess," came his stock reply, accompanied with a shrug of his bone-sharp shoulders. "Nobody's gonna eat less'n I fix it. Sure like to have you over. I

ain't never had a friend to dinner." We took a few more steps
toward the Dowdys' in silence.

"Okay," I said.

There was a slight clearing in the sawgrass in front of their
shanties. On either side of the trail there was marsh, and the
shanties had been elevated on stilts, with ladders leading to the
interiors and planks forming a network of safe paths. One shanty
was for cooking and eating, and the other for sleeping. Usually
there were equal numbers in each shanty, either sleeping, or
playing by the boards in what passed for a yard. The interior
of each shanty was dim. They depended on the light that filtered
in through the numerous cracks in the tarpaper framework. One
particularly large rip just over the stove served for both the overhead light and the escape hole for smoke and the fumes of cooking. The flour sack, the same as Broward's fish sack, slumped
next to the stove like a dumpy old man. The humidity in the
central Florida air caused the top half-inch of flour to cake over.
The bulging bottom was gnawed open and here and there lay
conical deposits, like anthills. Broward set the still-flopping sack
on the floor by the stove. The flies that had followed us from
the inlet and those that had been waiting, blackening the pools
of watermelon juice on the table, now bombarded the sack.
Broward's mother, who had been in the other shanty when we
arrived, came back.

"You get them things the hell out of here, you hear?" she
shouted from her slumped position at the head of the ladder.
"And you hand me my pack Luckies on the table."

"Yes, ma'm," Broward answered softly, and slid the cigarettes
across the floor.

"When I say I want my cigarettes, I mean for you to *hand* them
to me if you ain't too stupid, that is. Ain't you worth nothin'?"

"Yes, ma'm," he replied quietly as he ripped a brown paper
bag open and spread it on the table. "Hand me them fish," he
directed.

"On the table?" Flies settled in my eyes.

"Sure." I laid it on the table.

"Now dump 'em," he said. I opened the top and tilted the
sack downward, and the fish came sliding and squirming out. A

little turtle, clamped onto the largest fish, started to walk away, dragging his prize behind. "Goddamn it," Broward hissed, "that right there's just exactly what I was sayin'." He scooped it up and shook the fish from its beak. He slammed it furiously to the floor, as though it were a tiny coconut, then fired it against the wall until at last, mercifully, the bottom shell snapped off. I couldn't bear the sight; it looked, I imagined, like a frog turned belly-up, white and helpless; but then an almost nauseating vision of the secret nether-parts of the turtle, half frog, half snake, took hold and when he asked me to come over and look, I only waved my arms frantically around the fish and around my head, to clear my face of flies. He tossed the remains underhand into a clump of sawgrass.

"Here," he said, handing me his pocket knife. "While's I'm lightin' the fire y'all scrape the leeches off and start choppin' up the fish."

"How?" I asked. My father had been an angler, with artificial lures and a casting rod. He loved to fish and my mother had always done the cleaning.

Broward laughed. "Y'all just watch. First stick the knife under here, see," indicating the area under the gills, "and then just cut through. Then you slit his belly and dump out all this. Got it? Then make sure there ain't no leeches in the meat."

"Y'all get a mudfish?" his mother asked.

"No, ma'm."

"Then how the hell you expect to feed your fambly? How can anybody be so goddamn dumb is what I want to know."

"Don't get mad. We couldn't help it. I ast everybody that come in from the lake if they got anythin' they was throwin' out, like a mudfish, and there weren't nobody even heard of one. They was all Yankees anyhow."

"If you wanted to get one, you could have," his mother retorted.

"Ma, I tried, honest. Now I got me a friend to dinner."

"Ain't enough you don't bring home no food, but you gotta bring home another mouth to feed. Tell me this—you see him invitin' us up there? Not for nothin'."

"They would. Maybe not all of us, but me anyhow, and you and Pa too." He looked to me for support.

"Sure," I said weakly. My mother would die, cooking for migrants.

"Anyhow we ain't losin' any food. Val said she's sick again and she don't want nothin'."

"She ain't sick any more'n I am. She's fixin' to run off is all. I know what she's sick from," she laughed. "They gets to be her age and all of a sudden they's regular young ladies they think and their fambly ain't good enough for them no more and this place just don't suit them—it ain't elegant like Waycross is. Or they starts thinkin' how grand they can live in Leesburg and go to pitcher shows ev'ry night. Well, that ain't the way you was raised, and it ain't the way anybody was intended to be raised, and they all gone to the devil, ever single one. There ain't no more my children goin' to school, you hear that Mr. Smarty? Any body thinks they're too good for this house is free to sashay out and all it means is they ain't any goddamn good theirselves."

While she was speaking Broward had been stacking wood around the burning paper. Then he came back to the table and took the knife from me.

"I'll go, Broward. It's not fair."

"Now you're stayin'. Now it's fer sure you ain't leavin'."

After the fish had been cleaned, or at least cleaned to his standard, Broward took out a cleaver from inside the flour sack and began chopping the fish into half-inch squares. Then he dusted the diced fish with a handful of gray flour and dropped the pieces into the oiled skillet. They spattered and spewed and smoked and occasionally the flames from under the skillet curled around and ignited the oil. The flames shot roofward, nearly lapping the paper ceiling. He smothered them with the wet fish sack, and then the frying settled down to the noisy gurgle of flour in boiling oil.

The smell of frying fish never changes no matter how you cook it. You forget how you cleaned it, what kind of sorry fish you caught, and begin to look forward to eating it. Broward took the stack of dishes from the end of the bench by the table—plates with bright purple designs, the kind you get at service station openings—and placed them evenly, seven to a side.

Meanwhile, the odor of frying fish had attracted the other Dowdys to the kitchen entrance. They seemed not to notice me, as though I were one of them, and Bruce even waddled up and hugged me around the legs. By the time the fish was lifted and in its place at the center of the table, the family had all assembled in an evidently prearranged pattern on the benches. Broward stood at the end nearest the stove, while Bruce and I occupied the last seats on either side.

They all sat quietly about the table. All eyes were on the tall, thin, and red-cheeked father. His face was lined from sleep and his weak blue eyes were bleary from the light. He rose, bowed his head, and folded his hands piously. The children remained seated, but also folded their hands and closed their eyes as hard as they could, so that each face was a mass of folds and wrinkles.

"Lord," the father shouted as though He were sleeping in the next shanty, "Thou hast been truly good to thine sheep. We thank Thee that we have this delicious food on our humble table, health in our fambly, and that Thee, that guards all our blessings hast kept our name and blood untainted." All the family followed with an "amen."

"Brow'd, you take care of Bruce's food, now, hear?" his mother ordered. "You know he ain't fixin' to eat less you cut it up. I reckon your friend there can handle his own."

"Yes, ma'm." Bruce looked up at his brother and smiled his thanks.

"Here, y'all hold your fork like this and bring it up to your mouth." As soon as Broward let Bruce's hand go, the fork clattered to the floor. "Oh, it just ain't no use," Broward said, looking at his mother. Bruce looked up smiling, with his mouth open.

"You feed that baby, you no good—"

"Wayc, you do it," Broward pleaded. "He don't remember from one meal to the next and anyhow I got me a friend to dinner." Waycross Dowdy, who was fourteen and already taller than his father, and blubbery, scowled at Broward, then down at Bruce. Then he picked up the fish on Bruce's plate and stuffed it into his own mouth, and no one said a word.

On Wayc's other side sat Stuart. He never looked up from his plate, and was eating his fish with his fingers, cleaning them with a smack, then a swipe against his pants. Stuart often fished with Broward and me, and of the children, he bore the closest resemblance to Broward. Next to Stuart sat Starke, one half of a twin combination. Though much younger, he was built on the order of Wayc, with a low forehead and wide neck, and muscles already thick on his arms and shoulders, that jumped with the slightest movement of his hands. As I looked from the children to the parents, particularly to the mother, I noticed something of the final maturity of Waycross Dowdy in nearly all of them, made all the more terrible for its softened femininity. Starke's twin sister Willamae, the only girl at the table, except for a baby in her mother's arms, was a wisp of a girl whose eyes never focused on any object for more than a few seconds, and whose speech was so heavily "cracker" that I couldn't understand it. She wore a pair of purple earrings which she kept swinging with a flick of her long red fingernails. Next to her was Henry, still wearing the cutout underwear of infancy. He was loud, a brat, and particularly antagonistic to his sister, whose earrings he kept trying to pull off.

"Wayc, you make Henry quit pickin' on Willamae," Mrs. Dowdy ordered. Wayc swung over the bench and lumbered up to his brother. Henry's fingers were on Willamae's earring when he was sent headfirst into the edge of the table by a slap on the back of the head. He shrieked. Willamae's earring now lay in his hand, and Willamae, seeing it, shrieked with pain and de-layed outrage. She dashed from the table, out of the kitchen, towards the other shanty, holding both hands over her ear. Henry's forehead, scraped a watermelon-red, was already purple in a long narrow band. Waycross went back to his seat, and Broward went over to Henry, whose face was red from crying. He looked down, then ran his finger across the cut. Then he took Willamae's plate and dumped her uneaten fish into his own.

"Take a little?" he asked Henry, who didn't reply.

Broward came back to his seat and offered some more to me, which I refused. Then he scraped half the remaining fish into the skillet and kept the rest for himself. After a few minutes Henry quit crying and shuffled over to his mother.

"Ma—Wayc, he hit me."

His mother looked at the bruise. "You know he didn't mean to go and do it," she comforted. "Y'all go back and eat up your dinner."

As he walked back, he stopped for a moment behind Wayc, who didn't turn. I thought he was going to hit him back, and half hoped, half feared that he would. Henry waited for everyone to quit eating before he said, "Anyhow, you didn't hurt me at all."

Letters from my father came once a month, from Somewhere in the Pacific. During the sweltering nights of my ninth summer, my mother and I sat on the porch in the dark, with the burlap rolled up, listening to the Orlando station on the battery radio, to the network news.

Her face aged that summer, and her body grew thin on the fish I caught. She would read me parts of the letters and told me when to listen closely to the news, and very slowly I realized that the Pacific Theater was a battleground and not what it sounded like, and that men were dying and my father could be one of them. It seemed that men were dying all over, everywhere but home, and I would cry out to my mother, "Why doesn't he come back to us?" and she would answer, "Pray that he will."

My memory of him blurred, although now we had a picture of him holding a coconut in his hand and grinning just like he did at home—looking happier in fact—surrounded by much younger men in shorts, wringing out their shirts. In his letters he called me "little soldier" and always ended with an order for me to look out for my mother, and not to forget him, and he said that he missed us very much. Those orders I took seriously, and the fishing every day with Broward became in my imagination something of a tactical maneuver.

Broward knew nothing of the War, and asked me many times where my father was but never understood. He merely fished for food, but I reconstructed assaults and casualties. Turtles became tanks, and were thrown on tiny fires until—half cooked—the re-

tracted parts surrendered; dragonflies were Zeros, and downed
with a deluge of water; and the endless wriggling hordes of
bream were Japs and their numbers hacked with glee. My father
had been a driver for the citrus trucks going to port, and every
so often he'd write that "this island I can't name" would be a
great place for growing oranges.

But the summer was an idyl. Whenever Broward and I
roamed the woods we felt that unutterable sensation of being
the first who had ever felt or heard the music of the place. For
hours we would run along the beaches of the lake, prying our
way through the twisted vines and stunted underbrush, skimming
the ankle-deep runoffs, and building lookout blinds along the
beach where we could watch the Yankees in their rowboats and
hear their strange accents plainly over unruffled water. Alone, I
would gaze over the water; the sun, piercing the calm surface
of the lake, fluoroscoped the top two or three feet of lime-tinted
water, often exposing a gator drifting like a log, or schools of
bream dancing in the warm water like swarms of May flies. I
would think that there was just the lake, the beach, and me; then
I would be startled by the splash of water from the swamp behind, and turning quickly, I'd often catch a glimpse of brown
and know that I, or a prowling cat, had disturbed a deer and
sent it in fearful bounds deeper into the forest. Then September
arrived, and we received notice from the government that we
were to be resettled in South Carolina in special quarters for
servicemen's dependents. And with September came time for
the Dowdys to leave the summer moss-picking grounds and head
back up to the pecanfields of Georgia.

"You know, this is the time of year I like best," Broward confided the last time I ever saw him. "When we get up north, we're
right near a big city and all kinds of things happen that don't
happen here. Last year they made Wayc and me go to school
and I can almost read now. Pa says there ain't no reason to go to
school, but I know there ain't nothin' you can't do if you can
just read and write, ain't that so?"

Before the Dowdys could leave, they had to get their sole pos-
session, the old Dodge truck, ready to roll. Over the humid summer months, rust had set in and a thorough oiling was needed.

Naturally it was Broward who had been ordered under the truck to oil the bearings. The last I saw of Broward Dowdy were his legs, pale and brilliant against the sour muck, sliced cleanly by the shadow of the truck and the shanties beyond.

RELIEF

Those with radios were safe from hurricanes, in their snug bunga-
lows on landscaped streets. They nailed their shutters down,
parked their cars under protection, and threw a card party till
the storm blew over. In the morning, bleary-eyed but fresh with
adventure, they'd drive down the cluttered streets, detouring
around power lines, trees, temporary floods, then go home to
sleep. Schools closed, and the kids gathered behind the fallen
trees, firing kumquats at the clean-up crews of Negroes. The next
day, blue skies and an autumn coolness returned; the town appeared cleaner, almost freshly painted. Errant hurricanes did
that when they chanced across the state—made the townsfolk
feel akin for a day to the blizzard-struck residents of upper
New York who had also licked the adversity with candles, forti-
tude, and a supply of good hard liquor.

But with us things were different. We had no radios back in
the swamps by the lake. Even if we had, what could we have
done? Warn the moss-pickers who were the nearest humans?
Tell them—on a hot, still day—that a voice from Miami had
warned that a hurricane was coming tomorrow? Impossible. And
in those days, had we known in advance, it might have been
crueler. Had we known a storm was coming, we might have sat,

terrified, a longer time, tempted to flee the flimsy shelter we had.
On normal days Lake Oshacola was an inland sea—not like
Okeechobee, that shallow infinite puddle further south. Oshacola
seemed fresh, moving, and deep; we could see ten miles across
to the hamlet of Oloka, but the transverse shore, nearly thirty
miles away, was hidden in perpetual haze. It seemed that we
commanded an arm of the ocean, and we believed the lake con-
tained the sharks and monsters of the sea. Of gators there was no
doubt; I'd seen them at a distance pulling themselves up the rise
over the Florida Central tracks, from the sawgrass sloughs on
either side where they nested. We lived among the gators; little
kids had to be kept in sight, and tied-up hounds were lost if
the water rose.

That was thirty-five years ago. Now those shanties have been
plowed over and the hollows are getting filled. Bounty hunters
have driven the gators back to the swamps with the otters and
moccasins. Sprayers have killed the mosquitoes and the townsfolk are building cabins where I was raised, and their children
have safer, drier yards to kick the can in, free of reptiles and migrant workers spoiling their fun.

But just before the War, those tracts between the lake and
the highway, the sandy enclaves rising slightly above the
swamps, were still untamed. We had pumas then, and wildcats
that shredded your wash if you left it out overnight. We were
isolated from the town and separated from nearly everyone by
the impenetrable channels of the lake that made the land we
lived on a peninsula. On the same neck of land with us, but over
the tracks and virtually in the permanent swamps, lived the
family of migrant moss-pickers in two shanties raised on stilts.
And on the inlet, Leon Sellers at his boat landing, living alone.
Maybe there were people on Sem'nole Island about two miles
off shore, but they'd be colored or Indian, so we didn't speculate.
On school mornings, three days a week, I walked up to the highway with my father and waited with him for our separate buses.
He worked for the packing plant, dyeing oranges for shipment
north by the Chamber of Commerce. He caught the Orlando bus
into Hartley; I took the school bus going the other way.

Our schoolroom was a gray shanty car that had been part of a hobo jungle—now joined to a few others, a convoy of tin chimneys. Inside, the Migrant Agency had nailed in some orange crates for the dozen of us from Buck's Cove. There was a teacher's desk that looked like a vanity dresser, and a blackboard so tiny she could only squeeze on a quarter of the alphabet at a time—even now the alphabet divides itself into fourths whenever I recite it. There were other cars near ours, to take care of the Negroes and Seminole kids who lived in the other direction, but whom we sensed behind us in the swamps and never saw. The accumulation of shanty cars, a gas station, and a store was called Camp Hollow, Florida.

Inside that car, winter or spring, it was a caldron, because of the peat-burning stove which was never banked. Since I was the only nonmigrant taking instruction, and since I was able to read, I was allowed to sit up front to aid Miss Hewitt, and I would notice the beads of sweat on the slope of her breasts, for she usually wore revealing sun dresses that made school in such weather a little more tolerable. She was young, and fresh from St. Petersburg.

One morning in October, when the heat of day was just beginning, she announced that maybe there'd be no school the day after tomorrow.

"How come?" asked one of the littler ones.

"They say there's a hurricane coming," she explained. All of us stood up and peered out the high screened windows. The sky was blue, a little hazy.

"Ain't no storm comin', ma'm," I said.

"You just wait you, Lester," she said. "The radio said a hurricane is maybe coming tomorrow plumb through here." We still looked out the window, smiling as we shook our heads.

"Ain't no storm comin', ma'm." My reading assignment that morning had concerned a frontier family cut off by a blizzard, and their near-starvation before relief had come. "Like this here storm, Miss Hewitt?" I asked.

"Worsen that," she said.

I told my mother about the storm that afternoon, when innocent clouds were overhead. "What kinda stuff they teachin' you?" she demanded, as she set out her wash. The clothes hung dead and took the longest time to dry, even when the sun came out. When my father came home, as he washed his arms of dye, he told us it was fixing to storm bad, with all this moisture in the air.

There was no school the next day, so I woke up early, slipped into my jeans, and left the cabin while my parents were still asleep. The sun had risen but was invisible, just a smudge under steaming clouds. Though I wore no shirt, sweat collected in the hollow of my spine. I headed down to the lake, following the slimy boards strung over the slough, then over the Florida Central tracks, then over more boards that the migrants used. They lived behind some cypress, where the puddles never dried. Several of their kids were running from one shack to the other.

When I got to the landing, Leon Sellers was bailing out his boats. He was a thin, pale man who smoked all day in what he called his office and lived on occasional boat rentals. A colored woman sometimes visited him, according to the migrants. Two Yankees were standing by Leon, waiting for a boat. They were fat, sunburned men with tackle boxes and felt hats festooned with flys and hooks. They rubbed their arms with mosquito oil. Leon bailed a long time.

The Yankees paid and stepped aboard. They paddled out the inlet and Leon headed back to his office. His workshirt was stuck all over. The inlet was calm; ripples from the boat froze into creases on the surface. But in the cypress tops, the wind rattled. I took a cane pole from the rental rack, then went around back to the tray of coffee grounds where Leon raised the worms. I unknotted a few, wrapped them in paper, then ran to his wooden dock where I baited up.

There were whitecaps on the open lake. I fished and paid no more mind.

Leon Sellers got no more customers, and in a while fried bacon smell lay heavy on the air. I could even smell his cigarette, as though he were beside me. There were bass in the inlet that I tried for but never got, and a few gar and moccasins that I'd tap with the pole-tip when they drifted by. The inlet, where it spread into the cypress groves, formed a shallow lake and while I fished alone I heard the splash of larger things—gators and otter—walking in the water, whacking their tails. I sat there many hours and caught a few dozen bream.

Some kids from the migrants' shacks came down to fish. They wore tattered shorts. "Lake's dryin' up," one of them said. I noticed my string of fish, tied to the pilings, had lifted, and the top fish were out of water. The green, underwater part of the pilings was dry. I lowered my fish and several minutes later they had surfaced again. I quit fishing, walked off the dock, and peered into the swamp behind Leon's. There were puddles, but the drainage to the lake was pasty, cut by little run-offs.

"Shacks is all dry underneath," said one of the moss-pickers. "Fetch yourself some minnies. Jist pick 'em offn the ground." He didn't seem excited—not the way I became when I heard. I looked out on the lake and thought of running to Oloka, knee-deep in dying fish.

"It can't dry up," I said. Leon Sellers had told me once the lake had a little tide, so small we couldn't notice unless we were boatmen, since it was connected somehow to the ocean. That's why it had sharks, too, he said.

"It's a tide."

"What's a tide?"

"Something that makes the lake go up and down, only you can't see it."

They laughed. "That's loony," said one. I stood with them till the inlet muck emerged in glistening peaks, and the turtles, like stubby snakes, poked their heads out of their nests.

"There's a fierce wind, too," the oldest kid said. "She's kickin' up waves." We looked out again, beyond the inlet which now was guarded by logs that had been submerged. On the open lake the wind blew whitecaps off the tops of swells. There were ripples now on the inlet. The stench of mud, as it dried, made even the migrants back off. The inlet—now shrunk to the outline of its deepest depressions—roughened, and the congregations of fish frothed to the surface, drinking in air with little gasps. We stood at the end of the dock and looked into the water. There were boats, far below, long sunk, housing bass and larger turtles. We hadn't known that the inlet was so deep.

Leon Sellers came out. His boats had dropped from view, I guess, when he had wakened after breakfast.

"Can the lake dry up, sir?" I asked.

"That teacher yourn," he snapped. "Ask her can the lake dry up."

"She don't know."

"I seen her onct. Tell her from me I'll give her a boat all day free for nothin', hear?"

"She don't fish, I don't think."

"You kids, help me with my boats," he called to the moss-pickers. We all gathered on the bank, braving the odor. Leon Sellers in hip boots eased himself into the water.

"Them your boats, sir?" a migrant asked, pointing to the sunken ones still below the surface.

"Ain't mine. Them sunk a long time ago."

"Won't see me in that water," said the oldest migrant. He scratched his chigger bites all the time with one hand no matter what else he was doing, and he blinked a lot. "Ain't no tellin' what's in that water now."

"Nothin' that weren't there before," said Leon Sellers. "It's jist kindly squeezed together more."

There were three of Leon's boats still in the water; we worked an hour securing them on land. We dragged them to the side of Leon's shanty where he kept a tarp. When it came time to speak, we had to shout.

"She ain't fallin' anymores," he said, after checking the water level. "If I was y'all"—he pointed to the migrants—"I wouldn't stay back there today. She's fixin' to rise again. And you—ain't no need you hangin' round her neither. You go home." He went back to the shanty, lowered the shutters from inside, and brought in his tray of worms.

The wind, as though reacting on signal, suddenly snapped the branches off the higher cypress, sending a shower of twigs and moss down on the inlet. The nest of a buzzard was blown apart and Oloka vanished in the rising of waves and the coming of rain.

The water was rising now, visibly, as it relinked the standing pools, then covered up the mud. Rain pelted the inlet. The migrants gathered their fish and raced back to their shanties, afraid as I was now of something more powerful than our curiosity. I followed them as soon as I had gathered my dead fish, and ran over the boards that were freshly slick. Back in the swamp, where our paths split and I was left alone, I saw the rest of the migrants running into the larger shack and rolling down the burlap for protection.

The sloughs on either side of the path were filling up. I kept to the center of the path, in case anything hiding might try for the fish. I didn't look up until I came to the rise before the tracks. Then I froze. Churning the mud just a few feet in front of me were two gators. They couldn't see me, but I heard their snorting and was stung by the mud their tails threw up.

I dropped to my knees. The water was rising rapidly, inching up the sawgrass stalks. I kept turning, all directions, and I whimpered. The gators reached the tracks; if they turned, they would see me. I couldn't see them now. I waited as long as I dared, till snorts and hisses filled the slough, then traced their slimy ruts up to the tracks. Slowly I stood, and saw the path was clear to our cabin. I threw the fish behind me, and dashed numbly over the boards till I collapsed in the clearing, just outside our door.

My father came out and fetched me. He'd been sent home as soon as he arrived at the packing plant. "It's a hurricane," he said, as he carried me inside.

The eye of the storm was to pass near Hartley by early evening. It was well past noon now, and the sky was purple, screened by lower clouds that looked like smoke. I told my father that the lake had fallen and now was rising.

"It's like to keep right on. I seen it onct down on Okeechobee. We lost everthin' then. But Oshacola ain't big enough to flood us here."

"It's flooding the migrants."

"Them's migrants."

"Leon Sellers sent two Yankees out in a boat this morning."

"I wouldn't take one of his boats acrost that li'l biddy inlet."

The winds now cut across the clearing, causing the palmetto fronds to collide, or setting up little pockets of equipoise. The rain struck in gushes, letting up for several seconds as though suspended by the wind. Puddles formed in the sand, collared with yellow scum.

"This here's just the beginnin'. Just the beginnin'," said my father. Land tortoises scurried across the clearing, up from the tracks. Inside, the crevices of the cabin grew cold and moist. From the east, the clouds were black.

"I'm checkin' the water level," my father decided. He threw on a slicker and took off his shoes. "I'll be down by the tracks!" he yelled. We lost sight of him quickly, as the rain darkened him into a shadow. He came back several minutes later, with leaves plastered to his slicker and his face lashed red. "She's still risin'," he said. "Near up to the tracks on the far side. Them friends of yourn—they're gettin' wet."

"Reckon she'll reach the clearin'?" my mother asked. I helped her arrange pans and glasses under the leaks.

"Can't say. High's a man's waist down at them moss-pickers'."

"Let's get out," I cried. "Up to the highway while there's time."

"Ain't no sense runnin'. Nobody's outn the highway anyhows."

"I'm scared. I don't want to drown in *that*. I seen what's in that water."

"Shut up. Ain't nobody drowndin' here."

"Lookit!" my mother suddenly cried. "Lookit out yonder!" Two gators hustled across the clearing, and battered into the under-brush, where they disappeared.

"I told you—it's them same two!"

"Probably ain't all," my mother added. Then she turned to the puddle at the corner of the kitchen. "I wonder can them cinder blocks melt?"

I kept silent. I had seen the new look in my father's eyes, after the gators crossed our yard.

We were stranded that night on a tiny skirt of threatened sand. All depressions were water-filled; the privy had blown away and the stench alternated with the wind. We had lanterns, and by sitting on the bed we could remain reasonably dry. The water inside was a few inches deep. We dared not go out, with the moccasins stretched like nightcrawlers in the clearing. The only food was a few oranges my father had swiped when he learned of the hurricane.

At the far end of the clearing there were other lights, set on the ground in a half-circle. The migrants had strayed up to the dry land, set their lanterns down, then huddled around them to keep the flames going. They didn't bother us. The wind had slackened, but that allowed the rain to drive down cleanly. Hours later, the lanterns hadn't moved, so we figured the lake had stopped rising, despite the rain. I fell asleep.

Around midnight we were awakened by a kicking at our screen door. It was the father of the migrants, holding a lantern near his face so we could see he was white.

"Can we borry some kerosene? Our lamps done give out," he asked when my father and I came to the door.

"Ain't got none to spare," my father said.

"I reckon could the missus and me get warm by your stove then? She ain't got a wrap and she's suckin' a baby."

"Just her then."

"I gotta come too. Can't her go off alone."

"Just her," my father said. "It's you come by my door at midnight."

"There's niggers out there. I heard them. What are we gonna do if they come on us in the dark? We ain't got no knives even. There was niggers on Sem'nole Island."

"I didn't make it flood."

"Give us a little food."

"What I got is two oranges. I got a wife and boy."

"My boys, they know yourn. They gotta ride together on that there bus."

My father motioned me back to the kitchen, but I turned away slowly. The migrant went on talking, in a new tone. "That's three of mine to one of yourn."

"Wait up," said my father. He sloshed to the kitchen with a scowl, and poured half an inch of kerosene in a milk bottle. Then he took a pan of leakwater and leveled off the bottle with it. "There any niggers on Sem'nole Island?" he whispered before handing back the oily water.

"I seen smoke onct."

The moss-picker took the bottle and hurried back over the puddles to the flickering lights at the far end of the clearing. A few minutes later, they flared, then went out. My father double-latched the door, and we lay awake for a long time.

We woke at daybreak. There was a thumping on the door, and my father took a butcher knife with him before opening up. Standing in a black slicker and rain hat was a woman, with several people behind her, each holding a lantern. Two trucks were parked in the clearing. It was raining softly.

"Miss Hewitt!" I cried. She introduced herself to my father, first as head of relief for Buck's Cove, then as my teacher. She brought us out to the clearing, to the rear of one truck which was loaded with sandbags and boxes of food. An old lady was serving coffee. The other truck was brimming with Negro kids that had been rescued from the flood. They weren't allowed down, and didn't try to get out. Several of the migrant kids got shirts to cover themselves, then took positions by the tailgate, where they could toss little pebbles into the truck. The colored kids moved deeper inside. The oldest migrant boy was bruised all over his back, and his shoulder was cut and swollen. Two of the volunteers swabbed the cuts and helped him into the truck with all the food. They said his shoulder was broken.

"We picked up a dozen children during the night," Miss Hewitt told my mother, and the migrants' father, as they blew on their coffee. "We have just no way of knowing how many drowned. It was terrible further east, where the flooding was higher. I'm afraid dozens were lost."

"Well—" said the moss-picker. My mother nodded, with a smile broadening around the lip of the cup. "We could have used y'all last night," he said. He pointed to the truckful of colored kids. "They found us last night, like I knowed they would. They fixed it so we couldn't see them comin'. But we still laid it on them heavy. Musta killed one them sons-a-bitches. I guarantee you won't find no more of *them* back here."

"Who, sir?" Miss Hewitt asked. "Who are you talking about? Because if you are referring to colored, there is not a Negro within five miles of here." Her voice was categorical. "You must try living with the meaning of that."

"Says you," he chuckled, smiling at my mother. "I know different."

"There's the boatman," said my mother. "Down at the inlet."

I followed them to the inlet. The trail stank now, but the water had receded, leaving everything coated with scum. The other side was still flooded out. The migrants' shacks were toppled, and their Dodge truck was windshield-deep in water, with little waves breaking against its doors. We could see clear through the swamp now to the open water.

"You said there was someone else over there?" Miss Hewitt asked me.

I tried to gauge where the inlet had been. Finally I spotted the bow of a boat pointing up, and the peak of a tin chimney.

"It's there, under the chimley."

"God," cried Miss Hewitt. "Can't you people—"

"Ain't nothin' we can do here," said one of the helpers. We walked back to the clearing. Miss Hewitt said I should have warned the boatman, at least. The sun was up now, looking raw and tired, just over our cabin. They piled sandbags around our door, to keep out snakes. "Don't drink anything that isn't boiled first, *please,*" Miss Hewitt told my mother. "And see that you get your outdoor commode repaired. We'll leave you some food now, enough till you get into town."

The migrant family was led into the grocery truck. "We'll take this boy to the clinic," she said to the father. "And there's shelter for you in town."

"We're comin' back," he promised.

My father carried the box of groceries in. The two trucks, filled with crying children, sputtered from the clearing.

A few days later Leon Sellers showed up. He had waited out the storm Seminole-fashion fishing from a frogboat deep in the swamps, with his tray of worms for bait. The Yankees were never heard from. Our school cars were destroyed, and after a few weeks they found room for me in Hartley. The migrants did come back a few days later to work on the truck, which eventually started up. They loaded everything the water hadn't lost, and pulled out one night very late. Someone cut our screens that night, and since copper became scarce during the War, mosquitoes plagued our sleep for the next three years until we too moved to Hartley and gradually forgot those years on a promontory, threatened by swamps.

THE FABULOUS EDDIE BREWSTER

Etienne was my father's only brother, old enough to have enlisted in the Canadian army in 1915 when my father was only six. After the War, Etienne had stayed in France as an interpreter for the Americans. Finally he married, fathered an intemperate New World brood of children, and in the thirties dropped from family correspondence, after notifying my aunt Gervaise that he had been elected mayor of his village. During those same years, my father drifted off the Broussard family farm, near Baie Comeau, to a hardware store in Montreal. In 1938 he married my mother, *une anglaise* from Regina. Eye trouble harbored him in Montreal when the new War broke out, and precipitated my arrival a few months after Dunkirk. When the War ended, my father took us into the States, where, he surmised, a fortune waited. He had relatives all over New England—Gervaise and Josephine were living with their husbands in Vermont—and none of them was breaking even, but my father easily explained their lack of success. "They're afraid," he said, "afraid to leave *Québec.*" Just *habitants* by his standards, whose children would be raised on beans and black bread for Sunday breakfast. My father wasn't afraid; he'd learned good English and sensed the future flow of money was southward, far southward. And so we ended in Hartley, a north-central Florida town of five thousand Crackers, where he started selling jalousie windows and doors. We waited several months for a break while my father bronzed in God's own sun, caught his fill of bass, and cultivated a drawl around his *canadien* twang. Then we heard from Etienne.

Louis, mon cher, mon seul frère: Forgive me, my dear brother, for all these years of silence. All was well until the war took it away. Thinking of you all these years, believe me. I was the mayor and they put me in prison. My Verneuil-le-chétif is no more, just some buildings . . . everything is taken from me. My boys, fine boys Louis, only two left and they fight in Indochine. My girls gone from me, two in the Church, God keep them. Louis, help me, whatever you can send—I will not beg but as your only brother, I ask for help. The food is not so good in this camp, but with money I can buy little things on black market. . . . Louis, if I could only see you now, my boy, my dear, dear boy. Bless you, Louis, your own brother Etienne.

Immediately, my father cabled two hundred dollars. A few weeks later came a second letter blessing us, thanking us, and asking if it were possible for him to return to America and maybe find work in the States? Could we perhaps sponsor him until he could get a start? He included a snap taken next to a prison shed. He wore prison grays and stood Chaplin-fashion, with hands at his side, feet out, a look both forlorn and astonished in his eyes. The picture did it; thirty years of estrangement instantly healed. My father condemned his own good health, his youth, our relative comfort, then decided to bring his brother over.

"Not to live here," said my mother. "Not with Frankie needing his own room—"

"He needs rest, Mildred. After a while, he gets fattened up, rested, I'll find him work."

"What could he do, Lou? We don't know a soul who would hire an old refugee—no matter what he's been. He just wouldn't be happy."

But Etienne's letters came more frequently: twice a week. He was in a DP camp outside Paris. "Everyone but French here," he wrote, "with everyday the Russians and the Germans and the British identifying refugees and taking them back—if they want to go or not. Good food costs money like hell. For myself I buy nothing, but there are others here, from Verneuil. Chocolate for the old women, tobacco for the old men, shoes for the kids. I am still their mayor, *non?*"

Finally my mother relented and the government granted permission for my father to bring Etienne over. Etienne in the DP camp had collected nearly five hundred dollars in three months, wiping out our first year's savings in the States. "Either forget him, Lou, or bring him over," said my mother. "God knows it's a rotten choice."

"Maybe we could afford a hundred a month. I could write him."

"Send him a hundred and he'll squawk. But I don't like getting drained long distance. If he's taking our money, I want him under my nose."

"Mildred—he's suffered. We can't imagine how he's suffered. Those Germans—they're not human."

"Well, maybe suffering's made him hard," said my mother. "And how do we know what they imprisoned him for, eh?" Suspicion was instinctive with my mother, but that suspicion extended finally to herself. "Oh, Lou, don't just listen to me. He's your brother, if you think you should bring him over, then bring him. One look at this place and he'll head back to Paris anyway, if he has any sense."

"And I don't know him at all," my father muttered. "That's what makes it bad. Why did he come to me?"

But it was decided. My father wrote his sisters in Vermont, and somehow they persuaded their husbands to share Etienne's passage three ways. They all met their brother in New York, in February 1947. Down in Hartley, my mother transformed my toy- and map-strewn room into a study, suitable for a refugee mayor who had suffered but was accustomed to finer things. I slept the next year on the living-room sofa.

Hartley in 1946 was yet undiscovered by the prophesied boom.

Inland towns in the north of Florida had no special interest in the tourist trade, being citrus regions intent on keeping the land in local, unreconstructed hands. It was small-town America with a Southern warp: proper and churchly, superstitious and segregated. As the only outsider in the school, I was a vulnerable freak and not allowed to forget it; as the only Yankees in town (the term outraged my mother—she remembered overturning Yankee cars in 1914 when the States had ignored their higher duties), we were treated cordially by the weekly *Citrus-Advocate* and Welcome Wagon lady, but suspiciously by the neighbors and businessmen. Once the Klan warned us to move after an interview with my mother had been aired on the radio (". . . well, I think certain social changes are desirable and inevitable, yes . . ."). The night of the Watermelon Festival, the Klan had staged an unmasked parade down Dixie Highway with the unhooded mayor and sheriff leading the way.

Etienne was much heavier than the prison snap prepared us for. He had bought a sale-priced summer suit in New York, so all traces of his displacement had been left in port. He was silverhaired, very short, and classically fat, with the hard unencumbering fat of middle-aged Latins, even polar Canadian ones. Though he looked much older than my father, who was trim and darkhaired, the resemblance was arresting, and one was somehow certain they were brothers, not father and son.

"So—your lovely wife!" he cried, taking my mother in his bulging, tattooed arms. "Louis tells me this was your idea, bringing an old man over. Bless you, bless you. You've saved my life!" He lifted her, pivoting her on his belly, then kissed her loudly as she settled down. She was three inches taller.

"This is Frankie," said my father, urging me forward. I held out my hand.

"Kid," he announced, taking my hand in both of his, "it's good to see you. I'm your uncle Etienne and I've come around the world to see you."

"You're home now, Etienne," said my father.

"I feel it, Lou. I sure as hell feel it." He carried in two belted suitcases—scuffed and greasy, plastered with stamps and permits —then showered while we met in the kitchen.

"Some DP!" said my mother. Her cheek was still red where Etienne had kissed her.

"He surprised me too, Mildred. But don't go by his English— he learned it all in the army, so it's pretty rough. But he's proud of it. He doesn't even want to speak French anymore. Says he wants to be accepted by you and the town. He doesn't even want to hear it."

"Why, for heaven's sake? He's the first Frenchman I've ever met ashamed of French."

"Well, he's not a normal Frenchman."

"I'm watching him," said my mother. "A special Frenchman doesn't have to be a typical American."

"What do you want? He suffered *some*, but he wasn't tortured. I asked him that and he got offended. He asked me what kind of prisoner I thought he was. His family got scattered, but I don't think any got killed. His boys are fighting now in Indo-China. He was an important man and now he has nothing left."

"And what about his wife? Or did he have one?"

"He didn't say anything. I guess she might have died, or maybe they're separated. He's not in the Church anymore, so maybe they're divorced."

"Thank God for that," said my mother. "But what does he expect from us? He thinks it was me who brought him over. I'll tell him it was because we couldn't afford to keep him in France."

My father traced a pattern on the oilcloth. "That reminds me— he wants *you* to decide a proper allowance for him."

"He what?"

"Mildred—he's a grown man. He doesn't want to beg, but he wants some freedom in town. Little things. He came over with nothing. He thinks I'm too generous, so you're supposed to decide."

"Five dollars a week."

"Don't be cheap, Mildred. Ten at least. Even so, he'll be running short. He needs shoes, shirts, a razor, a bathrobe—things to be respectable around the house."

"You give him ten and all you're going to see for supper is this fat back and black-eyed peas, and that's a promise. Take your pick. Just settle it before you go back on the road again, because

I want everything to go smoothly with Etienne. I don't want him begging."

"It'll be settled," my father promised.

Uncle Etienne at first spent his days inside in front of the fan, listening to the news reports and reading the morning paper from Tampa which he walked downtown to get. While my father was on the road selling the jalousie windows, Uncle Etienne would tell us tales of their childhood in Baie Comeau: of inhuman poverty and his fatherliness towards *ti-Louis*. God, he'd had some times, though, just after the War, and it was clear to see why he had remained in Europe. His favorite story concerned the day the Americans, occupying a post next to the Canadians, had called for an interpreter. Young Broussard had scampered over, and for two weeks had been assigned to a young officer named Eisenhower. "That s.o.b. couldn't make a move without me," Etienne recalled. "What a man he was! I could have sent him anywhere—imagine—me a twenty-year-old kid. And did we get along! We were buddies, Ike and me. He wanted me with him when we hit Paris, believe me, but we got separated. Remind me to show you some letters from Ike. I always *knew* he was headed for the top. Always knew it. And the crazy joker couldn't even crap without word from me, and that's the God's own truth. . . ."

While my father was away, it had been customary for my mother and me to eat lightly: a salad and iced tea with a dish of ice cream after—all if the icebox were working. But with Etienne at the table, such informality was disallowed. First, there had to be bread, crisped in the oven, then meat, gradually potatoes, and—due to his stomach ailments—they had to be baked. He would help with the shopping too, picking up steaks and chicken after scrupulous comparing. The apartment grew hotter with the oven on (Hartley ovens went unlighted from April to October), and my mother's patience grew shorter. She refused to cook to his specifications any more, and he astonished her by not complaining.

"Right!" he said. "One hundred per cent right. Why should you cook when you've got a genuine French chef in the house? I'll cook. That's a bargain, eh, a real French chef for nothing?"

Small towns in central Florida, however, supply few of the staples of *haute cuisine*. Lamb was unheard of; similarly, all the more delicate vegetables. Hardiness was all a Florida cook demanded of her greens, that like paper towels they not disintegrate from oversubmersion. The new meals concocted by Etienne were no better-tasting, but the failures were more interesting: okra *parmesan,* a bouillabaise of large-mouth bass, turnip-heart salad. I retired to cokes and grilled-cheese sandwiches, and my mother tried bits of the main course, but concentrated on the salads. Etienne kept cooking for himself, undaunted by our disinterest and proud of his indispensability. When my father was home for the weekends, he ate enthusiastically in the steaming spicy kitchen.

Aside from the dinner hour, Etienne was now rarely home. It was a custom, he quickly discovered, for the town's older citizens to leave their respective dwellings very early, before the sun sucked the town to dust, and seek the public benches by the courthouse or under the commercial awnings along the Dixie Highway. By eight o'clock he would finish his tea and corn flakes at home and step out in his beige Panama with the tricolor *boutonnière.* If I happened to pass him during the day as I bicycled to the Lake Oshacola Park in search of shade and a coke, or to the air-conditioned drugstore to check the new comics, I'd wave, but he rarely waved back. His circle of cronies was wide, no matter where he sat: the retired locals at the courthouse, or the wretched Yankees on Dixie Highway who had shunned St. Petersburg and Winter Park, or heard tales of Miami Beach, and had finally selected—at not much saving and very little comfort—the grove of cabins on swampy Lake Oshacola. He'd then return late in the afternoon with his bundle of vegetables, baked goods, and meats, shopped for in the Parisian fashion at separate stores. He arrived in time for the news, the ugly news of Communist riots, and he would curse in French. After iced tea, he'd calm down. The local news and Fred Peachum's hillbilly music came on, and we turned it off.

"How was your day, Etienne?" my mother would ask.

"Nice, nice day. Talked to friends. Nice town—you really should know more people, Mildred. I mean it. Very nice people."

"Don't tell me about the people, Etienne. You had bad people in your village—we have them here. The majority."

"Naw, Mildred. I mean it. You don't take an interest is your trouble. Louie's too. He won't get ahead working for other people."

My mother agreed, but never said so. Though my father was making more selling the jalousie windows and doors in Florida than he had selling screws in Montreal, Florida had not been the gold mine he'd hoped for. I too missed the snow, hockey, French (which my mother barely spoke and Etienne refused to), and was uncomfortable in the heat. I'd forget to tap out my shoes for scorpions, I contracted foot worms, my allergies were stimulated, sand seeped in every place, and my mother's treasured Irish lace got mildewed. My father, however, was still hopeful. He greedily sought the sun, grew brown and striking, and felt at least that he had planted himself in fortune's path and had only to stay put and success would stumble across him.

But Etienne, we soon learned, had not been idle on those long afternoons. His cronies at the courthouse, or along the Dixie Highway, had a little power, a little influence, or at least helpful bits of information. One weekend, when my father had just returned from a lucrative venture into new territory—Mobile and New Orleans—Etienne mentioned that if *he'd* just made a thousand dollars, he'd know how to invest it.

"Property, Lou. Any town worth living in is worth buying up. Nobody advertises what's up for sale. If you got friends and if you're on the ball, you know what's up. Pay the taxes and it's yours. No one knows about it, so the mayor and his friends snap it right up. How you think he owns this town? Smart man, the mayor."

"What could I buy with a thousand dollars, assuming I wanted to invest it?" asked my father.

"Ah—that's the hitch, Lou. You couldn't buy. They wouldn't let you. It's exclusive, who they let buy. They don't know you."

"They know you, eh?" asked my mother.

"That's right. I'm not up there for nothing. If I had the money, I'd form a partnership with you. Land or business."

"What's to stop me going down tomorrow and buying up one of those places?" my father persisted. He was smiling, but dead serious, a gambler.

"They'd dump something on you that was half in the lake, Lou. The deedskeeper is the mayor's son-in-law. Fine boy named Stanley."

"Typically American," snapped my mother.

"You got to keep in touch," said Etienne. "Small town, after all. Naturally I'm telling you first, Lou, but I know you're not a rich man. Some of these others—the retired ones out along Dixie Highway waiting to die—they're rich. And they're dying to make a little more. There's a lot of them in town."

"Watch out for your visa, Etienne," said my mother. "There's nothing in it about investing while you're here."

"I'm not investing. I'm just advising. It's their money—or yours. I'd just have a job and maybe with a job they'd give me a visa. Maybe then old Ike would write them for me. I got to think of my future. My family—two boys getting shot at in Indo-China, that's no life for a boy, they get shot, crippled for life. Better I find them a place, maybe get them started. I got talents, Mildred, Lou, I may be bragging, but I got talents." He took out plates to the sink, ran the water, and sprinkled some soap. "Then my wife working like a slave in Paris," he added.

"You wife? What's this about a wife?" cried my mother.

"Sure I got a wife. Twenty-eight years married. What do you think? Her name's Arlette."

Now my father joined in. "How come you never told me about her?"

"Did you ever ask, Louie?"

"I thought maybe—the War."

"Would I be here then?" he charged. "Do I act like my wife is dead? She's working, that's all. A seamstress, like she was thirty years ago."

"Well," sighed my mother, "you take the cake."

"She was afraid you wouldn't bring us both over, or me alone if you knew I was leaving her back temporarily. She said, 'Go get well with your little brother in America and, maybe if you can, send me a little something back.' That's what I do with what you give me every week, send little things back she can't get in Paris. You think I spend it all on myself, maybe? I'm an old man, I don't need anything. Just a little safety, a little money so when I'm old they don't carry me off to the poorhouse. I've seen everything wiped out, Louie; I've got a few years left and I'm going to use them."

"You still should have told us, Etienne," said my father. "We would have been happy to bring her over."

"She's my responsibility," Etienne insisted. "Things will work out better this way. You think over what I said about your thousand dollars. In the morning, one way or another, I'm going into business."

"Etienne—what an American you are," my mother said.

My parents didn't invest with Etienne, and for several days the subject was dropped. The mention of Arlette had a softening effect on my mother, and the stories Etienne now told us of France included Arlette and were a little more suitable. Soon he received her letters at home instead of the post-office box he had been renting.

Then one night he asked, "What do you think of my cooking?"

"It's fine," said my mother. "It reminds me of Montreal, when Lou and I used to eat out."

This soured him; one thing he resented was those remote origins.

"Better than Montreal, Mildred. Etienne's really good," said my father.

"What I meant was, would you pay for it?"

"We *are* paying for it," my mother reminded.

"No—I mean at a restaurant, say. If I had all the right vegetables and the right meats, do you think people would pay for it?"

"I don't think so," she said. "There's no money here, let alone taste. This is the worst food on the continent, why?"

"I know a man. Met him last week, comes from New Orleans, named Lamelin. Wife is dead and his boy died in the War—"

"How sad—"

"—and he had this restaurant in New Orleans, see, then he

sold it when his boy was killed, and he came here when his wife up and died, so he's got money and he's itching to get back in the restaurant business. His wife was the cook, so he doesn't know much about that end. I do. He's the business type, see—has contacts all over, and lots of money."

"What are you thinking about, Etienne?" asked my father.

"A French restaurant here," he announced. "Outside Hartley, a few miles, near the main highway. More like a night club, really, with drinks, good food, entertainment."

"You're crazy," my mother said. "You know what they go for here? Hillbilly stuff."

"I'll give them something better."

"They don't want it. You could bring Chevalier and they wouldn't pay."

"I'll educate them. We start with Cubans since they're cheap and maybe move up to French. Believe me, I know lots of kids would come over. That camp I was in—full of them. Singers, dancers, pretty girls, kids with talent—I saw them."

"Lou—you tell him," my mother pleaded. "They don't *like* Cubans any better than they like Canadians. Look—all you can get on the radio is Havana; it even drowns out their hillbilly junk and they hate it. Etienne, as a businessman you'd fail utterly."

"I'm not a businessman," he reminded.

"But she's right, Etienne. You can't take any crazy chances here. Things are too expensive."

Etienne slammed the table. "So what do you know, eh? A window dresser? I don't see you making a big name for yourself. So, they want doors and windows and you supply them. Good, fine, the best of luck. But how bad does anyone want doors and windows? Not so bad they can't wait. Not so bad they got to have you and nobody else. But with me—I know what they need. Even if *they* don't know it yet, I know. French food, but not too French. Why waste it? Deluxe treatment. Beautiful girls—can you give them that? Maybe a chance to make a little money. I give them something just a little better than they got, but not so much better they feel bad they can't ever have it. And the entertainment—leave that to me. I'm not selling Havana music, I'm

giving them Havana girls. So I'll ask you one more time—you
want to back me up? Lou—what do you say?"

"Etienne, can't you see?" My father towered over him, speech-
less. "Christ, it's just crazy."

"I always thought the Germans were pigheaded, but you take
the cake, Etienne, believe me," added my mother.

"*Eh bien,*" he grumbled, "no more—all right? No hard feelings,
eh? You don't trust me with your money. That hurts me—once
five hundred people trusted me with their lives—their lives,
Louie—and I didn't let them down. No one was killed in my
town. I can't wait now, Lou—I'm taking back everything I had
and I'm taking it here. Let me stay here another month, that's
all, and I'll move out. No more trouble from me."

"Etienne, you stay with us. We insist," said my father.

My uncle started to his room. "No thanks, Lou—I wouldn't
feel right any more. I'll be keeping late hours anyway. It's best
like this." He came out in a few minutes, dressed in the best he
had.

"Just remember you had a chance," he said. "And now I'm off
to the radio station. They're interviewing me, so you listen, eh?"

"Radio!" exclaimed my father.

"On the local news. The 'Fred Peachum Show.' You be listening."

Peachum was Hartley's own hillbilly, whose show cut into the
network's "Swing Time from New York" each afternoon for
two hours of jamboree music: the Clewiston Cowboys and some
added talent from the pine flats of northern Florida. The local
news was a reading of the police blotter including all traffic
tickets, hospital records, court decisions, school awards, and crop
reports, interspersed with tales, interviews, songs, weather, ads,
and sports. We'd never listened to it in its entirety, except for the
time my mother had irritated the Klan with her predictions.
We waited that evening an agonizing hour for Etienne.

"Got a gentleman dropped in to say a few words here,"
drawled Fred Peachum, "and I reckon y'all gonna find him
right interestin'. Come right in here and pull up a crate, Eddie.
This here is . . . ah . . . Eddie Brewster I reckon is how you'd

say it, and he come to Hartley out of Paris, France. Tell the folks listenin' in how long you been in town, Eddie."

"Oh, jus' a mont'," said my uncle in a new accent, mellow as a *boulevardier.*

"Let's see here, accordin' to my information you got a brother in town permanent, don't you?"

"Yes, my brodder Louie. He sells door and window built special for Florida. He brought me over from France."

"What's happenin' over there now, Eddie?"

"Ooh—terrible. So much is destroyed. Everything was beautiful before, now not so beautiful. I think sometimes there is nothing left. In my village, just the church."

"Kindly like a miracle, ain't it?"

"Yes, many time I tell myself—a miracle."

"That fake!" my mother cried. "A miracle—"

"*Chou,*" hissed my father. "He's a little nervous is all."

"And how you makin' out in Hartley, Eddie? I reckon it's right peaceful, after the War and all. . . ."

"Oh, this town is very nice. Very nice—nothing in the world I like more than to settle down right here. And this town is ready for big things, you believe me. There's gonna be smart people come down here, once everything gets back to normal. My brodder Louie—he's a smart boy—he come all the way down from Canada. There gonna be others, you see."

"Like you say, Eddie, we got a nice li'l biddy town here. I'd kindly hate to see it change. But that's the reason you come by today, ain't it, Eddie, to tell the folks how you wanta change Hartley?"

"That is right. I want to give Hartley something for the way it has welcomed me. I think the best thing I can do is give the town something that is personal from me—a French restaurant, with entertainment. Everything cooked personal by me, and the entertainment is direct from Tampa, maybe even Cuba. My partner and me are looking for property now that is close to Hartley but near Gainesville too. It would be my little way of thanking Hartley and all the people."

My mother was up now, and yelling above Fred Peachum's long reminiscence about Cajun soup in New Orleans. "The hu-

mility of the man! Lou, he's crazy, he's out of his mind—he's going to show his undying gratitude by opening a restaurant, eh?
He's already announced it. Do you realize we're responsible for
him? What if he signs loans for ten thousand dollars? They can't
touch him—they'll come to his sponsor, that's who. Lou—you've
got to stop him. I thought he was sly, but I never realized he was
incompetent. He's a sick old man, Lou, and we never realized
it." My father bowed his head, and nodded.

Etienne was talking again. "We're just not free to give any
more information now. My partner and me hope to announce
everything next week. I appreciate letting me talk, Mr. Peachum.
You wait till you taste *my* turtle soup."

"All right! Eddie Brewster, folks, come in to give you the dope
on a gen-u-ine French restaurant right here in Hartley. You
check your paper for the big news next week, hear?"

Our phone rang and rang in the hours we waited for his return.
When he finally arrived, he brought with him Maurice Lamelin,
lately of New Orleans, and a portfolio of documents. They had
made a purchase and were business partners.

Lamelin looked as though he had suffered a double loss in the
past year; he looked also, as Etienne had said, greedy to rebuild
his fortune. He was a sallow little man, taller than Etienne, but
in no way powerful. Technicalities were his specialty: he spoke
with authority about vegetable distributorships, freezer consign-
ments, licenses, and fire laws. The building had been Etienne's
contribution; through contacts at City Hall, he had heard of the
old Sportsman's Club—a stucco structure with a tile roof, plazas,
and a courtyard—going for back taxes and an unspecified transfer
fee. The building was a local landmark, hastily erected in the
twenties for a boom that never came. It stood a few miles outside
Hartley on the main road to Gainesville. Landing the Sportsman's Club, my father agreed, was a shrewd move; it was the
only possible site for a night club in all north-central Florida.

"We've got a new name for it. The *Rustique*," said Etienne. "I
figured anyone can translate that. Come on out, we'll show it to
you tonight."

We drove out in Lamelin's new convertible. Cadillacs, the

Cajun apologized, were back-ordered for months, so he had settled for a Chrysler at the same price.

At night, by flashlight and matches, the old structure with its
faded mosaics, cracked beams, and resident lizards scurrying
ahead, seemed like a Hollywood imitation of everything it, in
fact, was: Fitzgerald and Gloria Swanson, darkies mixing drinks,
mannered but desperate poker games in the smaller rooms. Upstairs were rooms suitable for overnight accommodations. Lamelin planned to renovate them as soon as the kitchen equipment
was installed. Already, we learned, the freezers and special gas
ovens were on their way. Local merchants were providing furniture, thanks to the mayor's endorsement of Etienne's credit.

"How deep is the mayor's interest, Etienne?" asked my mother.

"He's nothing. Like a stockholder you might say. He has no
power in this operation."

"I'm the proprietor," said Maurice Lamelin, "and Broussard's
my chef."

"And impresario," added my uncle.

"We'll be set up in two months," continued Lamelin. "We're
gonna be the biggest thing between Jacksonville and Tampa."

"Well, you'd better put some screens up," said my mother.
"These mosquitoes are murder."

The next day we returned, at Etienne's bidding, "for a better
picture." Things had improved indeed; trucks unloaded in the
marshy lot, neon experts measured the gables, power saws
whinned, and new timber was stacked outside for paneling the
guest rooms and subdividing the ballroom. Lamelin prodded the
workers: a tiny man, expertly profane. Etienne took us inside,
showed us the kitchen area, the private dining rooms, the main
room and stage, and the smaller rooms—for gambling.

"But you can't have gambling here!" said my father.

"How do you expect a place like this to make money, then, eh?
You said yourself these people won't pay for food alone. So, let
them try to win some money—what's the harm?"

"*Mon Dieu*—it's against the law, that's what!"

"Louie, Louie, what's the matter, you a kid? It's all clear with
the law. All you need is a special license so the county can collect
some money too."

"You know it's under the table, Etienne," my mother charged. "Don't try telling me it's legal."

"All I'm saying is in Oshacola County it's as legal as selling doors and windows. It's called a Special Revenue Permit and we bought it and it's good till December 31."

"Etienne—you listen to me," my mother cried, "so far as I'm concerned, it's illegal and what you plan is wrong, all wrong. I don't want you around the apartment, understand? If you need money for a hotel room, I'll give it to you personally. But don't come around, because I don't want to expose Frankie to any more of your double dealings."

Etienne stepped back and held out his hands, palms up. "Louie, what is she talking about? Tell her I'm doing this to bring Arlette over. You think I like taking chances at my age? You think I like the Cajun even? Mildred—you're my family. I feel like a grandpa to Frankie. Would I do anything to—to corrupt a kid? Louie, Louie, tell her, you can't just throw me out on the street like a dog, not after what I've been through. Lou?"

My father grabbed my mother's arm and pulled her to him. "Why did you have to say such a thing, eh? Can't I have some peace as few times as I'm home?" Mother looked straight on, silent, her lips Scottishly tight. My father turned to his brother. "Look, why didn't you tell me about the gambling, eh? Hell, if I had known *that* . . . how do I know I'm not responsible for any bills you run up, maybe any crimes too? I sponsored you, but I sure as hell didn't think you'd start up a casino, not here. I'm trying to build something too, ever think of that? I'm new here too, I got a lot to lose too, only what I might lose is all in the future. So—"

"Lou, look at it like this. Let me stay till the restaurant's going good. After that I'll be working so hard I'll just stay in one of the rooms upstairs. Arlette will come over anyway. I don't want to sponge off you. Hey—where's she going?"

My mother yanked me with her to the car. We watched them argue awhile, and saw the screening go up; and the first tubes of neon. My father handed Etienne some money, then came back to the car, and without a word we drove home. "Don't you ever butt into my personal business again," he threatened as he let her out. "Now I'm taking him into Tampa. Just don't wait up for me."

That night we had salad and iced tea again, then we saw a movie: Margaret O'Brien. "Your uncle Etienne is a bad man, Frankie, understand? I want you to try to forget him."

The grand opening of the *Rustique* was publicized in all the area papers, and from most rural telephone poles in Oshacola County. For entertainment, Etienne had hired a flamenco guitarist and his troupe he'd found rolling cigar leaf in Tampa. Though Etienne rarely showed up in our apartment, my father often went out in the evenings before the opening to deliver mail or have a drink. He'd watch the floor show rehearse, and come back with tales.

"I saw girls, Mildred, nigger girls that bend over backwards so far that they go under a pole just *that* high off the ground." He held his hand at shin level. "Etienne was driving down to Orlando and he saw these niggers out in the celery field doing this crazy dance, see—"

"Don't call them niggers, please, Lou."

"So he watched awhile, then he went over and offered them fifteen dollars to do it at the *Rustique*. They almost fell over him, they were so glad, being Bahamian and all. So he figures he's got the best entertainment in Florida outside of Miami Beach, and it cost him about fifty dollars total. After that, he found some Greek girls in Ybor City that belly dance—"

"Good Lord, Lou, they'll close him down. He can't run a place like that in the middle of nowhere. What'll people say? The Klan —they won't stand for that."

"What do you mean? They know all about it."

We were presented tickets for the opening night; Etienne figured a thousand tickets offering concessions on food and drinks had been won in contests or given away all over north-central Florida. Hard-drinking veterans now dominated the fraternities at the university, and they flocked up from Gainesville for the opening to sample all the attractions, especially Etienne's "Normandy Knockout," a reported favorite of General Eisenhower's. Fred Peachum was the M.C. and many personalities (the mayor and Stanley the deedskeeper plus the sheriff) were interviewed by the tablehopping hillbilly. The whole operation was a huge success; even the guest rooms were rented by strung-out celebrators. My father came home high and happy but the next day cursed my mother for not letting him invest.

It wasn't long before the *Rustique* was returning an extravagant profit on weekends and breaking even most week nights. Etienne scoured the region for talent. The gambling—and even sportier—activities in the rented rooms were the proud secrets of the town. When the next winter came the tourists took an inland route, thanks to enticing posters as far north as Augusta and Macon. They stopped in Hartley nearly as often as Daytona. The whole town prospered, as the *Citrus-Advocate* pointed out, and new motels were frantically erected. There was talk of a northern citrus processor coming to Hartley with a new scheme for freezing orange juice. The representative came, and after several conferences which Etienne joined, the processor was politely refused and advised to go further south. Oshacola County, it was felt, could make its money from Yankees without the mixed blessing of their industries.

After the winter season, the business slowed down somewhat, enabling Etienne to return to France for a visit to bring back Arlette. With Etienne gone, Lamelin closed the *Rustique* for two weeks to allow for some remodeling and general expansion. Already, rooms were being reserved for next winter by Yankees who would never get further south, and a golf course was contemplated, along with an improvement of the docks.

Etienne and Arlette had been back in Hartley a week before they visited us. Arlette was my mother's height and, like my mother, pale in her features. She was *alsacienne,* her hair blond-gray, and her eyes the palest blue. Had she been in Hartley, one felt, Etienne would never have started the *Rustique*. Her English, contrary to Etienne's report, was perfectly Gallic: proper in every respect, but barely understandable. In her presence Etienne sat quietly and humbly, while she answered my mother's questions. They were staying in the bridal suite at the club, but she would try to find a small home on the lake—maybe even on the ocean, thirty miles away.

"We cannot thank you enough, Etienne and I," she said. "Life was without hope for us in France. Etienne couldn't work, and I could only support myself—" she looked down at her fingers, those of an overworked, perhaps unpracticed seamstress. "It seems all that is behind us. Thank God."

"Have you seen the town?" my mother asked.

"I have. It is very small, is it not? We lived in a village much smaller, of course, before the War, but very different, too. My husband was the mayor. But after the War things changed horribly. *They had no right,*" she cried suddenly, "Etienne did nothing wrong. He saved many lives."

"*Assez,*" he commanded. "It's all forgotten."

"How many would be killed? How many of our friends would they have killed if Etienne had not urged co-operation? One need not approve, in order to co-operate."

"I saved many lives. I know it," said Etienne. He stood, and placed his hands on Arlette's shoulders. She took his hands in hers, smiling, but not looking back. "It's all in the past. I've proved I was right. One year in America and I'm one of the richest men in the county and they'll let me stay." He looked over at us and said to my father, "Who needs them, the little men who judge you after the danger's past? They're the bad ones—the little men who were not in sight but suddenly become the judges. France is full of them."

Etienne and Arlette were silent, defensive, waiting for a response. Finally my mother said, "I imagine you'll be very happy here, Madame. You'll find no one to judge you here."

Ten years later, Etienne was elected mayor of Hartley. We were already North, predictably, a year before the authentic boom began. We sat out Etienne's salad days from dingy suburbs of Cleveland, Toronto, and Buffalo. We never heard from Etienne directly, but were sent clippings from the *Citrus-Advocate* (now a daily), third-hand from Gervaise. The winter my father introduced portable heaters for drive-in movies in Buffalo, his brother was able to bring over Gaspar and Gérard from Indo-China. A few months later, Gaspar married a local girl, a wealthy one, and at the moment he is sheriff of Oshacola County. Arlette, a woman I barely remember but for her fingers, died before their beach home was completed. Etienne has retired alone to a sumptuous home by the golf course on Lake Oshacola—a course he invited Ike himself to open. My father goes down each winter for fishing and golf with his brother; everything again is cordial.

After their divorce several years ago, my mother went back to Canada and now teaches history in Regina.

GRIDS AND DOGLEGS

When I was sixteen I could spend whole evenings with a straightedge, a pencil, and a few sheets of unlined construction paper, and with those tools I would lay out imaginary cities along twisting rivers or ragged coastlines. Centuries of expansion and division, terrors of fire and renewal, recorded in the primitive fiction of gaps and clusters, grids and doglegs. My cities were tangles; inevitably, like Pittsburgh. And as I built my cities, I'd keep the Pirates game on (in another notebook I kept running accounts of my team's declining fortune . . . "Well, Tony Bartirome, that knocks you down to .188 . . ." the pregame averages were never exact enough for me), and during the summers I excavated for the Department of Man, Carnegie Museum. Twice a week during the winter I visited the Casino Burlesque (this a winter pleasure, to counter the loss of baseball). I was a painter too, of sweeping subjects: my paleobotanical murals for the Devonian Fishes Hall are still a model for younger painter-excavators. (Are there others, still, like me, in Pittsburgh? This story is for them.) On Saturdays I lectured to the Junior Amateur Archaeologists and Anthropologists of Western Pennsylvania. I was a high school junior, my parents worked at their new store, and I was, obviously, mostly alone. In the afternoons, winter and summer, I picked up dirty clothes for my father's laundry.

I had—obviously, again—very few friends; there were not many boys like me. Fat, but without real bulk, arrogant but ridiculously shy. Certifiably brilliant but hopelessly unstudious, I felt unallied to even the conventionally bright honor-rollers in my suburban high school. Keith Godwin was my closest friend; I took three meals a week at his house, and usually slept over on Friday night.

Keith's father was a chemist with Alcoa; his mother a pillar of the local United Presbyterian Church, the Women's Club, and the University Women's chapter; and the four children (all but Keith, the oldest), were models of charm, ambition, and beauty. Keith was a moon-faced redhead with freckles and dimples— one would never suspect the depth of his cynicism—with just two real passions: the organ and competitive chess. I have seen him win five simultaneous blindfold games, ten-second moves— against tournament competition. We used to play at the dinner table without the board, calling out our moves while shoveling in the food. Years later, high school atheism behind him, he en- rolled in a Presbyterian seminary of Calvinist persuasions and is now a minister somewhere in California. He leads a number of extremist campaigns (crackpot drives, to be exact), against education, books, movies, minorities, pacifists—this, too, was a part of our rebellion, though I've turned the opposite way. But this isn't a story about Keith. He had a sister, Cyndy, one year younger.

She was tall, like her father, about five-eight, an inch taller than I. Hers was the beauty of contrasts: fair skin, dark hair, gray eyes, and the sharpness of features so common in girls who take after their fathers. Progressively I was to desire her as a sister, then wife, and finally as lover; but by then, of course, it was too late. I took a fix on her, and she guided me through high school; no matter how far out I veered, the hope of eventually pleasing Cyndy drove me back.

In the summer of my junior year, I put away the spade, my collection of pots and flints, and took up astronomy. There's a

romance to astronomy, an almost courtly type of pain and fas-
cination, felt by all who study it. The excitement: that like a
character in the childhood comics, I could shrink myself and dis-
miss the petty frustrations of school, the indifference of Cyndy
and my parents; that I could submit to points of light long
burned-out and be rewarded with their cosmic tolerance of my
obesity, ridicule from the athletes in the lunch line, and the
Pirates' latest losing streak. I memorized all I could from the
basic texts at Carnegie Library, and shifted my allegiance from
Carnegie Museum to Buhl Planetarium. There was a workshop
in the basement just getting going, started for teen-age telescope-
builders, and I became a charter member.

Each week I ground out my lens; glass over glass through
gritty water, one night a week for at least a year. Fine precise
work, never my style, but I stuck with it while most of the
charter enthusiasts fell away. The abrasive carborundum grew
finer, month by month, from sand, to talc, to rouge—a single
fleck of a coarser grade in those final months would have
plundered my mirror like a meteorite. Considering the winter
nights on which I sacrificed movies and TV for that lens, the long
streetcar rides, the aching arches, the insults from the German
shop foreman, the meticulous scrubbing-down after each
Wednesday session, the temptation to sneak upstairs for the
"Skyshow" with one of the chubby compliant girls—my alter
egos—from the Jewish high school: *considering all that,* plus
the all-important exclusiveness and recognition it granted, that
superb instrument was a heavy investment to sell, finally, for a
mere three hundred dollars. But I did, in the fine-polishing stage,
because, I felt, I owed it to Cyndy. Three hundred dollars, for a
new investment in myself.

Astronomy is the moral heavyweight of the physical sciences;
it is a humiliating science, a destroyer of pride in human achieve-
ments, or shame in human failings. Compared to the vacant
dimensions of space—of time, distance, and temperature—what
could be felt for Eisenhower's heart attack, Grecian urns,
six million Jews, my waddle and shiny gabardines? My parents
were nearing separation, their store beginning to falter—what
could I care for their silence, their fights, the begging for bigger

and bigger loans? The diameter of Antares, the Messier system, the swelling of space into uncreated nothingness—these things mattered because they were large, remote, and perpetual. The Tammany Ring and follies of Hitler, Shakespeare, and the Constitution were dust; the Andromeda galaxy was *worlds*. I took my meals out or with the Godwins, and I thought of these things as I struggled at chess with Keith and caught glimpses of Cyndy as she dried the dishes—if only I'd had dishes to dry!

The arrogance of astronomy, archaeology, chess, burlesque, baseball, science-fiction, everything I cared for: humility and arrogance are often so close (the men I'm writing this for—who once painted murals and played in high school bands just to feel a part of something—they know); it's all the same feeling, isn't it? Nothing matters, except, perhaps, the proper irony. I had that irony once (I wish, in fact, I had it now), and it was something like this:

In the days of the fifties, each home room of each suburban high school started the day with a Bible reading and the pledge of allegiance to the flag. Thirty mumbling souls, one fervent old woman, and me. It had taken me one night, five years earlier, to learn the Lord's Prayer backwards. I had looked up, as well, the Russian pledge and gotten it translated into English: this did for my daily morning ablutions. The lone difficulty had to do with Bible Week, which descended without warning on a Monday morning with the demand that we, in turn, quote a snatch from the Bible. This is fine if one's name is Zymurgy and you've had a chance to memorize everyone else's favorite, or the shortest verse. But I am a Dyer, and preceded often by Cohens and Bernsteins (more on that later): Bible Week often caught me unprepared. So it happened in the winter of my senior year that Marvin Bernstein was excused ("We won't ask Marvin, class, for he is of a different faith. Aren't you, Marvin?") and then a ruffian named Callahan rattled off a quick, "For God so loved the world that he gave his only begotten Son . . ." so fast that I couldn't catch it. A Sheila Cohen, whose white bra straps I'd stared at for one hour a day, five days a week, for three years— Sheila Cohen was excused. And Norman Dyer, I, stood. "Remember, Norman," said the teacher, "I won't have the Lord's Prayer and the Twenty-second Psalm." She didn't like Callahan's rendition either, and knew she'd get thirty more. From me she expected originality. I didn't disappoint.

"Om," I said, and quickly sat. I'd learned it from the Vedanta, something an astronomer studies.

Her smile had frozen. It was her habit, after a recitation, to smile and nod and congratulate us with, "Ah, yes, Revelations, a lovely choice, Nancy . . ." But gathering her pluckiness she demanded, "Just what is that supposed to mean, Norman?"

"Everything," I said, with an astronomer's shrug. I was preparing a justification, something to do with more people in the world praying "Om" than anything else, but I had never caused trouble before, and she decided to drop it. She called on my alphabetical shadow (a boy who'd stared for three years at my dandruff and flaring ears?), another Catholic, Dykes was his name, and Dykes this time, instead of following Callahan, twisted the knife a little deeper, and boomed out, "Om . . . amen!" Our teacher shut the Bible, caressed the marker, the white leather binding, and then read us a long passage having to do, as I recall, with nothing we had said.

That was the only victory of my high school years.

I imagined a hundred disasters a day that would wash Cyndy Godwin into my arms, grateful and bedraggled. Keith never suspected. My passion had a single outlet—the telephone. Alone in my parents' duplex, the television on, the Pirates game on, I would phone. No need to check the dial, the fingering was instinctive. Two rings at the Godwins'; if anyone but Cyndy answered, I'd hang up immediately. But with Cyndy I'd hold, through her perplexed "Hellos?" till she queried, "Susie, is that you?" "Brenda?" "Who is it, please?" and I would hold until her voice betrayed fear beyond the irritation. Oh, the pleasure of her slightly hysterical voice, "Daddy, it's that *man* again," and I would sniffle menacingly into the mouthpiece. Then I'd hang up and it was over; like a Pirates' loss, nothing to do but wait for tomorrow. Cyndy would answer the phone perhaps twice a week. Added to the three meals a week I took with them, I convinced myself that five sightings or soundings a week would eventually cinch a marriage if I but waited for a sign she'd surely give me. She was of course dating a bright, good-looking boy a year ahead of me (already at Princeton), a conventional sort of doctor-to-be, active in Scouts, Choir, Sports, and Junior Achievement, attending Princeton on the annual Kiwanis Fellowship. A very common type in our school and suburb, easily tolerated and easily dismissed. Clearly, a girl of Cyndy's sensitivity could not long endure his ministerial humor, his mere ignorance disguised as modesty. Everything about him—good looks, activities, athletics, piety, manners—spoke against him. In those years the only competition for Cyndy that I might have feared would have come from someone of my own circle. And that was impossible, for none of us had ever had a date.

And I knew her like a brother! Hours spent with her playing "Scrabble," driving her to the doctor's for curious flaws I was never to learn about . . . and, in the summers, accompanying the family to their cabin and at night hearing her breathing beyond a burlap wall . . . Like a brother? Not even that, for as I write I remember Keith grabbing her on the stairs, slamming his open hands against her breasts, and Cyndy responding, while I ached to save her, "Keith! What will Normie think?" And this went on for three years, from the first evening I ate with the Godwins when I was in tenth grade, till the spring semester of my senior year; Cyndy was a junior. There was no drama, no falling action, merely a sweet and painful stasis that I aggrandized with a dozen readings of *Cyrano de Bergerac,* and a customizing of his soliloquies . . . "This butt that follows me by half an hour . . . An ass, you say? Say rather a caboose, a dessert . . ." All of this was bound to end, only when I could break the balance.

We are back to the telescope, the three hundred well-earned dollars. Some kids I knew, Keith not included this time, took over the school printing press and ran off one thousand dramatic broadsheets, condemning a dozen teachers for incompetence and Lesbianism (a word that we knew meant more than "an inhabitant of Lesbos," the definition in our high school dictionary). We were caught, we proudly confessed (astronomy again: I sent a copy to *Mad* magazine and they wrote back, *"funny but don't get caught. You might end up working for a joint like this"*). The school wrote letters to every college that had so greedily accepted us a few weeks earlier, calling on them to retract their acceptance until we publicly apologized. Most of us did, for what good it did; I didn't—it made very little difference anyway, since my parents no longer could have afforded Yale. It would be Penn State in September.

I awoke one morning in April—a gorgeous morning—and decided to diet. A doctor in Squirrel Hill made his living prescribing amphetamines by the carload to suburban matrons. I lost thirty pounds in a month and a half, which dropped me into the ranks of the flabby underweights (funny, I'd always believed there was a *hard* me, under the fat, waiting to be sculpted out— there wasn't). And the pills (as a whole new generation is finding out) were marvelous: the uplift, the energy, the ideas they gave me! As though I'd been secretly rewired for a late but normal adolescence.

Tight new khakis and my first sweaters were now a part of the "New Look" Norman Dyer, which I capped one evening by calling the Arthur Murray Studios. I earned a free dance analysis by answering correctly a condescending question from their television quiz the night before. Then, with the three hundred dollars, I enrolled.

I went to three studio parties, each time with the enormous kid sister of my voluptuous instructress. That gigantic adolescent with a baby face couldn't dance a step (and had been brought along for me, I was certain), and her slimmed-down but still ample sister took on only her fellow teachers and some older, lonelier types, much to my relief. I wanted to dance, but not to be noticed. The poor big-little sister, whose name was Almajean, was dropping out of a mill-town high school in a year to become . . . what? I can't guess, and she didn't know, even then. We drank a lot of punch, shuffled together when we had to, and I told her about delivering clothes, something she could respect me for, never admitting that my father owned the store.

But I knew what I had to do. For my friends there was a single event in our high school careers that *had,* above all, to be missed. We had avoided every athletic contest, every dance, pep rally, party—everything voluntary and everything mildly compulsory; we had our private insurrections against the flag and God, but all that good work, all that conscientious effort, would be wasted if we attended the flurry of dances in our last two weeks. The Senior Prom was no problem—I'd been barred because of the newspaper caper. But a week later came the Women's Club College Prom, for everyone going on to higher study (92 per cent always did). The pressure for a 100 per cent turn-out was stifling. Even the teachers wore WC buttons so we wouldn't forget. Home room teachers managed to find out who was still uninvited (no one to give Sheila Cohen's bra a snap?). The College Prom combined the necessary exclusiveness and sophistication—smoking was permitted on the balcony—to have become the very essence of graduation night. And there was a special feature that we high schoolers had heard about ever since the eighth grade: the sifting of seniors into a few dozen booths, right on the dance floor, to meet local alums of their college-to-be, picking up a few fraternity bids, athletic money, while the band played a medley of privileged alma maters. I recalled the pain I had felt a year before, as I watched Cyndy leave with her then-senior boy friend, and I was still there, playing chess, when they returned around 2 A.M., for punch.

It took three weeks of aborted phone calls before I asked Cyndy to the College Prom. She of course accepted. Her steady boy friend was already at Princeton and ineligible. According to Keith, he'd left instructions: nothing serious. What did *he* know of seriousness, I thought, making my move. I bought a dinner jacket, dancing shoes, shirt, links, studs, cummerbund, and got ten dollars spending money from my astonished father. I was seventeen, and this was my first date.

Cyndy was a beautiful *woman* that night; it was the first time I'd seen her consciously glamorous. The year before she'd been a girl, well turned-out, but a trifle thin and shaky. But not tonight! Despite the glistening car and my flashy clothes, my new near-mesomorphy, I felt like a worm as I slipped the white orchid corsage around her wrist. (I could have had a bosom corsage; when the florist suggested it, I nearly ran from the shop. What if I jabbed her, right *there?*) And I could have cried at the trouble she'd gone to, *for me:* her hair was up, she wore glittering earrings and a pale sophisticated lipstick that made her lips look chapped. And, mercifully, flat heels. The Godwin family turned out for our departure, so happy that I had asked her, so respectful of my sudden self-assurance. Her father told me to stay out as long as we wished. Keith and the rest of my friends were supposedly at the movies, but had long been planning, I knew, for the milkman's matinee at the Casino Burlesque. I appreciated not having to face him—wondering, in fact, how I ever would again. My best-kept secret was out (Oh, the ways they have of getting us kinky people straightened out!); but she was mine tonight, the purest, most beautiful, the *kindest* girl I'd ever met. And for the first time, for the briefest instant, I connected her to those familiar bodies of the strippers I knew so well, and suddenly I felt that I knew what this dating business was all about and why it excited everyone so. I understood how thrilling it must be actually to touch, and kiss, and look at naked, a beautiful woman whom you loved, and who might touch you back.

The ballroom of the Woman's Club was fussily decorated; dozens of volunteers had worked all week. Clusters of spotlights strained through the sagging roof of crepe (the lights blue-filtered, something like the Casino), and the couples in formal gowns and dinner jackets seemed suddenly worthy of college and the professional lives they were destined to enter. A few people stared at Cyndy and smirked at me, and I began to feel a commingling of pride and shame, mostly the latter.

We danced a little—rumbas were my best—but mainly talked, drinking punch and nibbling the rich sugar cookies that her mother, among so many others, had helped to bake. We talked soberly, of my enforced retreat from the Ivy League (not even the car stealers and petty criminals on the fringe of our suburban society had been treated as harshly as I), of Keith's preparation for Princeton. Her gray eyes never left me. I talked of other friends, two who were leaving for a summer in Paris, to polish their French before entering Yale. Cyndy listened to it all, with her cool hand on my wrist. "How I wish Keith had taken someone tonight!" she exclaimed.

Then at last came the finale of the dance: everyone to the center of the floor, everyone once by the reviewing stand, while the orchestra struck up a medley of collegiate tunes. "Hail to Pitt!" cried the president of the Woman's Club, and Pitt's incoming freshmen, after whirling past the bandstand, stopped at an adjoining booth, signed a book, and collected their name tags. The rousing music blared on, the fight songs of Yale and Harvard, Duquesne and Carnegie Tech, Penn State, Wash and Jeff, Denison and Weslyan . . .

"Come on, Normie, we can go outside," she suggested. We had just passed under the reviewing stand, where the three judges were standing impassively. Something about the King and Queen; nothing I'd been let in on. The dance floor was thinning as the booths filled. I broke the dance-stride and began walking her out, only to be reminded by the WC president, straining above "Going Back to Old Nassau," to keep on dancing, please. The panel of judges—two teachers selected by the students, and Mr. Hartman, husband of the club's president—were already on the dance floor, smiling at the couples and poking their heads into the clogged booths. Cyndy and I were approaching the doors, near the bruisers in my Penn State booth. One of the algebra teachers was racing toward us, a wide grin on his florid face, and Cyndy gave my hand a tug. "Normie," she whispered, "I think something wonderful is about to happen."

The teacher was with us, a man much shorter than Cyndy, who panted, "Congratulations! You're my choice." He held a wreath of roses above her head, and she lowered her head to receive it. "Ah—what is your name?"

"Cyndy Godwin," she said, "Mr. Esposito."

"Keith Godwin's sister?"

"Yes."

"And how are you, Norman—or should I ask?" Mr. Wheeler, my history teacher, shouldered his way over to us; he held out a bouquet of yellow mums. "Two out of three," he grinned, "that should just about do it."

"Do what?" I asked. I wanted to run, but felt too sick. Cyndy squeezed my cold hand; the orchid nuzzled me like a healthy dog. My knees were numb, face burning.

"Cinch it," said Wheeler, "King Dyer."

"If Hartman comes up with someone else, then there'll be a vote," Esposito explained. "If he hasn't been bribed, then he'll choose this girl too and that'll be it."

I have never prayed harder. Wheeler led us around the main dance floor, by the rows of chairs that were now empty. The musicians suspended the Cornell evening hymn to enable the WC president to announce dramatically, in her most practiced voice, "The Queen approaches."

There was light applause from the far end of the floor. Couples strained from the college booths as we passed, and I could hear the undertone, ". . . he's a brain in my biology class, Norman something-or-other, but I don't know her . . ." I don't *have* to be here, I reminded myself. No one made me bring her. I could have asked one of the girls from the Planetarium who respected me for my wit and memory alone—or I could be home like any other self-respecting intellectual, in a cold sweat over *I Led Three Lives*. The Pirates were playing a twi-nighter and I could have been out there at Forbes Field in my favorite right-field upperdeck, where I'm an expert . . . why didn't I ask her out to a baseball game? Or I could have been where I truly belonged, with my friends down at the Casino Burlesque. . . .

"You'll lead the next dance, of course," Wheeler whispered. Cyndy was ahead of us, with Esposito.

"Couldn't someone else?" I said. "Maybe you—why not you?" Then I said with sudden inspiration, "She's not a senior. I don't think she's eligible, do you?"

"Don't worry, don't worry, Norman." I had been one of his favorite pupils. "Her class hasn't a thing to do with it, just her looks. And Norman"—he smiled confidentially—"she's an extraordinarily beautiful girl."

"Yeah," I agreed, had to. I drifted to the stairs by the bandstand, "I'm going to check anyway," I said. I ran to Mrs. Hartman herself. "Juniors aren't eligible to be Queen, are they? I mean, she'll get her own chance next year when she's going to college, right?"

Her smile melted as she finally looked at me; she had been staring into the lights, planning her speech. "Is her escort a senior?"

"Yes," I admitted, "but *he* wasn't chosen. Anyway, he's one of those guys who were kept from the Prom. By rights I don't think he should even be here."

"I don't think this has ever come up before." She squinted into the footlights, a well-preserved woman showing strain. "I presume you're a class officer."

"No, I'm her escort."

"Her *escort?* I'm afraid I don't understand. Do I know the girl?"

"Cyndy Godwin?"

"You don't mean Betsy Godwin's girl? Surely I'm not to take the prize away from that lovely girl, just because—well, just because *why* for heaven's sake?"

The bandleader leaned over and asked if he should start the "Miss America" theme. Mrs. Hartman fluttered her hand. And then from the other side of the stand, the third judge, Mr. Hartman, hissed to his wife. "Here she is," he beamed.

"Oh, dear me," began Mrs. Hartman.

"A vote?" I suggested. "It has to be democratic."

The second choice, a peppy redhead named Paula, innocently followed Mr. Hartman up the stairs and was already smiling like a winner. She was a popular senior, co-vice-president of nearly everything. Oh, poise! Glorious confidence! Already the front rows were applauding the apparent Queen, though she had only Mr. Hartman's slender cluster of roses to certify her. Now the band started up, the applause grew heavy, and a few enthusiasts even whistled. Her escort, a union leader's son, took his place behind her, and I cheerfully backed off the bandstand, joining Cyndy and the teachers at the foot of the steps. Cyndy had returned her flowers, and Mr. Wheeler was standing dejectedly behind her, holding the bouquet. The wreath dangled from his wrist.

"I feel like a damn fool," he said.

"That was very sweet of you, Normie," Cyndy said, and kissed me hard on the cheek."

"I just can't get over it," Wheeler went on, "if anyone here deserves that damn thing, it's you. At least take the flowers."

I took them for her. "Would you like to go?" I asked. She took my arm and we walked out. I left the flowers on an empty chair.

I felt more at ease as we left the school and headed across the street to the car. It was a cool night, and Cyndy was warm at my side, holding my arm tightly. "Let's have something to eat," I suggested, having practiced the line a hundred times, though it still sounded badly acted. I had planned the dinner as well; *filet mignon* on toast at a classy restaurant out on the highway. I hadn't planned it for quite so early in the night, but even so, I was confident. A girl like Cyndy ate out perhaps once or twice a year, and had probably never ordered *filet*. I was more at home in a fancy restaurant than at a family table.

"I think I'd like that," she said.

"What happened in there was silly—just try to forget all about it," I said. "It's some crazy rule or something."

We walked up a side street, past a dozen cars strewn with crepe.

"It's not winning so much," she said, "it's just an embarrassing thing walking up there like that and then being left holding the flowers."

"There's always next year."

"Oh, I won't get it again. There are lots of prettier girls than me in my class."

An opening, I thought. So easy to tell her that she was a queen, deservedly, any place. But I couldn't even slip my arm around her waist, or take her hand that rested on my sleeve.

"Well, I think you're really pretty." And I winced.

"Thank you, Norman."

"Prettier than anyone I've ever—"

"I understand," she said. Then she took my hand and pointed

it above the streetlights. "I'll bet you know all those stars, don't you, Normie?"

"Sure."

"You and Keith—you're going to be really something some-day."

We came to the car; I opened Cyndy's door and she got in. "Normie?" she said, as she smoothed her skirt before I closed the door, "could we hurry? I've got to use the bathroom."

I held the door open a second. *How dare she,* I thought, that's not what she's supposed to say. This is a date; you're a queen, my own queen. I looked at the sidewalk, a few feet ahead of us, then said suddenly, bitterly, "There's a hydrant up there. Why don't you use it?"

I slapped the headlights as I walked to my side, hoping they would shatter and I could bleed to death.

"That wasn't a very nice thing to say, Norman," she said as I sat down.

"I know."

"A girl who didn't know you better might have gotten of-fended."

I drove carefully, afraid now on this night of calamity that I might be especially accident-prone. It was all too clear now, why she had gone with me. Lord, protect me from a too-easy for-giveness. In the restaurant parking lot, I told her how sorry I was for everything, without specifying how broad an everything I was sorry for.

"You were a perfect date," she said. "Come on, let's forget about everything, O.K.?"

Once inside, she went immediately to the powder room. The hostess, who knew me, guided me to a table at the far end of the main dining room. She would bring Cyndy to me. My dinner jacket attracted some attention; people were already turning to look for my date. I sat down; water was poured for two, a salad bowl appeared. When no one was looking, I pounded the table. *Years of this,* I thought: slapping headlights, kicking tables, wanting to scream a memory out of existence, wanting to shrink back into the stars, the quarries, the right-field stands—things that could no longer contain me. A smiling older man from the table across the aisle snapped his fingers and pointed to his cheek, then to mine, and winked. "Lipstick!" he finally whispered, no longer smiling. I had begun to wet the napkin when I saw Cyndy and the hostess approaching—and the excitement that followed in Cyndy's wake. I stood to meet her. She was the Queen, freshly beautiful, and as I walked to her she took a hanky from her purse and pressed it to her lips. Then in front of everyone, she touched the moistened hanky to my cheek, and we turned to take our places.

I'M DREAMING OF ROCKET RICHARD

We were never quite the poorest people on the block, simply because I was, inexplicably, an only child. So there was more to go around. It was a strange kind of poverty, streaked with gentility (the kind that chopped you down when you least expected it); my mother would spend too much for long-range goals—Christmas clubs, reference books, even a burial society—and my father would drink it up or gamble it away as soon as he got it. I grew up thinking that being an only child, like poverty, was a blight you talked about only in secret. "Too long in the convent," my father would shout—a charge that could explain my mother's way with money or her favors—"there's ice up your cunt." An only child was scarcer than twins, maybe triplets, in Montreal just after the War. And so because I was an only child, things happened to me more vividly, without those warnings that older brothers carry as scars. I always had the sense of being the first in my family—which was to say the first of my people—to think my thoughts, to explore the parts of Montreal that we called foreign, even to question in an innocent way the multitudes of unmovable people and things.

When I went to the Forum to watch the Canadiens play

hockey, I wore a Boston Bruins sweatshirt. That was way back, when poor people could get into the Forum, and when Rocket Richard scored fifty goals in fifty games. Despite the letters on the sweatshirt, I loved the Rocket. I loved the Canadiens fiercely. It had to do with the intimacy of old-time hockey, how close you were to the gods on the ice; you could read their lips and hear them grunt as they slammed the boards. So there I stood in my Boston Bruins shirt loving the Rocket. There was always that spot of perversity in the things I loved. In school the nuns called me "Curette"—"Little Priest."

I was always industrious. That's how it is with janitors' sons. I had to pull out the garbage sacks, put away tools, handle simple repairs, answer complaints about heat and water when my father was gone or too drunk to move. He used to sleep near the heating pipes on an inch-thick, rust-stained mattress under a Sally Ann blanket. He loved his tools; when he finally sold them I knew we'd hit the bottom.

Industriously, I built an ice surface, enclosed it with old doors from a demolished tenement. The goal mouth was a topless clothes-hamper I fished from the garbage. I battered it to splinters, playing. Luck of the only child: if I'd had an older brother, I'd have been put in goal. Luckily there was a younger kid on the third floor who knew his place and was given hockey pads one Christmas; his older brother and I would bruise him after school until darkness made it dangerous for him. I'd be in my Bruins jersey, dreaming of Rocket Richard.

Little priest that I was, I did more than build ice surfaces. In the mornings I would rise at a quarter to five and pick up a bundle of *Montréal Matins* on the corner of Van Horne and Querbes. Seventy papers I had, and I could run with the last thirty-five, firing them up on second and third floor balconies, stuffing them into convenient grilles, and marking with hate all those buildings where the Greeks were moving in or the Jews had already settled and my papers weren't good enough to wrap their garbage in. There was another kid who delivered the morning *Gazettes* to part of my street—ten or twelve places that had no use for me. We were the only people yet awake, crisscrossing each other's paths, still in the dark and way below zero, me with a *Matin* sack and he with his *Gazette*. Once, we even talked. We were waiting for our bundles under a street lamp in front of the closed tobacco store on the corner. It was about ten below and the sidewalks were uncleared from an all-night snow. He smoked one of my cigarettes and I smoked one of his and we found out we didn't have anything to say to each other except "*merci*." After half an hour I said "paper no come" and he agreed, so we walked away.

Later on more and more Greeks moved in; every time a vacancy popped up, some Greek would take it—they even made sure by putting only Greek signs in the windows—and my route was shrinking all the time. *Montréal Matin* fixed me up with a route much further east, off Rachel near St-André, and so I became the only ten-year-old in Montreal who'd wait at four-thirty in the morning for the first bus out of the garage to take him to his paper route. After a few days I didn't have to pay a fare. I'd take coffee from the driver's thermos, his cigarettes, and we'd discuss hockey from the night before. In return I'd give him a paper when he let me off. They didn't call me Curette for nothing.

The hockey, the hockey! I like all the major sports, and the setting of each one has its special beauty—even old De Lorimier Downs had something of Yankee Stadium about it, and old Rocky Nelson banging out home runs from his rocking chair stance made me think of Babe Ruth, and who could compare to Jackie Robinson and Roberto Clemente when they were playing for us? Sundays in August with the Red Wings in town, you could always get in free after a couple of innings and see two great games. But the ice of big-time hockey, the old Forum, that went beyond landscape! Something about the ghostly white of the ice under those powerful lights, something about the hiss of the skates if you were standing close enough, the solid *pock-pock* of the rubber on a stick, and the low menacing whiz of a Rocket slap shot hugging the ice—there was nothing in any other sport to compare with the *spell* of hockey. Inside the Forum in the early fifties, those games against Boston (with the Rocket flying and a hated Boston goalie nmed Jack Gelineux in the nets) were evangelical, for truly we were *dans le cénacle* where everyone breathed as one.

The Bruins sweatshirt came from a cousin of mine in Manchester, New Hampshire, who brought it as a joke or maybe a present on one of his trips up to see us. I started wearing it in all my backyard practices and whenever I got standing room tickets at the Forum. Crazy, I think now; what was going on in me? Crying on those few nights each winter when the Canadiens lost, quite literally throwing whatever I was holding high in the air whenever the Rocket scored—yet always wearing that hornet-colored jersey? Anyone could see I was a good local kid; maybe I wanted someone to think I'd come all the way from Boston just to see the game, maybe I liked the good-natured kidding from my fellow standees ("'ey, you, Boston," they'd shout, "oo's winning, eh?" and I'd snarl back after a period or two of silence, "*mange la baton, sac de marde . . .*"). I even used to wear that jersey when I delivered papers and I remember the pain of watching it slowly unravel in the cuffs and shoulders, hoping the cousin would come again. They were Schmitzes, my mother's sister had met him just after the War. *Tante* Lise and Uncle Howie.

I started to pick up English by reading a *Gazette* on my paper route, and I remember vividly one spring morning—with the sun coming up—studying a name that I took to be typically English. It began *Sch*, an odd combination, like my uncle's; then I suddenly thought of my mother's name—not mine—Deschênes, and I wondered: could it be? Hidden in the middle of my mother's name were those same English letters, and I began to think that we (tempting horror) were English too, that I had a right, a *sch*, to that Bruins jersey, to the world in the *Gazette* and on the other side of Atwater from the Forum. How I fantasied!

Every now and then the Schmitzes would drive up in a new car (I think now they came up whenever they bought a new car; I don't remember ever sitting in one of their cars without noticing a shred of plastic around the window-cranks and a smell of newness), and I would marvel at my cousins who were younger than me and taller ("they don't smoke," my mother would point out), and who whined a lot because they always wanted things (I never understood what) they couldn't get with us. My mother could carry on with them in English. I wanted to like them—an only child feels that way about his relatives, not having seen his genetic speculations exhausted, and tends to see himself refracted even into second and third cousins several times removed. Now I saw a devious link with that American world in the strange clot of letters common to my name and theirs, and that pleased me.

We even enjoyed a bout of prosperity at about that time. I was thirteen or so, and we had moved from Hutchison (where a Greek janitor was finally hired) to a place off St-Denis where my father took charge of a sixteen-apartment building; they paid him well and gave us a three-room place out of the basement damps. That was *bonheur* in my father's mind—moving up to the ground floor where the front door buzzer kept waking you up. It was reasonably new; he didn't start to have trouble with bugs and paint for almost a year. He even saved a little money.

At just about the same time, in the more spacious way of the Schmitzes, they packed up everything in Manchester (where Uncle Howie owned three dry-cleaning shops) and moved to North Hollywood, Florida. That's a fair proportion: Hutchison is to St-Denis what Manchester is to Florida. He started with one dry-cleaning shop and had three others within a year. If he'd really been one of us, we'd have been suspicious of his tactics and motives, we would have called him lucky and undeserving. But he was American, he had his *sch*, so whatever he did seemed blessed by a different branch of fate, and we wondered only how we could share.

It was the winter of 1952. It was a cold sunny time on St-Denis. I still delivered my papers (practically in the neighborhood), my father wasn't drinking that much, and my mother was staying out of church except on Sunday—it was a bad sign when she started going on weekdays—and we had just bought a car. It was a used Plymouth, the first car we'd ever owned. The idea was that we should visit the Schmitzes this time in their Florida home for Christmas. It was even their idea, arranged through the sisters. My father packed his tools in the rear ("You never know, Mance; I'd like to show him what I can do . . ."). He moved his brother Réal and family into our place—Réal was handy enough, more affable, but an even bigger drinker. We left Montreal on December 18 and took a cheap and slow drive down, the pace imposed by my father, who underestimated the strain of driving, and by my mother, who'd read of speedtraps and tourists languishing twenty years in Southern dungeons for running a stop sign. The drive was cheap because we were dependent on my mother for expense money as soon as we entered the States, since she was the one who could go into the motel office and find out the prices. It would be three or four in the afternoon and my father would be a nervous wreck; just as we were unloading the trunk and my father was checking the level of whisky in the glove compartment bottle, she'd come out announcing it was highway robbery, we couldn't stay here. My father would groan, curse, and slam the trunk. Things would be dark by the time we found a vacancy in one of those rows of one-room cabins, arranged like stepping stones or in a semicircle (the kind you still see nowadays out on the Gaspésie with boards on the windows and a faded billboard out front advertising "investment property"). My mother put a limit of three dollars a night on accommodations; we shopped in supermarkets for cold meat, bread, mustard, and Pepsis. My father rejoiced in the cheaper gas; my mother reminded him it was a smaller gallon. Quietly, I calculated the difference. Remember, no drinking after Savannah, my mother said. It was clear: he expected to become the manager of a Schmitz Dry Kleenery.

The Schmitzes had rented a spacious cottage about a mile from the beach in North Hollywood. The outside stucco was green, the roof tiles orange, and the flowers violently pink and purple. The shrubs looked decorated with little red Christmas bulbs; I picked one—gift of my cousin—bit, and screamed in surprise. Red chilies. The front windows were sprayed with Santa's sleigh and a snowy "Merry Christmas." Only in English, no "*Joyeux Noël*" like our greeting back home. That was what I'd noticed most all the way down, the incompleteness of all the signs, the satisfaction that their version said it all. I'd kept looking on the other side of things—my side—and I'd kept twirling the radio dial, for an equivalence that never came.

It was Christmas week and the Schmitzes were wearing Bermuda shorts and T-shirts with sailfish on the front. *Tante* Lise wore coral earrings and a red halter, and all her pale flesh had freckled. The night we arrived, my father got up on a stepladder, anxious to impress, and strung colored lights along the gutter while my uncle shouted directions and watered the lawn. Christmas—and drinking Kool-Aid in the yard! We picked chili peppers and sold them to every West Indian cook who answered the back doorbell. At night I licked my fingers and hummed with the air-conditioning. My tongue burned for hours. That was the extraordinary part for me: that things as hot as chilies could grow in your yard, that I could bake in December heat, and that other natural laws remained the same. My father was still shorter than my mother, and his face turned red and blotchy here too (just as it did in August back home) instead of an even schmitzean brown, and when he took off his shirt, only a tattoo, scars, and angry red welts were revealed. Small and sickly he seemed; worse, mutilated. My cousins rode their chrome-plated bicycles to the beach, but I'd never owned a two-wheeler and this didn't seem the time to reveal another weakness. Give me ice, I thought, my stick and a puck and an open net. Some men were never meant for vacations in shirtless countries: small hairy men with dirty winter boils and red swellings that never became anything lanceable, and tattoos of celebrities in their brief season of fame, now forgotten. My father's tattoo was as long as my twelve-year-old hand, done in a waterfront parlor in Montreal the day he'd thought of enlisting. My mother had been horrified, more at the tattoo than the thought of his shipping out. The tattoo pictured a front-faced Rocket, staring at an imaginary goalie and slapping a rising shot through a cloud of ice chips. Even though I loved the Canadiens and the Rocket mightily, I would have preferred my father to walk shirtless down the middle of the street with a naked woman on his back than for him to strip for the Schmitzes and my enormous cousins, who pointed and laughed, while I could almost understand what they were laughing about. They thought his tattoo was a kind of tribal marking, like kinky hair, thin mustaches, and slanty eyes—that if I took off my shirt I'd have one too, only smaller. *Lacroix,* I said to myself: how could he and I have the same name? It was foreign. I was a Deschênes, a Schmitz in the making.

On Christmas Eve we trimmed a silvered little tree and my uncle played Bing Crosby records on the console hi-fi-short-wave-bookcase (the biggest thing going in Manchester, New Hampshire, before the days of television). It would have been longer than our living room in Montreal; even here it filled one wall. They tried to teach me to imitate Crosby's "White Christmas," but my English was hopeless. My mother and aunt sang in harmony; my father kept spilling his iced tea while trying to clap. It was painful. I waited impatiently to get to bed in order to cut the night as short as possible.

The murkiness of those memories! How intense, how foreign; it all happened like a dream in which everything follows logically from some incredible premise—that we should go to Florida, that it should be so hot in December, that my father should be on his best behavior for nearly a month . . . that we could hope that a little initiative and optimism would carry us anywhere but deeper into debt and darkest despair . . .

I see myself as in a dream, walking the beach alone, watching the coarse brown sand fall over my soft white feet. I hear my mother and *Tante* Lise whispering together, yet they're five hundred feet ahead ("Yes," my mother is saying, "what life is there for him back there? You can see how this would suit him. To a T! To a T!" I'm wondering is it me, or my father, who has no future back there, and *Tante* Lise begins, "Of course, I'm only a wife. I don't know what his thinking is—"), but worse is the silent image of my father in his winter trousers rolled up to his skinny knees and gathered in folds by a borrowed belt (at home he'd always worn braces), shirtless, shrunken, almost running to keep up with my uncle who walks closer to the water, in Bermuda shorts. I can tell from the beaten smile on my father's lips and from the way Uncle Howie is talking (while looking over my father's head at the ships on the horizon), that what the women have arranged ("It would be good to have you close, Mance . . . I get these moods sometimes, you know? And five shops are too much for Howie . . .") the men have made impossible. I know that when my father was smiling and his head was bobbing in agreement and he was running to keep up with someone, he was being told off, turned down, laughed at. And the next stage was for him to go off alone, then come back to us with a story that embarrassed us all by its transparency, and that would be the last of him, sober, for three, four, or five days . . . I can see all this and hear it, though I am utterly alone near the crashing surf and it seems to be night and a forgotten short-wave receiver still blasts forth on a beach blanket somewhere; I go to it hoping to catch something I can understand, a hockey game, the scores, but all I get wrenching the dial until it snaps is Bing Crosby dreaming of a white Christmas and Cuban music and indecipherable commentary from Havana, the dog races from Miami, *jai alai.*

That drive back to Montreal lasted almost a month. Our money ran out in Georgia and we had to wait two weeks in a shack in the Negro part of Savannah, where a family like ours— with a mother who liked to talk, and a father who drank and showed up only to collect our rent, and a kid my age who spent his time caddying and getting up before the sun to hunt golf balls—found space for us in a large room behind the kitchen, recently vacated by a dead grandparent. There were irregularities, the used-car dealer kept saying, various legal expenses involved with international commerce between Canadian Plymouths and innocent Georgia dealers, and we knew not to act too anxious (or even give our address) for fear of losing whatever bit of money we stood to gain. Finally he gave us $75, and that was when my father took his tools out of the back and sold them at a gas station for $50. We went down to the bus station, bought three tickets to Montreal, and my father swept the change into my mother's pocketbook. We were dressed for the January weather we'd be having when we got off, and the boy from the house we'd been staying in, shaking his head as he watched us board, muttered, "Man, you sure is crazy." It became a phrase of my mother's for all the next hard years. "Man, you sure is crazy." I mastered it and wore it like a Bruins sweater, till it too wore out. I remember those nights on the bus, my mother counting the bills and coins in her purse, like beads on a rosary, the numbers a silent prayer.

Back on St-Denis we found Réal and family very happily installed. The same egregious streak that sputtered in my father flowed broadly in his brother. He'd all but brought fresh fruit baskets to the sixteen residents, carried newspapers to their doors, repaired buzzers that had never worked, shoveled insanely wide swaths down the front steps, replaced lights in the basement lockers, oiled, painted, polished . . . even laid off the booze for the whole month we were gone (which to my father was the unforgivable treachery); in short, while we'd sunk all our savings and hocked all our valuables to launch ourselves in the dry-cleaning business, Réal had simply moved his family three blocks into lifelong comfort and security. My father took it all very quietly; we thought he'd blow sky-high. But he was finished. He'd put up the best, and the longest, show of his life and he'd seen himself squashed like a worm underfoot. Maybe he'd had one of those hellish moments when he'd seen himself in his brother-in-law's sunglasses, running at his side, knowing that those sunglasses were turned to the horizon and not to him.

THE SEIZURE

We are talking of southern Ohio, southwestern Pennsylvania, that segregated blade of West Virginia that inserts itself between the East and the Middle West. Where are we? North? East? Midwest? You cannot say. What exactly are these people? A college boy on Christmas holidays, working reluctantly at his father's store; a giant black man in a green uniform, standing over his boss, hammer in hand, a look so hurt and menacing on his face that—let us say—a state trooper suddenly bursting into the store would fire first and be pardoned later; the boss, a tight little man, bald, mustached, robust in the hairy way of the short and bald. (You've seen him a thousand times in clothing stores, used-car lots, hotels. Cigars, rings on pinky, gold watch band gleaming on a hairy wrist.) The name is Malick. There are Mullicks in India, Maliks in Russia and the Middle East, Meliks in Egypt, Mallochs in Scotland, Malicks universally in the garment trade. Even the boss traces nothing back further than two generations. His faith was inherited: the shortest, darkest Presbyterian in the town of his birth. Uncles of his in larger cities had kept a complicated faith, with demanding rituals and obscure saints.

They are stringing a wire, the giant driver and the short, sweating businessman.

Upstairs, a woman in high heels greets a customer.

Off-stage, alone in a suburban home back in the hills, Margaret Malick—Justin's mother, the boss's wife—breaks eggs for an omelet. She worries about a phone call, whether to uncradle the receiver now, or to answer it when it rings.

Expected any time now, from the library, Justin. Called Judd, a name he has hated since its first corruption into Jug and its later similarity to the Jeds, Jebs, and Jeps in the hills around him. Mornings in the library thirty miles away, afternoons in the store helping out. He lives for the school year to end, when he will decamp to France for his junior year. Justin Malick, six-feet-two and consumptively thin, with the olive complexion of his father and his mother's massive bones, will make a perfect Parisian Arab. He can see his name tacked up on a splintered door: *Justin Maliq.* He can picture himself in a left bank café reading, nervously puffing a rancid Gauloise. There is a *tabac* in Wheeling, thirty miles east, that sells Gauloises, Gitanes, and Celtiques. He's added a new word from this morning's reading: *fricoteur,* a procurer of illicit delectables. In Wheeling, a *Gitane* pimp. Near-compensation for the unpleasant duties at hand.

The mind of Delman, who holds the hammer over the boss's head, who drives the truck and delivers the goods, is vastly more complex than Junior's, or the boss's. To the son, it seems merely a dark humid cellar; littered, earthen, sealed upon itself; slow, fat flies buzzing incessantly against the screens. There is a dripping from somewhere.

Once, when he was just a kid, Delman saw a bunch of pictures in *Life* of what the Japanese did, first thing after entering a Chinese village. Got the mayor and all the local bosses, all the big-shot landowners and all the men between ten and fifty and a few girls to spice it up, and put them in a building and set it on fire. Soldiers sat around with machine guns covering the exits. Mowed them down as they came pouring out, shirts on fire, hands up. *Ooo-eee,* some fucking Bar B-Q. *Banzai!* Few years later *Life* got the shots of Mao hitting Shanghai, and then it was the big-shot landlords all over again, down on their knees

with their wives and kids, hands tied to paddles behind. All of
the kids with their hands tied, bending over. One second there's
a kid with his hair a little sticking up the way Chinese hair is
always sticking up, in a clean white shirt he probably took out
of the drawer that morning not ever knowing it would be his
last one, and his feet in good sandals and his mouth open to say
something to his father who's kneeling at the next paddle (saying *what*, he'd wondered as a young man: "Daddy, is it going to
hurt?" "Daddy, tell them to stop it . . ." "Daddy, are they really
going to shoo—") and a second later his brains are coming out of
his mouth and his hair is plastered on his father's shirt. First
time he saw it, he got a headache. But he never forgot.

"Just loop it over the doorframe, Delman," says the boss. At
six-six, Delman's got about a foot on the boss. "I'm sure as hell
grateful she thought of this," Malick says. "Some kind of time-
saver, huh? All those trips you used to have to make up from the
warehouse—think of the time you'll save! She figured two hours
a week—*easy* two hours a week. And think of all the work you'll
get done without us bothering you till we call."

Ooo-eee, just think.

"Hey—guess what it cost, the whole rig. Take a guess."

"I'm sure I'd be wrong."

"Go on, try."

"Oh, I'm sure I'd guess way too high."

"Nail it in up there, Delman. God, you're some kind of giant,
aren't you? What d'ya go—six-four? Six-five? You should've played
basketball, Delman, they're always looking for guys like you.
Now come on, take a guess."

I played, I played. All-State twenty-five years ago, driving a
truck all over those Jap-held islands a year later. Been driving
ever since. "You want a guess, Mr. Malick? O.K. Here's a guess.
I'd say shopping smartly you can pick up a two-way intercom
and about half a mile of cable for five ninety-five." And you could
see the boss wilting a little, as if you'd dropped the hammer
accidently on his head.

"Dammit, Delman, you're not stupid. Use your head and guess
again."

"*Ten* dollars?" Eyes wide.

"For your information, you're holding the latest intercom on the market. German-made, from Office Outfitters. Finest on the market. Twenty-nine bucks complete. Can't beat that. Now what I want to know is how come we didn't think of it before, huh?"

"Well, I don't remember being asked, Mr. Malick—"

"*We*—how come Missus Malick, how come she never thought of it, since she's suddenly so concerned about the store?"

"Missus Malick always walked down and got me herself."

"That's just like her. Walk down and leave the floor empty for ten minutes. That's what I call smart. How come it takes Mrs. Simmons one week on the job to tell me we need an intercom? I swear to God that woman takes more interest in this store than anyone we've ever had." The boss looks up lovingly at the sound of heels tapping their way back to the office. The squeal of casters as she settles again into his office chair. Delman keeps on nailing, the boss keeps on praising. Upstairs, Mrs. Simmons is placing a call. "She's smart, Delman. God, it frightens me how smart she is. Learned the whole routine, *everything*, perfect in a week. In a week! You know I've had experienced furniture men come to me and ask me where I found her. 'Don't let that one get away, Jerry'—that's what they say. And she's got energy. Sells like three experienced men."

"She's got that good experience all right." And Delman remembers where they found her—in an ad: "WANTED: AGGRESSIVE SALESWOMAN FOR THRIVING SUBURBAN FIRM." When Mrs. Simmons said "firm" you could feel her squeezing it; you could feel it break in her hand.

Mrs. Simmons: you've seen her too. Behind cosmetic counters in overcooled Florida drugstores. Receptionist in a cocktail lounge. She is sitting in the office, dialing Margaret Malick. Her voice is honeyed; hair, eyelids, lips, and nails all frosted. Figure, at forty-odd, stunning. A few wrinkles under the chin, around the mouth. One can imagine her, under the make-up, a girl of twenty from the hills around here, gawky. Uncertain. Accented. Tough and bony. One, two, three husbands later she owns a home, a bank account, a brutal confidence. The last husband has made her a widow; the first a mother; the second polished the diamond he'd taken away, only to lose her to an older, richer, and stuffier man.

A voice, weak and tentative: "Hello?"

"Hello, Margaret. How *are* you, dear?"

"I've asked you never to call. I've warned you. I'll tell Jerry."

"But *that's* why I'm calling, Margaret. If you have a message for Jerry, why don't you just give it to me? Now the reason I'm calling is so you won't be worrying about tonight, all right? Jerry will be taking me out to dinner after we close, and I just don't see *how* we can be free before midnight, all right? And I'd be positively *frantic* if the roads get all icy and I had to send him home all by himself."

"Please—"

"I mean, I absolutely couldn't forgive myself if I was to blame for anything happening to my boss, right?"

"Stop—all I want is for you to stop. Please. Stop."

"Well, Mrs. Malick, if *that's* the way you feel about a friendly little phone call, then I can certainly understand all the things Jerry tells me about you. I didn't *want* to believe them, but—"

She waited two minutes, then dialed again.

Mrs. Simmons was out to lunch when Judd arrived from the library. The intercom had been installed. Delman and his father were in the office going over a file. "You're late," his father said. "The deputy's already here."

There had been a cop car in the parking lot; something suspicious about its studious plain-blackness had made him look a second time. The driver, in khaki, had been on the two-way radio. Then another patrol car—this one decked out in white doors, township crest, and revolving light—had pulled into the parking lot, and the two cars had rubbed against each other as the deputies talked. Like copulating worms, he'd thought at the time, each pointed in opposite directions.

"O.K., if we're ready now. You remember Szafransky?"

"She the lady with the tattoo?" Delman asked.

"What tattoo? He bought a ninety-six-inch sofa, a bedroom suite, lamps, rugs, and three tables. Hutch, sideboard, six chairs."

"On her elbow. Ooo-eee, a little blue star right smack on her elbow."

"Well, we're repossessing on sheriff's orders and he's sent a deputy to go out with you. I want you to take out every stick of furniture on that order, got it? And make sure you get the louse's signature when you leave."

"Right. Get the deputy's signature."

"Cut it out. You may think it's funny, and *him,* he's probably laughing to himself seeing his old man losing money, but I've got four thousand dollars tied up in that son of a bitch. Cheating a man who gives you credit—that's the lowest thing in the book. A rotter, that's all. By God, I'd rather be selling to niggers than bohunks like him. No offense, Delman. Prison's too good, too good. I want you in and out of there as quick as possible and if he tries anything, let the deputy handle it. Deputy's costing me fifty bucks an hour."

"What do you mean—*if he tries anything?*" asked Judd.

"I mean exactly what I said. If you touch anything but the furniture, it's assault. If they touch you, it's interference. I don't want either one of you saying a word to those people, got it?"

"Gotcha."

"I know *you* won't. It's the boy I'm worried about. He's good at some things, but it would be like sending his mother in there and trying to come out with anything. Just try to get it into your head that this is business and those people got charity from me and they abused it and try not to be like some kind of god-damn social worker when you deal with bohunks, O.K.? And if the merchandise is damaged, I want you to write out a descrip-tion on the spot and the deputy will sign it. He's got the forms."

"Right."

The deputy tailgated in the unmarked car. Delman thought of other men he'd sat with in the cabs of delivery trucks: white and black, college boys, drunks, racists, ex-cons, weaklings, queers. Relatives, scabs, junkies. All the faces and all the names he'd had to learn, all the home towns, all their bitches with the world. All the waste. But no matter what else, they all looked right for the job. They dressed right. They sat right in the cab.

They looked capable and barely strong enough. If they talked, it was about the right things for delivering furniture. But Junior sat hunched against the door with both legs up on the seat between them. Reading a French book and cutting the pages. Delman had warned him when they left: look, this ain't no T-Bird with kiddie-locks, sit straight! Truck doors can give way, especially when your old man buys them third-hand and they're already dented. All I need is losing Junior out the door when I'm driving.

"So, how're they treating you up there?"

"They leave me alone. After your freshman year you can do pretty much whatever you like."

They turned off the state highway, onto a county road that dipped towards a creek and bridge. If you go one way, curling up along the ridges and back down a valley or two, you come to some expensive homes, the boss's among them. But if you stick with the county road down along the "run," you come to a string of dead-end villages clinging to a railroad spur that used to carry coal. The road is snow-banked and cindered, barely covering the abandoned cars. The high ridge beyond the creek is white and studded with black trees. Good hunting, once. The road narrows to a one-lane bridge, then leads in front of a cluster of shanties at the other end. The water is black, with snow-topped rocks in the middle. A couple of old women in *"babushkas"* slog along the broken sidewalk. There is a discount gas station marked with a rusted, hand-painted billboard, "GAS 26.9," next to a foodstore that looks closed.

"God, this is foreign," said Judd. "It's like a painting, you know?"

In front of the store stood a State Historical Marker, but Delman didn't slow down.

"What's the marker for?"

Delman knew it well but said only, "You don't like to lose a single edifying experience, do you?" Then he laughed, "Ooo-eee, as we Knee-Grows say, you're somethin' else, Junior. Somethin' else." It marked the deepest northern penetration of Confederate troops, where a raiding party and some local copperheads linked

up in 1862 for their own special reasons and raided this hole of a
then-black hamlet called Enoch. They burned it down because
by 1862 it was one hundred per cent black and free although
just a handful had their legal papers. After gutting the town
they took some people back over the river into Virginia and
Kentucky, while the local citizens contented themselves with rape
and murder and scattering the rest of the blacks into the hills.
Those were Delman's people, hill-niggers that roamed free, shooting coons and squirrels until basketball and the War intervened.
By then the Polacks had come and taken over whatever was
left. And with the Polacks the whole thing hadn't changed in
forty years. Of course the Historical Marker didn't say a thing
about blacks and Polacks. It read: "FIRST ENGAGEMENT
WITH CONFEDERATE FORCES ON UNION SOIL, Burning of Enoch, 1862."

The Szafransky house was partly up the ridge and connected
to the creek road by a driveway lined with painted rocks and
red reflectors. It was too soupy for the truck, so Delman parked
a little off the road, making sure to block the drive. They waited
in the cab for the deputy to come around. He was a small
sallow man with a high husky voice that sounded deep South.
Half the voices in this region are Southern. He squinted; his
uniform was soiled.

"This it? Up that drive?"

"That's where I brung it last spring. They could have moved
since, but that's the place."

"Well, the residence appears occupied," said the deputy.
"Smoke in the chimley. Let's get it over with."

"We'll just wait here for the all-clear, seeing's how you got
the badge."

The deputy squinted, cocked his head. "No, sir, you get on
down and come up there with me. This here's your mess, not
mine. I'll be right behind if there's any ruckus. And don't think
you can start giving me orders, neither."

In front of the cottage stood a rusty mailbox with "szafransky"
painted in lower case. Delman snickered and pointed it out.
"Reckon they been reading their e e cummings?" he asked, then
turned his head quickly as though he hadn't said a thing. *Oh,*

*yes, there is some shit I will not eat, and that was the truest poem
anyone had ever written.* Junior was walking with one eye on
the house, slightly behind him, because this was mountaineer
country where everyone hunted and every so often, especially
near Christmas, a man would shoot his family and then a couple
of neighbors and barricade himself inside to shoot it out with
the State Patrol. But they reached the door without a movement
from inside.

Judd looked around the yard and kept away from the screen
door. Delman rattled it. The summer porch was crammed with
wooden tables, smashed cane chairs, and crushed toys under a
dusting of snow. There was a main door beyond, but the screen
door was latched.

"Deputy, open up!" the little man shouted, but his voice didn't
carry. He kicked the screen door hard against the frame.

Pump a few rounds into the kitchen, thought Delman.

A child lifted the curtain on the inner door. Then a tall,
wide-shouldered man with a run-over blond crewcut, dressed
in overalls and a red flannel shirt, opened the door. He smelled
of unbrushed teeth. He said nothing, but his eyes settled on
Judd.

"Well, I done my piece," said the deputy. "Get it over with if
you're going to do it."

Judd's voice came out clear. "We're from Malick's. The deputy
has the papers for picking up the furniture."

"What kind of papers gives you the right to come barging in
my house and taking off my furniture in Christmas week?"

Meubles gagés: French kept occurring to him at the oddest
times. He couldn't think of it in English. It was a good Célinesque
word, something he'd been reading that morning. "We're seizing
the furniture against your unpaid account. You were sent a
notice."

Szafransky was joined by his wife. She had a mannish face,
but a narrow body, and she linked one arm with her husband's,
keeping the other on her hip. The effect was insolent and almost
exciting. She looked suspicious and submissive, like a captured
woman in occupied territory.

"Let's see them papers you got," said Szafransky, walking over the broken toys to the screen door. His hands, Judd noticed, were red and scaly, the stubby fingers stretching the skin like boiled Polish sausages. He made a show of studying the papers, then said, "Reckon it's legal."

Inside, Judd smelled cabbage and watched the kids scatter. The ceilings were low; only the deputy fitted in. They were like a giant tribe in undersized quarters; everyone stooped, and Judd wanted to shield his head from something falling. Two boys and two girls pointed at Delman behind his back.

"Son of a bitch didn't leave us no time to pay up," Szafransky told the deputy. "Been out of work four month." The place was steaming hot, the children coughed as they whispered, and piles of toys, dishes, papers, and clothes littered the space between the television and the miniature chairs.

Quelle porcherie!

"Son of a bitch sends me a Merry Christmas card saying he's taking us to court, and me with four kids. Where'm I getting a fancy lawyer can standt up to Mr. J. Fucking Malick? Trusts me for a couple thousand dollar then he takes it back 'cause I miss five hundred. Make sense to you?"

"I don't make the rules," said the deputy.

I do, thought Judd. *God help me.*

The dining room table, the chairs, and a hutch, were already beyond repair. Delman was writing it down. Mrs. Szafransky slowly cleared the table of milk cartons, cereal bowls, paste, and coloring books. Globs of glue had blistered off the finish; the milk rings were plastic-hard. The chairs had nail gouges from the children's run-over shoes, and the fancy knobs and railings of the colonial hutch had broken off. Delman stacked the three side chairs and took them to the truck.

"Well, I reckon a cup of coffee won't hurt nobody," said Mrs. Szafransky to the deputy. "I know you ain't a part of this."

"Don't put yourself out none."

In a minute she brought a kettle of boiling water and a green glass mug with a spoonful of instant coffee in the bottom. The kettle and cup went directly on the table. "Reckon no need to put a placemat down is there?" she said and left a generous ring of boiling water around the cup.

"You?"

"No, thank you."

"Better watch who you're talking to," said the deputy. He smiled over the lip of the cup. "That there fine young man you're talking to is none other than the boss's son. That right there is Mister Malick Junior."

"Funny," she said, "I kinda had the other one figgered for the boss's son. The nigger one."

The deputy, blinking and smiling, took a long loud suck on his coffee, making it sound as thick as soup. Delman came back from the truck.

"Got in much hunting yet?" Szafransky asked the deputy. "Got me a nine-point buck back in the freezer."

"Just some squirrel is all."

"Looks like good coon shooting 'round here," said Szafransky.

"Ain't never seen a bigger one," said the deputy.

"Just tip that hutch over," said Delman to Judd. "I can get the rest of it on my back."

"Well-trained, too," said Szafransky.

"That's a plenty good helper you brung along, mister," said the deputy. Then he added to Szafransky, "Didn't you hear what I told your missus? That-there is Mister Malick Junior."

Szafransky squinted, then asked, "Reckon he'd come back later without his nigger?"

"Don't hardly think so."

"Sort of a queer-lookin' little cocksucker, ain't he?" he asked of his wife.

"You leaving these people a pot to piss in, boy?" asked the deputy.

"You have the list."

"Seems like damn near everything to me."

"Look—me and the wife can use some fresh air after cocksuck and the nigger been here. Gotta buy us a Christmas tree and some furniture down to the shopping center. Just close up the house when you're done." Szafransky passed close to Judd, who wanted to run. He pinched Judd's chin in his red sausage fingers. Judd trembled. Szafransky cleared his throat. "Naw—not this time. You ain't even worth spittin' on, you know?" His wife got her coat and scarf. "You kids be good and don't touch the stove, hear? We'll be back direct." They walked down the driveway, past the furniture truck and the deputy's car. Judd heard laughter.

Judd began stripping the bed. Parts of the sheets stuck to the mattress, then ripped away. The odors made him dizzy, the heat and closeness, the essence of the Szafransky life. If all this afternoon's business had a meaning, it lay somehow in these sheets. But what it was, exactly, he didn't know. The deputy, smirking, stood beside him. He's here to protect them, Judd thought.

"The bed goes too, huh?" he asked. "Kid's beds too? I seen you watching the lady—wouldn't you just like to settle out of court, huh? Wouldn't you and the nigger like to knock off a piece of that, huh?"

Judd folded the sheets, so cold and damp, and dropped them with the pillows on the floor. "Maybe if I pulled a gun on Szafransky, so's you and the nigger could have a go at her, nice and safe and legal, huh?" There were spots on the mattress so dark that they looked like grease puddles. The buttons had all been sprung and the welt was pulling loose. The *use* it must have had!

"But then I guess it don't bother you none, does it, taking their bed right out from under them. I mean look at the mattress—it ain't worth a nickel now 'cept maybe for charging admission. What about it, boy—a nickel a sniff for all your friends? Whang off on it for a dollar?"

Delman came back and started knocking the bedframe down. He and the deputy exchanged man-of-the-world, interracial smiles at the state of the mattress. *Me too,* Judd wanted to shout, *don't you think I know? Don't you think I can imagine them at night, the two of them in the middle, on the sides, sitting, rocking, pumping, bucking . . .*

"You was giving her the eye too—I seen that," the deputy said as Delman carried the frames past him.

"Can't control myself with them tattooed women," he laughed back. "You catch that little blue star just above her elbow? Oooeee!"

Judd and Delman picked up the box spring and carried it out. Stuck to its underside were pairs of undershorts and dozens of clumps of pink tissue paper. Judd started to pry them off with his pen, but Delman stopped him. "Your daddy said he wanted everything, and by God I'm going to give it to him."

Each time they carried out a new article, Judd prepared himself for something violent. A rifle shot from the garage, Szafransky lunging with a butcher knife. Delman didn't seem at all concerned and he should know. Would Delman have fought, or even killed, under these same conditions? he wondered. What if some whites came to take his Italian Provincial bedroom suite? Or would Delman have repossessed from Negroes? Would Negroes have let him? And why such sudden acquiescence from a man like Szafransky? When can you predict? When can you take furniture from an unemployed hunter and walk out unharmed, and when is some sleepy gentle schoolteacher going to blow your head off? There was something so vulnerable in the testimony of Kleenex parachutes, that he wanted to return the furniture, to apologize, to buy Szafransky a suit of clothes and resurrect him—give him and Delman a job on the floor. To be twenty years old and still not have the answer to anything, to have no one to turn to except the Negro at your side whom you respect and fear, and who, you suspect, hates your guts. The whole world was winking behind his back.

He took a last look around. The deputy was standing near the children, pouring them cereal as they sprawled on the floor in front of the TV.

"We're going," said Judd.

"Checked the list?" he asked.

"Don't need to," said Delman. "Everything's ours except the appliances. Just need your initials, since the man cut out."

"Then you've done your damage. So why not get the hell out? I'll sign your paper and then I'll personally chase off the first one of you that ever tries to enter this house again."

Delman liked driving a full truck: the skill it required, the drag of something behind him—he especially liked being an obstacle on the inclines, grinding up the hills at ten miles an hour. He would have preferred doing it alone. He liked talking to himself, and now he had Junior in the cab and the boss's big ear and the boss's piece of tail hooked into his warehouse.

"Oooo-eeee, I tell you," he suddenly burst out, and if he had been alone he would have left it there, but with Junior he had to finish it. "That was something else."

Junior looked mad. Said nothing, held a book, but wasn't reading.

"You pissed off at something?"

"Just thinking."

"Want a beer?"

"I said I was just thinking."

"Just thinking," he repeated, tapping his forehead. "Give yourself a headache, all that thinking," he shouted over the racket. A metal-racket of an ancient engine straining against a governor, the uninsulated hood, the shaking, whining, ungreased metal. "You're on a vacation, man," he yelled. "You're going to Europe in four–five months, and you got a set-up going here that's always going to keep you in bread, and you're only twenty years old, man. What the hell you always thinking all the time for?"

And you're a white boy, Junior. Your old man picks up five hundred on a bad day, five thousand on a good one. I've seen him sell ten thousand dollars on a single afternoon. When Delman thought too hard of the boss and Junior, he thought of the Czar and all the little czarevitches, how they must have worried too. Always worrying about where to go and how to spend it. Then: *plunk-plunk-plunk*. Delman's fantasies hovered between being a Cossack and being a revolutionary soldier. He was in the Red Army today, no doubt about it, with his heart in the basement of Malick's Furniture or, better yet, in the warehouse where he'd made a room of his own for lunch and dinner. Father and Son, hands on paddle, kneeling. And for Mrs. Simmons—what? There must have been times when nothing was slow and ugly enough.

"What's that you're reading?"

Over the whining and clatter of gears, Judd began to speak, then to shout: "It's not what I'm reading. It's not just a single book. Reading this book is like going to the Szafranskys day after day—are you listening, Delman? Can you hear me over the motor? It's like confronting something purer than your own situation, you know? This book happens in Paris fifty years ago, but it's today, it's me, it's you. Delman, listen: Haven't you ever seen something so close that it frightened you—or disgusted you? So much so that you had to turn away from it, thankful that it wasn't your situation? Haven't you ever felt that at last you've seen something *final*, the end of something, some definitive corruption, only to return to your own little world and see that it's just slightly less pure, less corrupt, less crystalline? Only slightly? Haven't you? That's how I feel about myself and about the store. That's how I feel about those poor fucking people we took the furniture from. As though everything that I can understand is radiating out from this little book, embracing more and more things that I can't understand, and I want to look away from all of it. Delman"—and now he was shouting, slapping the dashboard so that Delman would at least look his way and quit smirking for just a second—"I feel like it's drowning me. I feel like we've all died a little bit today. Delman, do you understand?"

NOTES BEYOND A HISTORY

She lived on the same curve of the lake as we did, but in a stone cottage that was a good eighty years old and set far back, because Oshacola had not been tame in those days. She had not wanted to see the lake—what was it but an ocean of alligators, the breeder of chilling fevers? She didn't need the water. Her wealth, back then, had been a Valencia grove two miles square, planted in her youth. Yet all that remained, by the time we arrived, were the two hundred yards of twisted trees between her door and the matted beach. Cypress and live oak had replaced her untended citrus. From where she used to sit on her porch, I doubt that she had even seen the lake in thirty or forty years. Her name was Theodora Rourke and she was ninety-two. The year was 1932.

We were the second year-round residents on the lake, having built a fine Spanish-style home of tawny stucco in 1928, set about fifty yards from the beach with a rich Bermuda lawn reaching to the water in front and to the hedge at the side that separated us from Theodora Rourke. By '32 there were other residents, not yet neighbors, but none so well-established. It was still a risky five-mile drive into Hartley over sand trails given to flooding or sifting, and no one but my father trusted his car enough to drive in daily. When I say we were the second family most Hartleyans of today would be suprised; we've always been known as the leading family and one of the oldest. Theodora Rourke, however, was the first by such a gulf that a comparison with anyone else is absurd. I should divide the history of Oshacola County into "Modern Era" and "All Time" so that both the Rourkes and the Sutherlands could enjoy their prominence, like Cy Young and Early Wynn, with no one confusing the equivalence of the records they set. We were the first family of Lake Oshacola, then; the Rourkes had come with the place.

She was Catholic. That was important, for we had no admitted Catholics in Hartley, and since she was the lone example of an absent conspiracy, we were taught that everything strange about her must be typical of the faith. My mother—poor tormented woman—was a south Georgia disciple of Tom Watson, and what she told my brother Tom and me about Catholics (especially the Black Sisters, which Theodora must have been) was enough to keep us awake, sweating together under our sheets. Black Sisters walked in loose black robes, two at a time in the day, and then at night they shed their robes and took to flight on the black leathery wings their robes had hidden, invisible on moonless nights but for their white human faces and their cruel white teeth for sucking blood. My mother's full-time job, aside from raising Tom and me to love each other, Florida, F.D.R., and the Christ of her choice, was collecting the goods on Theodora Rourke. Who delivered food to her and her daughter? What shape of clothes were drying from the trees, what black people visited and were taken inside, and what language did they speak?

My father was a Hartley man with education; being that, he had been mayor three times, school teacher, principal, state senator, and judge. Thirty years ago in Florida that was omnipotence. He was an old father to Tom and me (his first wife had died and he remarried at fifty), and his bent walk, white suits, stoutness, and eclectic learning have forever merged wisdom with self-righteousness, justice with legality, and history with just a little priggishness. He left us a great gift, however: an assurance that we need never answer for anything he did. It freed me for my manhood, this history, as it did for Tom, and his rockets.

I have never stopped wondering what it was that made my brother a builder of rockets—Apollo moon probes—and left me here in Hartley, a teacher.

My office is air-conditioned, wrapped in tinted glass, eight floors up on the main quadrangle overlooking the lake. Eight floors more than commands the lake. Oshacola is beautifully landscaped now—a pond on some giant's greens. The city of Hartley and its suburbs are gleaming white among the smoky citrus groves. More smoke rises from the processing plants—the stench of orange pulp—and the Interstate slices west from here in an unbroken line to the Gulf. That haze that never lifts, way way to the west, it could be Tampa; fifty miles isn't far and if eight floors of perspective can do *this* to Oshacola, why shouldn't Tampa be creeping slowly to my front lawn?

Oshacola was always this small, I'm forced to admit, but never this humanized. I was smaller then, of course, and places are always remembered as larger and more unruly—but *why* precisely? I've only grown six inches in the past thirty-five years; why then does my memory insist on an Oshacola too broad to be seen across, on whitecaps that would swamp a weekend cruiser, on softshell turtles Tom and I could only drag with ropes, on clusters of snakes threshing mightily on Theodora Rourke's warm sand beach? Not only has the lake been civilized, but so has my memory, leaving only a memory of my memory as it was then. I'm not a shrewd man (and more than a little bit my father's son), but I have a probing memory and what I see with my eyes closed, books shut, was also true, also happened, and Oshacola was once that inland sea and the things in it and around it would startle an expert today, men like my colleagues on the first seven floors.

Hartley had a population of forty-three hundred in 1932, approximately three thousand of whom were white. My father knew them all. Hartley had one main street, and cars were still so rare that even a lost Yankee could make a U-turn in broad daylight with the sheriff looking on and chances were he wouldn't be stopped. We had a movie house open on Wednesday for Negroes and on the weekends for us. The buildings were mostly dark brick—those were the days before we learned we were in the tropics and should show off everything in pink and white.

A few weeks ago I went roaming through the old Main Street section and couldn't find much I remembered. It's now on the fringes of a Cuban and Negro ghetto, and there are a few used-car lots, *casas del alimiento*, laundromats, and *tavernas*. The real center now is east, creeping towards the complex at the Cape. A year or two from now the first Hartley outpost, a pizza stand most likely, may find itself on national television at blast-off time.

Hartley now is—I can't describe the difficulty of adding to that phrase—*bigger*. One hundred thousand white souls, ten thousand black, and seven thousand Cuban exiles. The power is still in local hands, the boys from my class at Hartley High, despite the eighty thousand Yankees now among us, and though they no longer wear white suits or practice oratory they've not improved on my father's generation. They're a measly, brainless lot, owned ear-high by the construction, citrus, and power companies. And not a one of these local boys has an accent or curries a drop of character. As the wisest of all wise men said, the more things change, the worse they remain. The reason of course is that *change* merely reflects the unacknowledged essence of things. That's what history is all about.

In 1932 I delivered a Jacksonville paper to the row of cabins that were strung along the beach road that ran past our back door. A bundle was delivered to the courthouse and my father would have a janitor take the pile to the drugstore, where I would pick it up after school. Then I'd ride home with my father, eat, and Tom and I would later carry them down the road by kerosene lamp. Sometimes, when it rained, we didn't deliver till the next morning.

Big Mama—Theodora Rourke—was ninety-two; her daughter Lillian was in her middle seventies. It was the daughter who sent me a note one day (it took four days to reach us by customary post though she lived but sixty yards away): *Please to have*

Boy commence the Paper for Big Mama and Me. L. Rourke (Miss).

My father handed it to me discreetly; it would never do for my mother to know I was trafficking with witches, visiting at night, and taking part of their hoarded treasures. The fear of personal contact actually did delay my collecting until after Christmas. Their two months' bill had hit a dollar and there was always the chance of a tip.

One day I showed up at the foot of the steps to Big Mama's back porch. I wasn't going to climb up or go inside.

"Paper boy, ma'm," I managed when the younger old woman answered the door. From the bottom of the stairs, she looked dark and immense.

"How much are it?" she asked.

"Ma'm?"

"Mind to me what I say."

"A dollar and a dime," I said, guessing what she wanted. She turned away, black behind the ancient screen, leaving me to wonder if I had asked for too much. Should she complain, I was willing to take a fifty-cent cut.

Then Big Mama appeared and shuffled to the door. Her daughter opened it and Big Mama started down towards me, her spotted brown hand trembling on the wooden railing. I took a step backwards, wanting somehow to accommodate her presence. She straightened up when she reached the bottom step and I noticed she didn't even challenge my chin. I was looking down on the oily, brownish-pink swath of her scalp, the clumps of cottony hair stuck amateurishly, it seemed, to its flesh. My mother had said the Black Sisters were bald as buzzards under their bonnets—she was right.

Then she looked at me. Her skin was tarnished and wrinkled on a thousand planes; her eyes simply colorless—not even the rheumy blue I had expected. Her nose seemed to have receded into her face and her jaw had almost melted away. It was a long time (it seems now an eternity that I looked into her face!) before I noticed she was holding her cold fist on my arm. I looked, and she opened it.

Her palm was pink, darkly lined. I'd never seen such coins as she held. Two round, golden ducats lay flat and heavy in her hand, like the hammered heads of copper spikes. She brought them closer and I took another step back; they were medals, I thought, charms to mesmerize me.

"You never seen these here things before, have you, boy?" she asked, looking behind me with those pale, opaque eyes.

"No, ma'm."

"Take aholt of them."

"No, ma'm."

She dropped them on the sand at my feet and I jumped back, half expecting them to leap at me, like snakes from Aaron's rod. The daughter, watching from the porch, laughed. "You skeered, boy?" she called down.

"You just owe me for the paper," I said.

"Boy, I done paid you for the rest of your life. Now pick up what I throwed. Them is genuine ten-dollar gold pieces—" she finished in midsentence, as though she had decided I was not worth the rest, and when she ceased talking, she seemed to shrink.

The pieces were half buried in the sand. I picked them up; they were cool, half coated with sand where her moist palm had held them. But wasn't it magic, I wondered, that both the coins had dug edge-first into the sand instead of landing flat? I was still cautious.

"Would you be wanting a bite of cake?" the daughter suggested suddenly. She held the screen door open. "You can have it on the porch."

"No, ma'm."

"Johnnycake?"

I climbed to the porch, then followed Big Mama inside, but not into the house. I could see into the parlor and it was filled unlike any room I have ever seen since, except perhaps an auction house. Paintings and photos lined the walls with a single desire to be displayed; the tables were piled with metal and porcelain objects that reflected the pale sunlight like the spires of a far-off, exotic city. How I wanted to step inside, and I might have, but for a gold cross centered above the sofa and its remarkable crucified Christ whose face was lifted in agony to the door where I was standing.

Around the Christ several paintings were hung and they now caught my eye, for even in the dullness they were vivid. Wildlife scenes, water colors or India ink on white stock. The artist had wisely allowed the white itself to animate the studies of birds, fish, and smaller game of Florida . . . not like the murky, quasi-fabulous things my father collected, the overworked paintings by those New England gentlemen in floppy straw hats who merely observed the shoreline from the deck chairs on St. Johns River steamers. . . . These fish and bird and otter's eyes seemed to stare into mine and follow as I glanced away. Their scales and pelts and feathers were eternally moist, eternally in the sun.

"I see you are coveting my daddy's paintings," Miss Lillian noticed as she handed me the plate of cake.

"They're right nice," I said. "They are the nicest things I've ever seen."

"He executed them in the winter of eighteen hundred and fifty-seven."

I ate the cake silently. Christ's head, it seemed, had nodded.

"You live just over yonder, don't you, boy? I seen you."

I picked up the last piece of cake and underneath it was a fine gold crucifix, the type a schoolgirl might wear on a light gold chain. I pressed the last crumbs into a wafer and let it drop back on the plate.

"Now you kiss the Lord, boy," the daughter commanded. "Put your lips on Him and tell Him you are sorry for all you done."

"No," I cried. "I ain't going to!"

"You have got to, else He will follow you. You have accepted the gift of His immortal body and so now you must be forgiven." She lifted the crucifix as though she might a dime, and thrust it in my face. I could see the faint outline of a Christ, head bowed, dripping blood, vague as an Indian head on an old penny. Had it been worn from so much kissing? The daughter held it now to her thick, puckered lips. Her eyes were closed and her lips were quivering with prayer, forming sounds I couldn't understand. Magic! And that was my only chance to get away before she could drain my blood into a cup. I don't think she opened her eyes until I slammed the door, but as I threw my-self into the brier hedge between our properties, I heard her crying out, "Remember, He's a-goin' to foller you. . . ."

> *Facts:* Theodora (?) parents unknown; birthplace (pre-sumed), Oshacola County, Florida, 1840 (c.). d. 1937.
> Bernard Rourke, b. C. Galway, Ireland, 1822. Arrived New York, 1838. Buffalo, 1839–44. Mexico and Califor-nia, 1845–52. New York, 1852–55. Sent to Florida on canal crew, 1856. Married Theodora (?), 1858. Cap-tain, CSA. State Senator, 1882–84. Judge, 1886–88. Died, Oshacola County, Florida, 1888.
> Children: (records incomplete, but births recorded):
> Lucretia (d. infancy, 1859).
> Lillian (1859–1946). Barren.
> Bernard, Jr. (1866–1902). Issue suspected; unknown.
> John Ryan (1870–1894). Issue suspected; unknown.

Theodora Rourke, parents and birthplace unknown, according to the records I'm at the moment responsible for. But I know where she came from, though my *History of Hartley* will never record it, and therein lies the rest of my story.

Her birthplace is in Oshacola County, probably now within the city limits of Hartley. I've often looked for the exact spot, but the traces of the old canal have been filled in and chewed over for at least twenty years. Perhaps from a helicopter I could spot it: something subtle in the pattern of streets, a patch of parkland primordially rich, a shack or two that no one thought of re-moving. But from a car all Hartley is the same.

A word, historically, on the old canal scheme. Some states are driven by dreams—gold, oil, timber, ore—but Florida (long be-fore the sun and oranges counted for much) was weaned on a dream of the Mighty Ditch. The maps show why: the St. Johns is wide and navigable from Jacksonville down; central Florida is blessed with a chain of deep, virtually continuous lakes, and there are a dozen accommodating estuaries on the Gulf side, the best perhaps at Tampa. To the early speculators it looked as though nature herself had merely lacked the will or Irish muscles to finish what she had so obviously begun. Cuba was Spanish, and the Keys were often treacherous—and a canal through Florida offered no natural or diplomatic barriers. A guaranteed safe passage between New York and New Orleans. Nature had never smiled so sweetly on the schemes of capital. Not only that, certain local politicians reasoned, the canal would be a natural divider between the productive and enlightened north of Florida and the swampy, pestiferous south. We could sell the rest to Spain, give it to the freedmen, or make it a federal prison—"What Siberia is to the Tsar of Imperial Russia," a local editor once wrote. A dozen companies had been involved in a thirty-year period, to effect the cut from Atlantic to Gulf, and at least a couple had sent crews down to dynamite the forest and butcher the indigenous tribes—all before Bernard Rourke's arrival in 1856. Theodora, we can assume, had been born some sixteen years earlier to an unmarried mother of unknown origins, and an Irish father similarly anonymous. By 1856 the heroic age of the canal was actually over; not many of the crew sent to Florida from New York ever saw the North again.

The summer of the year I had run from the Rourkes' stone cottage, I made a discovery that determined my life. My brother Tom, the builder of rockets, must have been affected too.

One morning in August we were fishing from the frogboat we had tied to our dock. A political fish-fry was coming up, so we were keeping everything edible: shellcrackers, warmouth, some channel cats, and dozens of bream. The boat was filling. We quit awhile and stuffed a burlap sack with fish, then tied it to the dock.

"Look!" Tom cried.

We saw a black, blunt tub rounding the arm of the cove, with a tall man in black robes poling furiously towards us. He was close to the shore, at poling depth, and we huddled behind the dock, afraid that he would see us. A man who would pole a frogboat like it was a canoe, in black robes, in August, from Lord knows where—terrifying! The visitor swung beyond us, not looking, and then put it on Rourke's scummy beach and made his way through the jungly orange grove to their cottage.

"The devil hisself," Tom whispered.

And he looked it—a dark leathery face, sideburns, black cape and white collar, and a white sleeve with ruffles showing under his robes. He even carried a little black bag. It was a priest, I told Tom, a Catholic priest.

He was inside about an hour. We heard no noises from the stone cottage, no shrieks, no moans. When the priest emerged, we noticed that he had taken off his hat and robes, and he proceeded to pole out into the lake in his ruffled white shirt, without a look backwards or to us. We had a better look at him this time. Tom shook my arm, but I was already nodding. The priest had Negro blood; which meant, we knew in a flash, that Big Mama did too.

We had to follow—I wonder *why* we did; Tom would say, as he does of the moon, because it's there—but how did we ever find the nerve? He was already rounding the cove, poling rhythmically. We only wanted to keep him in sight.

About a mile from our place, Buck's Cove got sealed in with lily pads. Beyond the pads a stagnant creek emptied in. We'd never explored it—the pads repulsed a boat like rubber, and the mosquitoes hummed above creek like a faraway power saw—but the priest was prying his way through the pads, into the mouth of the creek. We followed.

Cypress overhung the mossy water. In the shade, the water was brown, the color and tepidness of tea. Mosquitoes hummed. The water was the calmest I had ever seen, rich with moss and minnows. The ripples died so quickly we barely left a wake. I could feel the bass and turtles knocking against my pole, but I couldn't see six inches underneath the surface. There was no real shoreline, just a thicker and thicker tangle of cypress and floating mangroves, and the heat was increasing as all the breeze died down. Our breath came hard, but when we tried to catch it, we sucked in gnats. The sweat rolled off my nose and chin, and my arms were spotted with flies, drinking in the salt. I looked up and the priest was out of sight.

I poled half an hour, never catching him. The creek curved and branched, trees thinned and thickened, birds hooted and then were gone. There were pockets of breeze, then deadness; places where the water dimpled around my pole and pushed with a sudden current, and places where I felt I was sliding on a thicker surface. Then a consistent current came up, and the mosquitoes died down. The water was deeper. I thought we were coming to another lake.

Up ahead I spotted a bright yellow cloth draped from a cypress whose roots overhung the water. To the right of the marked tree there was a broad, open ditch that emptied into the creek at right angles to where we were. The ditch, about thirty feet wide, was lined with a high dike of mud and crushed limestone and stretched before us straight as an avenue. We took it.

It was deep, very deep; we couldn't pole, so I paddled. I told Tom I could *feel* the fish knocking against my paddle and knocking on the bottom of the boat just like someone was hammering. Bass were jumping all around us, and a few gar were floating in the middle.

"Somebody made this," said Tom.

But where did they come from, I was wondering. We shouldn't be here, I thought; my father told terrifying stories of Seminole bands, still wild on the hummocks, that had never signed a treaty. They stole white boys and fed them to their hunting gators.

"Reckon it's Indians made it?" he asked.

I kept paddling. Seminoles or something—I couldn't picture white men so deep in nature. *Maybe niggers,* I'd wanted to say to Tom, but my voice was gone.

"Look, smoke!" Tom cried. We smelled it as soon as we saw it, and it wasn't just a campfire; it was lumber mill smoke. *Jackpiners,* I thought with relief. The ditch was narrower, and beginning to curve.

There were voices, children's and women's, not far away. We couldn't make out anything, but we smiled.

"I'm getting me a coke as soon as we get down," said Tom.

"I'm getting me *two,*" I said.

The settlement was just ahead. *Work crew,* I thought as soon as I saw the gray shanty shapes behind the dike. Two boys, our age, were squatting in the water on either side of the dike, dragging a seine and netting our way. They were thin blondish boys and Tom laughed suddenly, for they weren't wearing a stitch of clothing. I waited for them to spot us but they didn't look up from the water. "Hey, y'all," I finally shouted, "what you call this place?"

They stood up slowly, still holding the corners of the seine. They didn't move towards us. I looked down at Tom and I saw his smile begin to sag, and his eyes grow wide and frightened. He held that look for several seconds, and then he began to retch. Then he screamed.

"There's something wrong with them," he cried, his voice high and quivering, "there's something wrong with them—they ain't . . . they ain't. . . ." The boys dropped the tips of their net and pinned it in the mud with sticks. They were as light as we were but not the way we were, and their hair was light but it wasn't blond, it was just colorless. And then I seemed to be looking into the opaque, colorless eyes of Big Mama, and into the bleeding side of Jesus, and I could hear Miss Lillian commanding me to kiss Him, *kiss Him*. . . . The boys' hair was fair and kinky, and we could see they weren't any whiter than the priest we'd been following. They were only lighter.

"Let's get out of here," Tom wailed, his voice already breaking. I started paddling backwards as the boys climbed their respective sides of the dike and approached us slowly from above.

I looked up one last time and saw far behind them a gold cross on top of a pink stucco building, then it dropped from view.

"Say something to them," Tom cried. He held the useless pole, ready to defend himself somehow. Then one of the boys let out a hoop. People came running.

We were reeling backwards now, as fast as I could paddle and Tom could slash. I tried to stay near the middle, but what good was it—ten feet on either side—when the rocks started flying?

"No!" Tom was screaming. "I didn't do nothing—quit it!" He was ten years old; he didn't know it wasn't, finally, a game. I knew, but I couldn't believe it was happening. He curled himself under the poling ledge where I was sitting.

Each rock, as it struck me, took my breath away before it started burning. Tom was praying, *dear God, get me home,* and

I paddled with one arm and then with both, dodging what I could, trying to protect my head. They didn't have rocks, nothing big, just limestone gravel, but I remembered the story of David and the picture I loved of Goliath with blood between his eyes. Once more I looked up, hoping they'd see how young I was, how frightened, but all I could see were swarms of children, all the color of dirty sand, and darker adults screaming down at me, "*Morte, morte!*" and others, "Kill, kill!" They followed us to the end of the ditch, to the cypress hung with yellow, and then there was no place for them to stand as the dike and dry land petered out. We were suddenly back on the creek and I fell to the bottom of the boat, crying. We drifted awhile, until the current died, and then I poled and Tom paddled the rest of the way home.

The records show no settlement of mixed-blood Catholics in Oshacola County in 1932, or at any other time. The parish records, begun in 1941 by Father Enrique Fernandez, of Tampa, show no significant Spanish or Creole population this far east of Tampa. Theodora Rourke and Lillian are both listed as "white" on their death certificates, as was Bernard, Jr. (John Ryan Rourke, who died in 1894, was apparently buried privately without any record being kept), and since Big Mama's estate later endowed a public park and Bernard Rourke's paintings hang in the State Galleries, there is no great enthusiasm in Hartley to investigate. Nor am I concerned about her genes in any quasi-legal sense—only historically. Theodora Rourke and her line are dead, unless the suspected issue of her sons Bernard and John could ever be traced; but she is one of many who have left scars on my body and opened a path that time has all but swallowed up. If my instincts are correct, her race degenerated into whiteness and melted back to Hartley, or Tampa, or anywhere a lost people congregate. And the two children who discovered them a few years too early, before the transformation was complete, they too are only wanderers.

A passage I once marked from a story of Henry James reads, ". . . the radiance of this broad fact had quenched the possible sidelights of reflection. . . ." I too am a partisan of the broad sweep, of mystery that sweetens as its sources grow deep and dim. I live in the dark, Tom in the light; I wonder, to return to the original question, if my experience that afternoon thirty-five years ago did not compel me to become an historian—and prevent me from becoming a good one. And made Tom, eyes skyward in St. Louis, indifferent to it all—the broad facts and the sidelights—and everything else around us crumbling into foolishness.

HOW I BECAME A JEW

Cincinnati, September 1950
"I don't suppose you've attended classes with the colored be-fore, have you, Gerald?" the principal inquired. He was a jockey-sized man whose dark face collapsed around a graying mustache. His name was DiCiccio.

"No, sir."

"You'll find quite a number in your classes here—" he gestured to the kids on the playground, and the Negroes among them seemed to multiply before my eyes. "My advice is not to expect any trouble and they won't give you any."

"We don't expect none from them," my mother said with great reserve, the emphasis falling slightly on the last word.

DiCiccio's eyes wandered over us, calculating but discreet. He was taking in my porkiness, my brushed blond hair, white shirt and new gabardines. And my Georgia accent.

"My boy is no troublemaker."

"I can see that, Mrs. Gordon."

"But I'm here to tell you—just let me hear of any trouble and I'm going straight off to the po-lice."

. And now DiCiccio's smile assessed her, as though to say *are you finished?* "That wouldn't be in Gerald's best interest, Mrs. Gordon. We have no serious discipline problems in the elementary school but even if we did, Mrs. Gordon, outside authorities are never the answer. Your boy has to live with them. Police are never a solution." He pronounced the word "pleece" and I wanted to laugh. "Even in the Junior High," he said, jerking his thumb in the direction of the black, prisonlike structure beyond the playground. "There are problems there." His voice was still far-off and I was smiling.

DiCiccio's elementary school was new: bright, low and long, with greenboards and yellow chalk, aluminum frames and blond, unblemished desks. My old school in Georgia, near Moultrie, had had a room for each grade up through the sixth. Here in Cincinnati the sixth grade itself had ten sections.

"And Gerald, *please* don't call me 'sir.' Don't call anyone that," the principal said with sudden urgency. "That's just asking for it. The kids might think you're trying to flatter the teacher or something."

"Well, I swan—" my mother began. "He learned respect for his elders and nobody is taking that respect away. Never."

"Look—" and now the principal leaned forward, growing smaller as he approached the desk, "I know how Southern schools work. I know 'sir' and 'ma'm.' I know they must have beaten it into you. But I'm trying to be honest, Mrs. Gordon. Your son has a lot of things going against him and I'm trying to help. This intelligence of his can only hurt him unless he learns how to use it. He's white—enough said. And I assume Gordon isn't a Jewish name, is it? Which brings up another thing, Mrs. Gordon. Take a look at those kids out there, the white ones. They look like little old men, don't they? Those are *Jews*, Gerald, and they're as different from the others as you are from the colored. They were born in Europe and they're living here with their grandparents—don't ask me why, it's a long story. Let's just say they're a little hard to play with. A little hard to like, O.K.?" Then he settled back and caught his breath.

"They're the Israelites!" I whispered, as though the Bible had come to life. Then I was led to class.

But the sixth grade was not a home for long; not for the spelling champ and fastest reader in Colquitt County, Georgia. They gave me tests, sent me to a university psychologist who tested my memory and gave me some codes to crack. Then I was advanced.

Seventh grade was in the old building: Leonard Sachs Junior High. A greenish statue of Abraham Lincoln stood behind black iron bars, pointing a finger to the drugstore across the street. The outside steps were pitted and sagging. The hallways were tawny above the khaki lockers, and clusters of dull yellow globes were bracketed to the walls, like torches in the catacombs. By instinct I preferred the used to the new, sticky wood to cold steel, and I would have felt comfortable on that first walk down the hall to my new class, but for the stench of furtive, unventilated cigarette smoke. The secretary led me past rooms with open doors; all the teachers were men. Many were shouting while the classes turned to whistle at the ringing *tap-tap* of the secretary's heels. Then she stopped in front of a closed door and rapped. The noise inside partially abated and finally a tall bald man with furry ears opened the door.

"This is Gerald Gordon, Mr. Terleski. He's a transfer from Georgia and they've skipped him up from sixth."

"They have, eh?" A few students near the door laughed. They were already pointing at me. "George, you said?"

"Gerald Gordon *from* Georgia," said the secretary.

"Georgia Gordon!" a Negro boy shouted. "Georgia Gordon. Sweet Georgia Gordon."

Terleski didn't turn. He took the folder from the girl and told me to find a seat. But the front boys in each row linked arms and wouldn't let me through. I walked to the window row and laid my books on the ledge. The door closed. Terleski sat at his desk and opened my file but didn't look up.

"Sweet Georgia," crooned the smallish, fair-skinned Negro nearest me. He brushed my notebook to the floor. I bent over and got a judo chop on the inside of my knees.

"Sweet Georgia, you get off the floor, hear?" A very fat, coal-black girl in a pink sweater was helping herself to paper from my three-ring binder. "Mr. Tee, Sweet Georgia taking a nap," she called.

He grumbled. I stood up. My white shirt and baggy gabardines were brown with dust.

"This boy is *not* named Sweet Georgia. He *is* named Gerald Gordon," said Terleski with welcome authority. "And I guess he's some kind of genius. They figured out he was too smart for the sixth grade. They gave him tests at the university and—listen to this—Gerald Gordon is a borderline genius."

A few whistled. Terleski looked up. "Isn't that *nice* for Gerald Gordon? What can we do to make you happy, Mr. Gordon?"

"Nothing, sir," I answered.

"Not a thing? Not an itsy-bitsy thing, sir?"

I shook my head, lowered it.

"Might we expect you to at least look at the rest of us? We wouldn't want to presume, but—"

"Sweet Georgia crying, Mr. Tee," giggled Pink Sweater.

"And he all dirty," added the frontseater. "How come you all dirty, Sweet Georgia-man?" Pink Sweater was awarding my paper to all her friends.

"Come to the desk, Mr. Gordon."

I shuffled forward, holding my books over the dust smears.

"Face your classmates, sir. Look at them. Do you see any borderline types out there? Any friends?"

I sniffled loudly. My throat ached. There were some whites, half a dozen or so grinning in the middle of the room. I looked for girls and saw two white ones. Deep in the rear sat some enormous Negroes, their boots looming in the aisle. They looked at the ceiling and didn't even bother to whisper as they talked. They wore pastel T-shirts with cigarette packs twisted in the shoulder. And—God!—I thought, they had mustaches. Terleski repeated his question, and for the first time in my life I knew that whatever answer I gave would be wrong.

"*Mr. Gordon's reading comprehension is equal to the average college freshman.* Oh, Mr. Gordon, just *average?* Surely there must be some mistake."

I started crying, tried to hold it back, couldn't, and bawled. I remembered the rows of gold stars beside my name back in

Colquitt County, Georgia, and the times I had helped the teacher by grading my fellow students.

A few others picked up my crying: high-pitched blubbering from all corners. Terleski stood, scratched his ear, then screamed: "Shut up!" A rumbling monotone persisted from the Negro rear. Terleski handed me his handkerchief and said, "Wipe your face." Then he said to the class: "I'm going to let our borderline genius himself continue. Read this, sir, just like an average college freshman." He passed me my file.

I put it down and knuckled my eyes violently. They watched me hungrily, laughing at everything. Terleski poked my ribs with the corner of the file. "Read!"

I caught my breath with a long, loud shudder.

"Gerald Gordon certainly possesses the necessary intellectual equipment to handle work on a seventh grade level, and long consultations with the boy indicate a commensurate emotional maturity. No problem anticipated in adjusting to a new environment."

"Beautiful," Terleski announced. "Beautiful. He's in the room five minutes and he's crying like a baby. Spends his first three minutes on the floor getting dirty, needs a hanky from the teacher to wipe his nose, and he has the whole class laughing at him and calling him names. Beautiful. That's what I call real maturity. Is that all the report says, sir?"

"Yes, sir."

"You're lying, Mr. Gordon. That's not very mature. Tell the class what else it says."

"I don't want to, sir."

"You don't want to. *I* want you to. *Read!*"

"It says: '*I doubt only the ability of the Cincinnati Public Schools to supply a worthy teacher.*'"

"*Well*—that's what we wanted to hear, Mr. Gordon. Do you doubt it?"

"No, sir."

"Am I worthy enough to teach you?"

"Yes, sir."

"What do I teach?"

"I don't know, sir."

"What have you learned already?"

"Nothing yet, sir."

"What's the capital of the Virgin Islands?"

"Charlotte Amalie," I said.

That surprised him, but he didn't show it for long. "Then I can't teach you a thing, can I, Mr. Gordon? You must know everything there is to know. You must have all your merit badges. So it looks like we're going to waste each other's time, doesn't it? Tell the class where Van Diemen's Land is."

"That's the old name for Tasmania, sir. Australia, capital is Hobart."

"If it's Australia that would make the capital Canberra, wouldn't it, Mr. Gordon?"

"For the whole country, yes, sir."

"So there's still something for you to learn, isn't there, Mr. Gordon?"

The kids in the front started to boo. "Make room for him back there," the teacher said, pointing to the middle. "And *now*, maybe the rest of you can tell me the states that border on Ohio. Does *anything* border on Ohio?"

No one answered while I waved my hand. I cared desperately that my classmates learn where Ohio was. And finally, ignoring me, Mr. Terleski told them.

Recess: on the sticky pavement in sight of Lincoln's statue. The windows of the first two floors were screened and softball was the sport. The white kids in the gym class wore institutional shorts; the other half—the Negroes—kept their jeans and T-shirts since they weren't allowed in the dressing room. I was still in my dusty new clothes. We all clustered around the gym teacher, who wore a Cincinnati Redlegs cap. He appointed two captains, both white. "Keep track of the score, fellas. And tell me after how you do at the plate individually." He blew his whistle and scampered off to supervise a basketball game around the corner.

The captains were Arno Kolko and Wilfrid Skurow, both fat and pale, with heavy eyebrows and thick hair climbing down their necks and up from their shirts. Hair like that—I couldn't believe it. I was twelve, and had been too ashamed to undress in the locker room. These must be Jews, I told myself. The other whites were shorter than the captains. They wore glasses and had bristly hair. Many of them shaved. Their arms were pale and veined. I moved towards them.

"Where *you* going, boy?" came a high-pitched but adult voice behind me. I turned and faced a six-foot Negro who was biting an unlit cigarette. He had a mustache and, up high on his yellow biceps, a flag tattoo. "Ain't nobody picked you?"

"No," I hesitated, not knowing if I were agreeing or answering.

"Then stay where you're at. Hey—y'all want him?"

Skurow snickered. I had been accustomed to being a low-priority pick back in ball-playing Colquitt County, Georgia. I started to walk away.

"Come back here, boy. Squirrel picking you."

"But you're not a captain."

"Somebody *say* I ain't a captain?" The other Negroes had fanned out under small clouds of blue smoke and started basketball games on the painted courts. "That leaves me and you," said Squirrel. "We standing them."

"I want to be with them," I protested.

"We don't want you," said one of the Jews.

The kid who said it was holding the bat cross-handed as he took some practice swings. I had at least played a bit of softball back in Colquitt County, Georgia. The kids in my old neighborhood had built a diamond near a housing development after a bulldozer operator had cleared the lot for us during his lunch hour. Some of the carpenters had given us timber scrap for a fence and *twice*—I remember the feeling precisely to this day— I had lofted fly balls tightly down the line and over the fence. No question, my superiority to the Arno Kolkos of this world.

"We get first ups," said Squirrel. "All *you* gotta do, boy, is get yourself on base and then move your ass fast enough to get home on anything I hit. And if I don't hit a home run, you gotta bring me home next."

"Easy," said I.

First three times up, it worked. I got on and Squirrel blasted on one hop to the farthest corner of the playground. But he ran the bases in a flash, five or six strides between the bases, and I was getting numb in the knees from staying ahead even with a two-base lead. Finally, I popped up for an out. Then Squirrel laid down a bunt and made it to third on some loose play. I popped out again and had to take his place on third, anticipating a stroll home on his next home run. But he bunted again, directly at Skurow the pitcher, who beat me home for a force-out to end the inning.

"Oh, you're a great one, Sweet Georgia," Squirrel snarled from a position at deep short. He was still biting his unlit cigarette. "You're a plenty heavy hitter, man. Where you learn to hit like that?"

"Georgia," I said, slightly embarrassed for my state.

"Georgia? *Joe-ja?*" He lit his cigarette and tossed me the ball. "Then I guess you're the worst baseball player in the whole state, Sweet Georgia. I *thought* you was different."

"From what?"

"From them." He pointed to our opponents. They were talking to themselves in a different language. I felt the power of a home-run swing lighten my arms, but it was too late.

"I play here," said Squirrel. "Pitch them slow then run to first. Ain't none of them can beat my peg or get it by me."

A kid named Izzie, first up, bounced to me and I tagged him. Then a scrawny kid lifted a goodly fly to left—the kind I had hit for doubles—but Squirrel was waiting for it. Then Wilfrid Skurow lumbered up: the most menacing kid I'd ever seen. Hair in swirls on his neck and throat, sprouting wildly from his chest and shoulders. Sideburns, but getting bald. Glasses so thick his eyeballs looked screwed in. But no form. He lunged a chopper to Squirrel, who scooped it and waited for me to cover first. Skurow was halfway down the line, then quit. Squirrel stood straight, tossed his cigarette away, reared back, and fired the ball with everything he had. I heard it leave his hand, then didn't move till it struck my hand and deflected to my skull, over the left eye. I was knocked backwards, and couldn't get up. Skurow circled the bases; Squirrel sat at third and laughed. Then the Jews walked off together and I could feel my forehead tightening into a lump. I tried to stand, but instead grew dizzy and suddenly remembered Colquitt County. I sat alone until the bells rang and the grounds were empty.

Every Saturday near Moultrie, I had gone to the movies. In the balcony they let the colored kids in just for Saturday. Old ones came Wednesday night for Jim Crow melodramas with colored actors. But we came especially equipped for those Saturday mornings when the colored kids sat in the dark up in the balcony, making noise whenever we did. We waited for too much noise, or a popcorn box that might be dropped on us. Then we reached into our pockets and pulled out our broken yo-yos. We always kept our broken ones around. Half a yo-yo is great for sailing since it curves and doesn't lose speed. And it's very hard. So we stood, aimed for the projection beam, and fired the yo-yos upstairs. They loomed on the screen like bats, filled the air like bombs. Some hit metal, others the floor, but some struck home judging from the yelps of the colored kids and their howling. Minutes later the lights went on upstairs and we heard the ushers ordering them out.

A second bell rang.

"That burr-head nigger son-of-a-bitch," I cried. "That goddamn nigger." I picked myself up and ran inside.

I was late for geometry but my transfer card excused me. When I opened the door two Negro girls dashed out pursued by two boys about twice my size. One of the girls was Pink Sweater, who ducked inside a girls' room. The boys waited outside. The windows in the geometry room were open, and a few boys were sailing paper planes over the street and sidewalk. The teacher was addressing himself to a small group of students who sat in a semicircle around his desk. He was thin and red-cheeked with a stiff pelt of curly hair.

"I say, do come in, won't you? That's a nasty lump you've got there. Has it been seen to?"

"Sir?"

"Over your eye. Surely you're aware of it. It's really quite unsightly."

"I'm supposed to give you this—" I presented the slip for his signing.

"Gerald Gordon, is it? Spiro here."

"Where?"

"Here—I'm Spiro. Geoffrey Spiro, on exchange. And you?"

"Me what?"

"Where are you from?"

"Colquitt County, Georgia."

He smiled as though he knew the place well and liked it. "That's South, aye? Ex-cellent. Let us say for tomorrow you'll prepare a talk on Georgia—brief topical remarks, race, standard of living, labor unrest and what not. Hit the high points, won't you, old man? Now then, class"—he raised his voice only slightly, not enough to disturb the colored boys making *ack-ack* sounds at pedestrians below—"I should like to introduce to you Mr. Gerald Gordon. You have your choice, sir, of joining these students in the front and earning an 'A' grade, or going back there and getting a 'B,' provided of course you don't leave the room."

"I guess I'll stay up here, sir," I said.

"Ex-cellent. Your fellow students, then, from left to right are: Mr. Lefkowitz, Miss Annaliese Graff, Miss Marlene Leopold, Mr. Willie Goldberg, Mr. Irwin Roth, and Mr. Harry Frazier. In the back, Mr. Morris Gordon (no relative, I trust), Miss Etta Bluestone, Mr. Orville Goldberg (he's Willie's twin), and Mr. Henry Moore. Please be seated."

Henry Moore was colored, as were the Goldberg twins, Orville and Wilbur. The girls, Annaliese, Marlene, and Etta, were pretty and astonishingly mature, as ripe in their way as Wilfrid Skurow in his. Harry Frazier was a straw-haired athletic sort, eating a sandwich. The lone chair was next to Henry Moore, who was fat and smiled and had no mustache or tattoo. I took the geometry book from my scuffed, zippered notebook.

"The truth is," Mr. Spiro began, "that both Neville Chamberlain and Mr. Roosevelt were fascist, and quite in sympathy with Hitler's anticommunist ends, if they quibbled on his means. His evil was mere overzealousness. Public opinion in the so-called democracies could never have mustered against *any* anticommunist, whatever his program—short of invasion, of course. *Klar?*"

He stopped in order to fish out a book of matches for Annaliese, who was tapping a cigarette on her desk.

"*Stimmt?*" he asked, and the class nodded. Harry Frazier wadded his waxed paper and threw it back to one of his classmates by the window, shouting, "Russian MIG!" I paged through the text, looking for diagrams. No one else had a book out and my activity seemed to annoy them.

"So in conclusion, Hitler was merely the tool of a larger fascist conspiracy, encouraged by England and the United States. What *is* it, Gerald?"

"Sir—what are we talking about?" I was getting a headache, and the egg on my brow seemed ready to burst. The inner semi-circle stared back at me, except for Harry Frazier.

"Sh!" whispered Morris Gordon.

"At *shul* they don't teach it like that," said Irwin Roth, who had a bald spot from where I sat. "In *shul* they say it happened because God was punishing us for falling away. He was testing us. They don't say nothing from the English and the Americans. They don't even say nothing from the Germans."

"Because we didn't learn our letters good," said Morris Gordon. The matches were passed from the girls to all the boys who needed them.

"*What* happened?" I whispered to Henry Moore, who was smiling and nodding as though he knew.

"Them *Jews*, man. Ain't it great?"

"Then the rabbi is handing you the same bloody bullshit they've been handing out since I went to *shul*—ever since the bloody Diaspora," Spiro said. "God, how I detest it."

"What's *shul*, Henry? What's the Diaspora?"

"Look," Spiro continued, now a little more calmly, "there's only one place in the world where they're building socialism, really honestly *building* it"—his hands formed a rigid rectangle over the desk—"and that's Israel. I've seen children your age who've never handled money. I've played football on turf that was desert a year before. The desert blooms, and the children sing and dance and shoot—yes, shoot—superbly. They're all brothers and sisters, and they belong equally to every parent in the *kibbutz*. They'd die for one another. No fighting, no name-calling, no sickness. They're big, straight and strong and tall, and handsome, like the Israelites. I've seen it for myself. Why any Jew would come to America is beyond me, unless he wants to be spat on and corrupted."

"*Gott*, if the rabbi knew what goes on here," said Roth, slapping his forehead.

"What's a rabbi, Henry? *Tell me what a rabbi is!*"

"What*ever* is your problem, Gerald?" Spiro cut in.

"Sir—I've lost the place. I just skipped the sixth grade and maybe that's where we learned it all. I don't understand what you-all are saying."

"I must say I speak a rather good English," said Spiro. The class laughed. "Perhaps you'd be happier with the others by the window. All that *rat-tat-tat* seems like jolly good fun, quite a lift, I imagine. It's all perfectly straightforward here. It's *your* country we're talking about, after all. Not mine. Not theirs."

"It's not the same thing up North," I said.

"No, I daresay . . . look, why don't you toddle down to the nurse's office and get something for your head? That's a good lad, and you show up tomorrow if you're feeling better and tell us all about Georgia. Then I'll explain the things you don't know. You just think over what I've said, O.K.?"

I was feeling dizzy—the bump, the smoke—my head throbbed, and my new school clothes were filthy. I brushed myself hard and went into the boys' room to comb my hair, but two large Negroes sitting on the window ledge, stripped to their shorts and smoking cigars, chased me out.

Downstairs, the nurse bawled me out for coming in dirty, then put an ice pack over my eye.

"Can I go home?" I asked.

The nurse was old and fat, and wore hexagonal Ben Franklin glasses. After half an hour she put an adhesive patch on and since only twenty minutes were left, she let me go.

I stopped for a coke at the drugstore across from Lincoln's statue. Surprising, I thought, the number of school kids already out, smoking and having cokes. I waited in the drugstore until the sidewalk was jammed with the legitimately dismissed, afraid that some truant officer might question my early release. I panicked as I passed the cigar counter on my way out, for Mr. Terleski was buying cigarettes and a paper. I was embarrassed for him, catching him smoking, but he saw me, smiled, and walked over.

"Hello, son," he said, "what happened to the head?"

"Nothing," I said, "sir."

"About this morning—I want you to know there was nothing personal in anything I said. Do you believe me?"

"Yes, sir."

"If I didn't do it in *my* way first, they'd do it in their way and it wouldn't be pretty. And Gerald—don't raise your hand again, O.K.?"

"All right," I said. "Good-by."

"*Very* good," said Mr. Terleski. "Nothing else? No *sir?*"

"I don't think so," I said.

The street to our apartment was lined with shops: tailors with dirty windows, cigar stores piled with magazines, some reading rooms where bearded old men were talking, and a tiny branch of a supermarket chain. Everywhere there were school kids: Jews, I could tell from their heads. Two blocks away, just a few feet before our apartment block, about a dozen kids turned into the dingy yard of the synagogue. An old man shut the gates in a hurry just as I stopped to look in, and another old man opened the main door to let them inside. The tall spiked fence was painted a glossy black. I could see the kids grabbing black silk caps from a cardboard box, then going downstairs. The old gatekeeper, a man with bad breath and puffy skin, ordered me to go.

At home, my mother was preparing dinner for a guest and she was in no mood to question how I got the bump on the head. The guest was Grady, also from Moultrie, a whip-thin red-faced man in his forties who had been the first of my father's friends to go North. He had convinced my father. His wife and kids were back in Georgia selling their house, so he was eating Georgia food with us till she came back. Grady was the man we had to thank, my father always said.

"Me and the missus is moving again soon's she gets back," he announced at dinner. "Had enough of it here."

"Back to Georgia?" my father asked.

"Naw, Billy, out of Cincinnati. Gonna find me a place somewheres in Kentucky. Come in to work every day and go back at night and live like a white man. A man can forget he's white in Cincinnati."

"Ain't that the truth," said my mother.

"How many niggers you got in your room at school, Jerry?" Grady asked me.

"That depends on the class," I said. "In geometry there aren't any hardly."

"See?" said Grady. "You know five years ago there wasn't hardly no more than ten per cent in that school? Now it's sixty and still going up. By the time your'n gets through he's gonna be the onliest white boy in the school."

"He'll be gone before *that*," my father promised. "I been thinking of moving to Kentucky myself."

"Really?" said my mother.

"I ain't even been to a baseball game since they got that nigger," Grady boasted, "and I ain't ever going. I used to love it."

"You're telling me," said my father.

"If they just paid me half in Georgia what they paid me here, I'd be on the first train back," said Grady. "Sometimes I reckon it's the devil himself just tempting me."

"I heard of kids today that live real good and don't even see any money," I said. "Learned it in school."

"That where you learned to stand in front of a softball bat?" my mother retorted, and my parents laughed. Grady coughed.

"And let me tell you," he began, "them kids that goes to them mixed schools gets plenty loony ideas. That thing he just said sounded comminist to me. Yes, sir, that was a Comminist Party member told him that. I don't think no kid of mine could get away with a lie like that in my house. No, sir, they got to learn the truth sometime, and after they do, the rest is lies."

Then Father slapped the fork from my hands. "Get back to your room," he shouted. "You don't get no more dinner till I see your homework done!" He stood behind me, with his hand digging into my shoulder. "Now say good night to Grady."

"Good night," I mumbled.

"Good night *what?*" my mother demanded. "Good night *what?*"

"Sir," I cried, "sir, sir, sir! Good night, sir!" the last word almost screamed from the hall in front of my bedroom. I slammed the door and fell on the bed in the darkened room. Outside, I could hear the threats and my mother's apologies. "Don't hit him too hard, Billy, he done got that knot on the head already." But no one came.

They started talking of Georgia, and they forgot the hours. I thought of my first school day up North—then planned the second, the third—and I thought of Leonard Sachs Junior High, Squirrel, and the Jews. The Moultrie my parents and Grady were talking about seemed less real, then finally, terrifying. I pictured myself in the darkened balcony under a rain of yo-yos, thrown by a crowd of Squirrels.

I concentrated on the place I wanted to live. There was an enormous baseball stadium where I could hit home runs down the line; Annaliese Graff was in the stands and Mr. Terleski was a coach. We wore little black caps, even Squirrel, and there were black bars outside the park where old men were turning people away. Grady was refused, and Spiro and millions of others, even my parents—though I begged their admission. *No, stimmt?* We were building socialism and we had no parents and we did a lot of singing and dancing (even Henry Moore, even the chocolatey Goldberg twins, Orville and Wilbur) and Annaliese Graff without her cigarettes asked me the capitals of obscure countries. "Israel," I said aloud, letting it buzz; "Israel," and it replaced Mozambique as my favorite word; *Israel, Israel, Israel,* and the dread of the days to come lifted, the days I would learn once and for all if Israel could be really real.

THE MARCH

My story is bound, in time and place, to the spring and summer of 1963, to a quadrant of North America that knows no borders, and to a mood that has vanished as surely as the spring snows of a dozen years ago. A determinist romance where transcendence lives a microsecond before it dims into nothing new. I am moved by that in art, in life; by the slow revelation of a larger design, the way we live one detail at a time and never know the depth and the extent—the meaning—of what we have made. Every life a universe unrevealed, as well as a simple, repetitive design. I am more patient with design now than I was ten years ago.

In the spring of 1963, Linda Feldman and I and two other couples shared an unheated frame house on Bank Street in Cambridge. Nick, Pete, and Pierre: three Harvard boys. Linda, Lois, and Penny: two B.U. girls and a Wheaton dropout. Three buddies from the same wing of the same freshman dorm; public high school boys who'd shown up that first September in greasy hair, starched white shirts, and undertaker suits with National Honor Society pins in the lapels. I'd been born with starch in my shirts. "Casual" had been the style to strive for, back in September 1959: Princeton haircuts, chino khakis, button-down collars, and Madras jackets. I'd never been casual a day in my life. Neither had Nick or Pete. It was natural, when we'd all found girls three years later, that we'd think of saving money by living together.

By the spring of 1963, the six of us were at each others' throats. Small talk outside the bathroom door at the same urgent moment every morning, then silence as we dumped five spoonfuls of instant coffee and Linda's tea bag in the same six mugs. Every morning we polished off eight "assorted" Danish, bought the night before. Nick and I took the seconds. I think we fought because we'd never adjusted to Harvard casualness. There was something in us that didn't take easily to that cool, natural Harvard sex. Deep down we were guilty. We should have been married, or at least living alone in a cheap Somerville apartment that would make us feel more married. And we were loyal to the memory of our old freshman friendship. Loyalty to my memories —an addiction.

We hated each others' women. Nick and Pete despised Linda. Linda hated Penny, who was an almost striking blonde but for a permanent crescent of pimples around her mouth. Linda was sturdier, chestnut-haired, her beauty was harder to define. She thought Nick was a racist. That was the worst thing she could think of anyone. I defended him for most of the winter—"He's a Chicago Greek. That's just the way he talks"—but I couldn't fool myself all the time: he was a racist. The Greeks I'd known in Manchester had all been like him—tough, sullen, smart . . . and racist, especially hard on Frogs like me. He'd never forgiven Linda for her involvement in civil rights, for lending the house key to certain friends from the neighborhood CORE. Then there was Pete's Lois: a Boston version of the Sicilian wife. Mousy and worshipful—our uncomplaining dishwasher. All this Pete attributed to his legendary potency. His potency was attributed to her raw, animal lust. Those first few mornings, when we'd all been friendly, he used to joke at breakfast, "Hope she didn't wake you up last night, Christ—!" and Lois would redden, Linda and I would quickly munch a Danish. By then we'd signed the lease.

The immediate cause of the final flare-up was a CORE worker

from Alabama who happened to be taking a shower one afternoon in April when Penny returned from shopping. She was putting things away when he came out. The poor man bolted himself back inside, begging for his clothes, but Penny had already
fled the house, screaming. On the third morning after, following two days of the blackest rage, just as Linda was reaching for
her accustomed pineapple Danish, Nick's eyes suddenly bulged
and he rushed from his chair and slammed her hand into the pastries, shouting: "Don't you ever bring another Spade into this
house when Penny's here alone!" Linda was dressed for her
teaching job—hair up, earrings on, wool suit and sweater—and
the sticky hand assaulted her dignity. With a smile to Penny
and a sneer to Nick (she must be a hell of a good teacher, I decided just then, even as I rushed to protect her), she slowly
licked her fingers and took a second Danish. Softly and sweetly,
lips puckering to a Penny-like pout, she said, "Fuck off, Nicky-
Pooh." I was standing between them, but Nick only whirled
and slammed the wall. Penny whined, between sobs, "You dis-
gusting bitch!" *Nicky-Pooh* was one of her names that we'd
overheard. And that was our final big scene. What else to do for
the next two months but lick our fingers, light cigarettes off the
gas burner, and try to keep up appearances until graduation?
Fortunately, we were very good at that.

I'd been trained in urban development, and my adviser, who
believed in roots, had set me an Honors Thesis topic of "Ten
Years of Development, Manchester, New Hampshire: 1890–
1900." So I spent a good part of my senior year commuting between sullen Bank Street and my parents' place in a dingy suburb of Manchester called Pinardville. I passed hundreds of
hours in the Hillsborough County Records Office going over
titles, transfers, and town council meetings of a full lifetime before. I read the preserved inanities of men whose names had
been handed down to us as parks, schools, and avenues; towards
the end of my studies I began to see the things that I couldn't
put into an Honors Thesis because they bore only on myself:
how generations of other semiskilled French Canadians from
basseville Quebec City had made my father's coming to Man-

chester inevitable; how nothing we had ever believed and no place that we had ever lived had truly been our choice. I knew nothing of America; I'd been kept out. I felt like a Dreiser, bitter in the pity of my understanding. If one high school counselor had not seen in me the image of his own wasted life and steered me on to Harvard (they were starting to look for mold-breakers like me, and Pete and Nick, even before it became too fashionable), I would have gone under like all my high school friends, married a week after graduation and stuck on a construction crew, with luck; three kids deep and far-gone in beer, all by the time I'd met Linda. I'd even had my chance. For one eventful high school year I'd fallen into a regular back-seat, country-road, borrowed-cabin entanglement with the matrimonially inclined Helen (later "Hooker") Lessard, her plans ruptured only by my announced departure for Harvard. My old classmates avoided me now in the South Elm bars where I'd have a beer or two while sorting my courthouse notes, waiting for the bus back to Boston.

After Helen, who was pliable and tiny, the women in my life have all been big: Linda was almost sculpted. Large but proportionate; not pretty, but sensual. Maybe she'd once been homely, later she'd be handsome, then still later striking, finally distinguished. You'd never use frilly words to describe anything about her. Some of those manor-born Harvard types, the ones who'd gone to prep schools and who carried those top-heavy last-name first names—the Baxters and Townsends—would appraise her and nod, "I like your woman, Pierre. She's fine."

She was a Boston girl who'd traveled. Norway on a high school year abroad. Israel for two summers. Junior year at a teacher's training college in Peru. And to my New England-sized imagination she was even more worldly than that—she'd lived ten years in Los Angeles before moving back to Boston. For me, California might as well have been Peking; I'd never been west of Valley Forge, courtesy of a high school field trip. And while I stewed over the choice of a future—grad school, Army, government service, Peace Corps, even going back to Québec where I'd been born to see if any part of me had been left behind—Linda had already made up her mind. She'd be off the day after she graded her final batch of high school Spanish papers, for a CORE project in Alabama. I knew I wouldn't be joining her.

That's how I had first noticed her: the girl in the CORE office at the front desk every weekend, hair hanging loose, sipping tea from a stained plastic mug, wearing a bulky B.U. sweatshirt that for all its thickness seemed to let in the light. Her smile was forthright and compassionate. I'd been sucked off the street to sign a petition. I didn't have a Harvard face—nose too long and a little bent, jug ears, a stubby body that obviously had never held a tennis racket—so she'd noticed me and been extra pleased. We started arguing mildly there in the CORE office, and it got louder at "Elsie's" over those thick roast beef sandwiches. The opening notes in our political concerto:

"What right do *I* have to go to another state to bring about change, however desirable?"

Oh, yeah? Her pugnacious mouth, the chestnut hair that softened its lines, the softer lines of that maddening sweatshirt: I'd never wanted anything removed, quite so badly. "How can *I* vote in Massachusetts if other Americans can't vote in Alabama?"

"All the more reason to vote wisely in Massachusetts."

"So—I've finally met someone who *admits* he doesn't like outside agitators." Then she asked with deliberate sweetness (her face saying *I want to make sure I get this straight*), "or is it just Negroes you don't like?"

It wasn't a question; she was waiting for a chance to slap my face and walk away. I always had that fear, even after she'd moved in with me. I'd be away in Manchester three days a week and I'd come back late to Bank Street and sneak up to the room, expecting to find a note on the door telling me she wasn't happy, hadn't ever been happy, and was running away with one of the CORE workers. But no, I'd find her things scattered about, or find her in the CORE office where she liked to grade her papers, and I'd feel a rush of desire for everything about her. I'd remember the thrill of having removed that sweatshirt for the first time. She took in everything with maximum seriousness, like a psychoanalyst, and being taken seriously made me uncomfortable. Back on that first day in "Elsie's," I hadn't known how to handle myself. I hadn't wanted to argue; I'd wanted to sit back and simply admire her. Probably I didn't mind agitators at all—it was outsiders I couldn't take. But that sounded too extreme. And since I wasn't too many years away from suspecting that Californians took nourishment through their toes, I had no right to dispute the corollary to all she'd been saying:

"Because, listen, mister, I'm an American and nowhere in this country is outside to me. I don't care if I've got Jesus Christ himself to vote for in Massachusetts—"

(*Fat chance,* I started to break in, *considering the Democratic primary,* but she was ferociously earnest, and I knew she'd take it badly.)

"—when other Americans don't even have a vote, let alone a choice."

We sparred a bit, there was no coming together. Thoreau on the brain, I thought. Had she seen Walden Pond lately? But she hadn't been reading. She'd barely read a thing. She was even more blindly ignorant than Penny, because Linda on principle hated books. She'd worked her way back to first beliefs the hard way. I was moved. I'd come from Manchester—*Union-Leader* country—it had been years since anyone in my hearing had followed a proud proclamation of citizenship with anything else than a threat or a boast. I cringed at the thought of changing the South. I didn't want its essence changed any more than I wanted Boston to become Chicago. I liked the pettiness of Boston, its rancid politics, I liked the whole ignorant small-mindedness of New England. I suppose that deep down I liked having remnants of an older vision still alive in the United States; it reminded me of Québec.

"Would you come South?" she asked.

"You mean *go* South? I've never been south of Philadelphia. Why should I?"

"Don't worry, they can see you're white—"

"Look. If I were a Southern white I hope I would have courage enough to be in a demonstration. And if I were a Southern white who didn't have courage, I hope I would move away. That's the best I can do." It sounded pretty cowardly, even to me. I really didn't know if I had the guts or not; it didn't seem

profitable to speculate. She was such a noble Yankee she made
me feel compromised and latently racist, merely discussing it.
She charged; I confessed.

"Personally," I said, "I don't think there's that great a need
for me anywhere—"

"What do you mean? We need everyone—"

I heard a slight accent creeping into my voice, the old Stage
Frog we'd done to death in Pinardville High. And I detected the
slightest weakness in her position. "The thing that amazes me
most about (*yes, say it,* I thought) *yewmericans* is how bloody
sure you are of always being needed and wanted wherever your
superior morality takes you. And if you want to know my name,
it's Pierre." I gave just that twist of authenticity. "Now tell me
who you are and quit acting so goddamned noble."

A stricken look passed over her face, like a proud and blame-
less Catholic informed of a new and serpentine form of sin. "My
name is Linda Feldman," she said. Then she began repeating,
"Pee-yair," like the name of a surprisingly good, unknown wine.
Peeyair: it was the first time my name alone had won an argument. She looked so mortified I wanted to console her.

"That's French, isn't it?"

My God. "Canadian," I said.

"I thought they spoke English."

"Some don't."

"I just got back from a year in Peru. I'm going to be teaching
Spanish at Newton High for my certificate." It was a litany, an
act of contrition. "I speak Spanish and some Hebrew and some
Norwegian, but I don't speak any French." I assured her it was
all right. "No," she insisted, "I had it coming. I did everything
we're not supposed to do. I just can't help arguing sometimes. It's
not our job to change anyone's mind—"

"Just to get his signature." I was trying to help.

"That's all they want—signatures." I could share her bitterness; I too would rather convince a single person of a truth than
collect a thousand signatures in support of it. I told her that, then
finally she smiled. We took off the rest of the afternoon; we
spent it with our sandwiches on the riverbank, then walked
back to my place.

Variations on a theme for the next ten months. Blood alone
moved the levers of social change, and better *her* bashed skull at
a Greyhound station than more little girls bombed in a basement. Linda was blind to danger, had no respect for anyone who
thought his own skin was more precious than racial justice.
Against that I had no principles, no morals, nothing to die for,
and little more than self-interest to guide me. I had regrets, pref-
erences, reservations.

My real interests had always been foreign, keeping up with
juntas, civil wars, and overseas investments. I cared more about
fixing South Africa and opening up China than I did about
improving the South. Alabama was as foreign to me as California
and both were stranger than Rio de Janeiro. Linda's commit-
ments, like partisan politics, stopped at the water's edge. For all
her traveling in the world, Libya remained Liberia, Toronto
wound up in Ohio, and she always had to ask if Taiwan was a
name for the mainland—or was that Formosa? And she didn't
know, *physically know,* America. I gave her an outline map of
the States and she got only seven states right. Not even Alabama.
I tried to teach her some basics, how geography imposed its
values, how the nuances between agricultural, black-belt Montgomery and red-dirt industrial Birmingham were still alive
and could save her life—or prematurely end it. Nothing. They
can't vote in Montgomery any more than they can in Birmingham, so what's the big deal? We were like broken halves of
some original harmony, each distrusting the other's knowledge.
Mere guts; mere learning. We never thought the other one had
quite gotten the point.

My head was slowly filling with postgraduate schemes. It was
Kennedy's high summer and even Ivy Leaguers were considering
ways of being less self-serving. One scenario saw me tearing over
the sand dunes on my Vespa, bringing the vaccine and saving
Malawi for social democracy. Bringing literacy, latrines, peace to
warring tribes. Trust me, little people. Even the Army didn't
seem too bad—I'd put in for language school in Monterey or
Army Intelligence in Europe, keeping tabs on wayward generals.

I didn't fear the future; the world was conspiring for my better-
ment. Government was an extension of Harvard, with money
and power and many of the same faces. If the thought of sacrificing three years grew suddenly offensive, there were scholarship possibilities on the Coast. And there was my insurance
policy against all painful decisions—Canada. I'd been born there
and that set me apart from Nick and Pete and even my classmates in Pinardville High. I still held the passport, I spoke the
language—I was the real thing. And for another six months I'd
continue to be both things: a draft-exempt bilingual Canadian,
and a bright-eyed American, ready to serve. Not that I seriously
considered going back for good—America had never been livelier,
Canada never more stagnant. Boston was truly The Hub. It
seemed that all the ground rules of America had changed overnight and the proletarian Ivy Leaguers with a shadow language
and identity were the boys to profit most. Little doubt, when it
came time to decide, which of my citizenships I'd gladly dis-
card.

Against all these differences, I loved Linda Feldman. We
wanted desperately to know each other, but even our ways of
knowing were different. We took each other to parental dinners.
Her father was a teacher-turned-contractor, the kind who hired a
hundred of my fathers on a daily basis. We acknowledged the
irony. It was a Friday *seder;* I wore a *yarmulka.* I liked him.
He said he never thought he'd see the day when a Frog could
teach a Jewish girl something about books and culture—but could
I try? Please, could I try? Her mother treated us all like overnight guests who'd stayed on several weeks past their welcome.
Her face said: *What did I do wrong?* But you knew from her
eyes that she'd stopped listening for answers. She hadn't spoken
to Linda in the past two years. Linda thought my parents were
sweet and well-meaning, which meant she hadn't understood
them at all. I judge my people infinitely stranger and less
knowable than hers. Then we found the place on Bank Street, I
invited the other couples, and the rest followed inevitably:
distractions, research, typists, commuting; the special moral slop-
piness of living intimately and devoting no effort. Nick helped

that day in April, squashing her hand into the pastries. He helped me see that we needed relief. Linda needed an outlet for all her convictions. I had visions of the longest forty miles in New England—Pinardville to Harvard Square—opening up to take me in.

Sometime that spring when I'd lost whatever easy rapport I'd had with my friends from freshmen year and with Linda, I decided to take advantage of the accident of my birth, at least to explore it and say finally, yes, it was only an accident. I would go to Québec for the summer. Linda had done that in Israel twice and ended up in trouble for turning pro-Arab. At least she'd had the satisfaction of knowing that there was a place in the world, at least for some of us, that had to take you in. I would go back the way Pete had gone to Italy just after high school, and maybe something of my new Americanness would lead to the kind of adventures that had made a man of him. To hear him tell it, the girls of Sicily had fallen on their backs to greet him. Only his dexterity and the gratitude of the girls themselves had saved him from marriage or assassination. And sometime during the summer I'd have to decide once and for all if I wanted to make the final leap from Pinardville into academic life, or do something secure and unselfish for the government. We parted, as they say, the best of friends. Pete drove me to the Everett Turnpike. I felt that if I'd met Linda anywhere but in Cambridge we couldn't have failed to be a kind of cast-in-bronze heroic couple. But she'd already slipped off by night a week before for Alabama. I'm sure for her it was something final, but I had that addiction to my memories, especially the imperfect ones.

New England was never the best place for hitchhiking: too many short roads, too much native suspicion, too few traveling salesmen. But a perfect place to sort out alternatives. Absolute self-reliance mixed with abject helplessness—hitchhiking as existential romance. I didn't mind the hours by a gas station trying to get to the fitful spurt of Interstate that sometime in the future promised to link Boston with everything Frostian. I was getting there, gradually. After Portland they cared more about my destination (even trying out their own childhood French) than my

Harvard pedigree. North of Skowhegan the forest encroached, lakes gleamed behind the pines, the black flies crawled the surface of my salty, bag-toting hand. Little bastards, raising welts; I'd forgotten about them. Those trickles of sweat turned out to be blood. A milk truck picked me up. I stood in the cab helping myself to half pints of buttermilk from little glass bottles. *Remember this*, I told myself: pretty soon glass bottles will disappear. The chime of the milkman. Pretty soon you'll be too old to hitchhike. We rattled along, dipping off the road every few hundred yards, down dirt ruts to cottages at the lakeside. It was a hot, cloudless day and the lakes had the burnished turquoise sheen that made you want to strip off your clothes and leap from the first high cliff. When I was dropped, at the end of the sixty-mile route, I stood on a hill refusing rides just to watch the cut timber scuttling down a narrow river a few hundred feet below me, then fanning out into a clogged, bowl-shaped lake. Tons of Rice Krispies. How good I suddenly felt, how right I had been to suspend my future and take this trip! A bright early summer day in the north woods, seventy degrees, twenty-one years of abysmal childhood behind me. It was the first day of my manhood. I wanted to shout into the Maine woods, the way Nick had into the winter nights of our first semester, after reading Thomas Wolfe: *"I'm young and drunk and twenty and can never die!"*

It was the drunken hitchhiker's pride that day near Jackman, Maine; I'd gotten myself into the middle of nowhere and I had no way of getting out, but I'd done it all on my own and I took full responsibility for every part of it. Full responsibility for no Hooker, no Linda, no draft board, no schools, no country. I regretted nothing. I knew a helluva lot. My life had been a miracle. And it would continue to be one. That oldest male desire, simply to drift and not say no to anything—to believe in the equivalence of disparate experience whether I picked apples in Québec, registered voters in Selma, enlisted, went to Berkeley—to drift with it all to see how far and how deep it will take you, even figuring (there, alone, with no Linda to tell me I was being immature) that that was the only way we were intended to live. Like a log, I thought, watching those sodden monsters bumping silently in the lake, and wondering if some unbookish knowledge were not coming to me for the first time, in symbols. Even if a planing mill lies at the end of it all. And I was glad it was Maine, where I had that north-of-Skowhegan face (a long fleshy nose and jug ears, all slightly bent and out of line), and the name and language to fit right in. Glad not to be hitching through Alabama with Harvard plates, where the cabins off the road might be black and hostile, or white and hostile, and the ride offered might kill me faster than the ride not given.

I stood in the silence for maybe half an hour, feeling that something profound was imminent. No cars passed. I heard nothing but the insect whine and the occasional crow. I'd never been so far away from another person. And then, so distant and so close to the sound of my own breathing, other noises started creeping in. A motorboat on a lake I couldn't see; chopping in woods far across this lake or another; lumber trucks changing gears on a grade miles ahead or miles behind—layers of human density, all being held back for me. The moment I began to hear them, the cars started coming and then the trucks, the campers, a border patrol. I was at Customs an hour later, then through the villages on the Québec side. Towns, suburbs, city, the slum I was born in—God! I reflected on that (bouncing along in a truck, trying to make small talk but not get involved), that I had known a few moments of grace. That I belonged somewhere off the streets and away from too much social complication. At that late June instant in 1963 I had known a mystical harmony and nothing was worth its shattering. The temperature must have stood at that precise degree and humidity where my sense of having a skin, a body, a pulpy involuntary self beyond my knowledge and control, had simply vanished. I had walked and felt a breeze upon my very bones and I was neither dead nor alive, neither Pierre Desjardins nor a collection of men: I was a harmony. My eyes had focused more clearly, and further, than ever before.

Two hours later I was sitting with my truck driver in a diner outside Vallée Jonction, and I was slowly (reluctantly) returning to my body, my own sober, mortal, and twenty-one-year-old self with urgent choices weighing him down, who'd stupidly removed himself from the very hub of Kennedy's world to a cross-roads *casse-croûte*, and would have to answer for it. The hamburgers were greasier than anything I'd had since moving to the States ten years before, and the vinegar over the French fries awakened giddy memories of pushcarts in *basseville* Québec. *Nostalgia*, stop it. *Je me souviens*. I was only sixty miles over the border and already being everything Linda liked to accuse me of: reactionary, romantic, and lazy. The trip up the ranks to Harvard and the promise of endless rewards had spoiled me. I wasn't hard enough for Québec, not ruthless enough for Boston, and I hadn't even given Alabama a second thought. My *camionneur* dropped me in Quebec City on the Grande Allée where the road broke off to the lower city. I didn't care to see *that* again until I'd settled myself into something clean and airy up behind the Château Frontenac where the breezes always blow.

It was five o'clock when I found a room on the Alley of the Drunkards. A simple name to explain: for three hundred years it had connected the old barracks at the top of the street to the taverns at the bottom. I'd gotten a gusty corner room with a good view of the *Conservatoire* and an endless heap of green copper roofs; the other window gave out on a giant maple in a churchyard. The alley could accommodate one car and a bit of parking: curbside tires on the sidewalk, a long line of tilting cars. Probably I couldn't really shake hands with tenants on the other side. Monsieur Vaillancourt, hairy-shouldered in an all-day undershirt, had scrounged for the furniture and managed it all for under fifty dollars. "You were taken," I said, seeing the standard dresser and night stand with chipped and blistered tops, a table with an oilcloth cover, and a wobbly, stiff-backed rocker that would not do for sitting. No reading lamp, of course, just two bracketed night lights with yellow parchment shades. A surprisingly wide, very loud, brass bed. At ten dollars a week, all I wanted. The cross-ventilation was bold on my sunburn and for my thin Boston shirt, but so fresh I didn't want to shut it off. Québec had cool summers; as a child I remember snow in early May and then again in late September. It felt like a sea breeze, and the sudden drop at the top of the street could have been

the shores of Gaspé instead of the tragic cliffs of Cap Diamant.
I'd taken a room a few hundred yards from where the drunken,
lucky Wolfe had challenged the cliffs and defeated the gallant
Montcalm (as I'd been taught), after which we'd become a
relic race.

I went downstairs to make one call. My father's oldest brother,
Achille, true to the laws of primogeniture, had inherited enough
land at just the right place under just the right corrupt regime
to sell it for an enormous profit. He'd bought an apartment building in town and started an appliance store. My father, inheriting
nothing, had learned enough about plastering and wallboarding
to become a general handyman in Manchester. He'd always
admired his older brother, even with my mother reminding him
of the undeserved (and unshared) advantages his brother had
had. Over the years, as Achille prospered, my father even endowed him with the most mysterious of attributes, a head for
business. And since I was the bright boy from the poor branch,
Achille's family had always felt a little sorry for me. There was
a girl cousin, Micheline, whom I'd once liked very much, and
having a likable girl cousin in a strange city is a great advantage.
All the other aunts and uncles had drifted away, to Montreal,
to California: only the successful ones kept in touch.

"Pierre," I was saying to my aunt, "*vot' neveu. Dezétas*—Manchester. *Mon-shess-tair.*" Should I invoke Harvard? My father?

"*Connais pas Pyarre.*" A pause. Should I hang up on this pest?
Sudden gasp of inspiration. "*C'est toi, Hector?*"

Hector: it sliced me under the knees. Forget Harvard, I was
ten years old in short pants and scabby elbows; I was *Hector*,
the first thing I'd thrown away when we got to the States—one
of the privileges of being reborn. But Hector I would always be
in Québec. I told her I'd be in town for a couple of months, and
gave her my address. "Michou will be glad to know," she said.
Despite what I'd said, she assumed I'd come back for good.

I went upstairs to empty my bag and then to rest. I'd left
Boston at six in the morning—twelve hours passing with the force
of a dozen years. I was hit by the absolute irresponsibility of all
I had done. Letting Linda go, not having followed through on
anything. Selfish bastard. Worse: coward. Where was she now?

In a tent city, on the floor of a Negro church? I could picture a pickup truck parked nearby, cans of gasoline in the back. Snipers, rapists, bombers—I could picture them all. *My Linda,* never as certain of herself as she tried to make out. I'd forced her to be more inflexible than she wanted to be. And the lover's other nightmare—not that she would die, but that she would thrive—hosts of lovers, from crewcut divinity types smoking pipes to giant Negroes in overalls, that not just her body but her childhood stories and her family secrets would be the property of others as well as myself—that our *entirety* can be transferred, not just our bodies. Could another person be enough like me to draw out the same admissions and embarrassments, the same occasional smile? I had come to know so much about Linda that I'd begun to interpret my own experiences in the light of hers, substituting all her travel for my own insularity, her family for mine, her disloyalties to Church and tribe for mine. Or was I already "this French-Canadian guy I used to know in Boston"? It was 6:30 P.M., the room was midday bright, and I was getting tired. Before I slept, I wrote a letter to Linda at Harmony House, Selma.

I told her about the trip up from Boston, the wild fluctuations in my moods. The fact that, apparently, I'd taken on a new name. I threw in the brightness, the cool breeziness, the cobblestones and leaded windows with rippling glass. And I closed regretting that I couldn't show this to her, that she'd never understand what it was like to have been born up here in a different century, that the great difference between us was her capacity for idealism. I wished I had it. I wrote the address, *Chez Vaillancourt,* the street name, even the date, in just the old French way I'd been taught as a child. Even my handwriting seemed to have changed just a little. I signed it with love, from Hector.

Before falling asleep, I noticed the caption of the one print framed on the wall just above the bed. "*Lourdes—La grotte miraculeuse,*" it said, dingy under dusty glass. The walls were fluffy with lint. How could dust cling to a vertical surface? I was home.

It was that purest sleep, keeping the mood but fleshing it out.
I was aware all along that it was late afternoon and that I was
only napping, that I was in Québec in an upstairs corner room in
the house of a Monsieur René Vaillancourt. But a party was going on. I heard conversations in French and English, music with
catchy tunes and clever lyrics, and Linda was talking to in-
teresting-looking men and women who seemed to be old friends
of mine. In fluent French she apologized for a trace of a Spanish
accent. A minute later she was sobbing into my shoulder that
she couldn't understand a word of what was going on. I reminded her of the *seder* she'd put me through and she winked
at me in my dream-room in Québec the same way she had in
her parents' kitchen, giggling as she had pinched the *yarmulka*
off my head after dinner: *you've come a long way, Charlie.*

More a vision than a dream, flattering but probable; I accepted it completely. Then perhaps I slept, the other obliterating
sleep. All the guests suddenly decamped, leaving only a sharp
light in an empty room behind. I tried to will myself from
waking up, wondering in fact how it would all turn out between
me and Linda and my attractive new friends, knowing on another level that it was still fairly early and I didn't have Linda or
any friends, and I'd have nothing to do for the rest of the night
if I couldn't sleep through it.

What sharp light?

A girl's teasing voice called from the waking world back into
my dream. It spoke French. "You drool a little when you sleep,
Hector."

In the dream I'd been Pierre. "And you've become *such* an
American to look at. Do you remember French at all?"

"Michou?" I asked, gurgling perhaps. Gauloise smoke, sharper
than the dream's, lay heavy in the room.

"He calls up and not one word about me! Mama says 'You'll
never guess who called today. Hector! And he wants a dinner.'"

The light and the voice and smoke came from a corner of
the room. It had to be Micheline, *ma cousine de fesse gauche.*

"*Toujours belle*, Michou?"

"*Psshou. Et toi, toujours sage*, Hector?"

"I asked you first."

"Just like an American. Really, Hector, I don't know why I came. Is that all you can say: *'Come to Kweebec and screw the pretty girls'?*"

Now I was sitting, looking through the bright beam of a high-intensity lamp at the reflection off a pair of glasses behind. "Pretty good English."

"I work in the Tourist Office."

"Know your enemy."

"I try my best." She was fumbling inside her purse, shaking a box of matches.

"How did you get in, Michou?"

The last time I'd seen her she'd worn a gray convent jumper and a starched white blouse, with a little gold crucifix tight against a very flat chest. An odd image to set beside Gauloise smoke and breaking and entering. "Old locks open with old keys," she said. "I used to know someone else who had this room. That's why I took this lamp from the store. You can take it back when you leave—"

I caught a meaning. "I'll be here a month or so."

"We'll see."

"Why do you stay in the dark?"

When she had finished her cigarette, she came over to me. She sat on the edge of the bed so softly that it didn't squeak. Still very small, a heart-shaped face not perfectly formed, yet more than childlike. She wore jeans and a navy-blue sweater (no crucifix, but her chest was flat; no matter), her hair was brown and wiry and her glasses almost rimless—French glasses. Her shoulders were so narrow I covered them entirely in my two cupped hands. I could even sense her bones and breathing underneath, like a bird's. She was so small and soft she seemed all curves, not like Linda whose shoulders and back were firm and flat. Michou seemed to be looking into my pillow, as though I hadn't quite satisfied her expectations. Then suddenly she dropped her head on my shoulder and I could feel her crying as I held her. Hugging, crying, she just kept saying, "Oh, Hector, it's so good to see you! I'm so happy, I'm so happy!" The brass bed creaked—what would Vaillancourt take me for? The crying and hugging were infectious; I hadn't cried in a good ten years, but suddenly—and for no good reason—I could feel good salt tears rolling down my cheeks, and I was hugging her madly and thinking, *Hot damn, we're an emotional race, we can feel deeply, we can love, that's what's been wrong with me the last four years.* Even with Pete, who'd driven me to the Everett Turnpike that very same morning, we'd gone through a kind of mock Harvard ritual. "Well, Pierre, be cool." "Yeah, Pete, well, thanks for everything." *Shit!* From now on, I'd be true to type. I gave a long last hug and tried to summon some appropriate words. But I was out of practice.

"Tonight I will introduce you to some of my friends," she said. *Tonight?* My God, it was only nine-thirty. I wasn't sleepy, it was like gaining a bonus day. "Especially girls, you'll like that, won't you." She was dimpled. Mousy and sexy; only the French can carry it off. I hoped she had a worthy boy friend. About her girl friends, I decided to drift.

The streets were still a little busy, though the evening had turned blustery with a threat of rain. The weather always changes suddenly in Québec. I shivered under my sweater. I'm not tall, but Michou came up only to my vaccination; even if she were a cousin, she was the kind of girl you want to contain, whose independence seems a provocation.

"Who am I going to meet? Your boy friend? Any girls?" I tried to be jaunty. Ivy casualness was a useful trait, but in short supply. It had been a very long day.

"I don't belong to any boy. These are just friends from Laval." We walked downhill all the way, near the old university quarters. The streets were dark and narrow.

The coffee shop was about the size of my rented room. It was named *Le Patriote,* and carried a wooden cutout of Papineau's men in stocking cap from the 1837 rebellion. It had the look of a student-run hangout. The walls were partially plastered, partially burlap. Some lathe-work and beams had been coaxed out of the walls and ceiling. Long tables occupied two walls, there were booths along a third, and half a dozen small tables clustered in the middle. The dream I'd had was still vivid and I wanted to get on with fleshing it out. Somehow Linda would have to leave

Alabama and join me here, and there'd have to be whitewashed rooms with handmade *habitant* furniture, some political posters in Chinese or Russian, and colorful cushions on the floor. There would be some august theoretician, European most likely, at the center. This blue-lit coffee shop, strangely quiet considering that it was nearly full, was an obvious detour.

We went to the long table at the back. "Robert," said Michou, to a sleek, smiling boy who rose to kiss her on the cheek, "my cousin, Hector. From Harvard." He didn't look my way; I hadn't yet offered my hand. He was blond and smooth-faced, with longish hair combed straight back. He looked as if he'd just climbed out of a pool after a difficult dive. It was a surprise to hear French, and not fraternity-boy English, pour from his lips. "Sorry, I don't speak English," he said.

Ah *ha*. "No one's forcing you," I said, and I could tell from his crooked smile that I'd just fallen into a baited trap. I made up my mind to forget all English.

Robert wouldn't let it drop. "Hey, did you hear? The American here says no one forces us to speak English." I could feel the rest of the table turn away from me, even those who'd looked up earlier with a ready smile.

"Hospitalité spoken here, boss."

"I've read the ads, thanks."

"Give tip, show girls?"

This was a college boy? "O.K. Enough." A dozen put-downs flashed through my brain, but all in English. I was twelve years old when we left Québec, a bright but obedient twelve. In French, I'd remained a child.

"Robert spends all day driving tourists around in a *calèche*," Michou explained. I tried to look mollified. "And Robert—you're behaving like a pig. Hector is one of us. He is like a brother to me."

He snickered.

"O.K., tell me," he asked, this time with a one-last-chance tone, "what would you call people who live on what the tourists throw them?"

"Pimps and beggars."

He seemed pleasantly surprised, quick to agree. "That's us,

pimps and beggars. And whores." He was easy to please. By straining for overstatement, I'd gained acceptance. But I was worse than Robert; I didn't want to drop it. "Is that what you call yourselves—pimps and beggars and whores?" I asked.

He shot me a look more animal then human; his eyes were burning with more passion than even Linda had ever shown. "We call ourselves patriots," he said.

For the next hour, I listened. I'd heard a bit about the separatist movement. Some bombs had gone off. No French Canadian is really immune to the call for independence; even from New Hampshire I'd sympathized. Québec had always been isolated, by choice. Separation seemed natural, especially in a country where separate-but-equal was a kind of national creed. It was so natural, in fact, that bitterness like Robert's seemed undignified. Why bother hating the English for being such sterling embodiments of precisely what they obviously were: unilingual, Protestant, bigots? Perhaps I sympathized all too easily, and loved too little. Only a few theorists knew that revolution was rooted in personal transformation, that the most entrenched enemies of change were the patterns of accommodation inside ourselves. Most of us thought it was a simple matter of registering voters and then collecting the ballots. We didn't understand the irrational, yet. At least Linda, like Robert, was combative. Like Robert, she assumed that gentlemanly differences were basically fraudulent, until they turned nasty.

I felt a welcome breeze, heard the hiss of rain outside. "Is this Hector?" Cold, strong, wet fingers grazed my neck. The girl hooked a soaked umbrella onto the back of Michou's chair. "Hi," she said, "I'm Christine."

"Kiki," said Michou, looking at me, and pointing to the girl.

I stood to shake her hand, mainly to see how tall she was. We were the same. Her hair was long, straight, and Iroquois black, tied in a loose ponytail. Her skin was as pale and her eyes as green as an Irish convent girl's. *Nice bones,* those cool Harvard boys would have said, more alert to the staying power of a girl's face than to the immediacy of her figure. I couldn't tell much about the figure; she wore jeans, a suède jacket now black from the drenching on the arms and shoulders. I'd always liked darkhaired girls in ponytails. "Michou has told me all about you," she said. "The Harvard boy, right?" Her fingernails were startlingly long, red, and unchipped. Otherwise, she seemed at ease with herself.

It had been so long since I'd even talked to an unattached girl that I was afraid I'd have nothing to say. The whole process of starting over again, trading life stories, learning tolerances and vulnerabilities and the million little differences that add up to friendship, seemed suddenly impossible. Like counting the stars at night, then looking away just once and finding you'd lost your place. Adjusting to Linda had changed me permanently; no one else seemed worth the effort. Kiki wedged a chair between Michou and me. What could Michou possibly have told her about me? A call went out for coffee, and a basket of good crusty bread was brought, the kind that in Manchester came with union stickers on the crust that ruined the best piece. Platters of French fries were dispensed like popcorn. There was enough starch on the table to stiffen all the sheets in the Château Frontenac. I was dreaming again, head swiveling to hear each speaker till I got dizzy. The oxygen content of *Le Patriote* was slipping dangerously. Kiki and I were the only people not smoking those ropy French cigarettes. She knew everyone, smiled at their jokes, offered none of her own, seemed aloof. I was glad to have her as a buffer. She ate French fries from my plate, laid her hand on mine when she leaned to talk across the table. It was becoming a dream setting, a cave of unanimity sealed off against the tourists, *calèches*, and the charming insipidness of the merely picturesque. A New World equivalent of a Left Bank *bistro*, minus the philosophers and carafes of Algerian red (fair enough, I thought, we're a French fries and Pepsi race and if we declare a *putsch* it will be from a *casse-croûte* and not a beerhall); I was probably the oldest person in the place, but I felt the least exposed to theory. I wondered what would have happened if we'd been in the States; forty bearded revolutionaries, plotting destruction of Queen and country, debating methods from massive obstruction to armed revolution. In Harvard Square, the cops used to raid the all-night cafeterias for no better reasons than the prevalence of beards. One summer in Manchester when I'd grown a beard, a carful of high school kids screaming "Castro, Castro!" had tried to crush me against a wall. Bearded, I was laughed at by the cops. I wasn't used to open discussions. Our talk of change, in Cambridge, had always been earnestly constitutional.

I felt I'd come in late on another vital argument. I couldn't share Robert's bitterness any more than I had been able to share Linda's guilt. "Ah, we know your kind," Robert sneered across the table. "Manchester spoiled you." I wanted to push his face into the French fries. You don't get spoiled on Dover Street, I wanted to shout. Michou purred, "Oh, Robert, you're getting impossible," which seemed to please him. In English, my thoughts raced on: when you're a French Canadian in *basseville* Québec and you don't want to die of drink or go crazy, you emigrate. Or co-operate. And if you emigrate, you find new ways of co-operating. That's what my father had done, and I was blaming him less and less. I had no way of answering Robert, only the simplest French that left me fuming inside. "You don't know me and you don't know my 'type'!" I cried, a few seconds too late. Perhaps only Kiki heard; it came out softer than I'd intended. Robert didn't even look at me. *Le Patriote* was stuffy with shared indignation.

Kiki had a low voice, she could talk to me without anyone else hearing. "Robert is just an amplifier, don't let him bother you," she said. "Other people's voices get fed into his ears and they come booming out of his mouth a hundred times louder."

"I know the type," I said, thinking of Nick, and maybe what I'd thought, at times, of Linda.

New people came in and no one left. I peeled off my sweater, down to my short sleeves. No one else had removed a jacket. By midnight they were standing, squatting, sharing chairs, and leaning on tables. They smoked Gauloise, Gitanes, Celtiques— esoteric fragrances that soon become a stench. Each time the door opened, a blast of the Latin Quarter must have rolled out into an empty rain-slick street (like the bars I had walked past as a child, threading my way back and forth just to catch a whiff of stale beer and manly laughter); things were so hot and noisy inside that only your ankles could tell when the door had been opened. The language and odors were French, but my feeling was Irish. I felt like a visiting Kennedy. Bottles of wine appeared from wrinkled bags, and I wondered if I'd fallen into a *Dubliners* story or maybe *The Informer*—some rancid bit of political masochism best left to the Irish, and American communists? The atmosphere was conspiratorial and cenacular, and I, as always, sat outside it. I wondered if someone among us might be spying, carrying names and dates to the Mounties. I could sense the bank of fog rolling in, fishnets drying, hawk-nosed men passing out manifestoes and quietly disappearing. I felt as guilty as a spy, simply because I couldn't share. They were discussing ways of garroting the Queen on her official visit the next year. I snickered, and Kiki turned to me as though to quiet me, for my own safety. A suicide squad got a few volunteers. "Abbott and Costello," I whispered. *Assassinate the Queen?* I tried to be reasonable. "Look," I said, "aren't you being foolish?"

"Why?" This was Robert, not one of the volunteers. "They'd be lost without their Queen."

I felt I'd fallen into a time-warp. While we in Boston were talking of Gandhi and Thoreau, people in Québec, supposedly educated, were plotting assassination, bombing, train derailment, like a bunch of Algerians. And no matter what they said, Montreal was not Algiers. "Look," I exploded, "who gives a shit about the Queen? *You'd* be lost without her. Having the Queen on the money and having the Union Jack flying over you is the greatest thing you've got going. Don't ever let them take it away." Naturally, they paid no attention; I wasn't even an irritation. I was a Harvard boy, I hadn't been there, I hadn't suffered.

Their grievances were circular, self-reinforcing. Every tourist proved himself a paragon of stupidity. What had happened to the Michou who'd wept in my arms?—now she was an encyclopedia of outrage. "My bunch today only took pictures of drunks," she said, everyone nodding. "All morning long they're taking pictures of guys staggering. Finally I took them to one of those bars down by the train station. I said, 'Go in there and take their pictures and ask them why they can't get work. Ask them who took their land and who took their jobs.' Then I just left them there. I don't care if they report me—"

"You'll get a promotion."

"I should."

Another chimed in, this time laughing. "Mine liked horse turds. Every time we passed a mound of horse shit in the street he'd train his camera down and snap a shot."

"Did you tell him *why* we keep *calèches* in the first place?" Robert cut in. "All for his fat-assed comfort. And the reason why we have the indispensable skill of driving a *calèche* in 1963 is because of *hospitalité* and the easy money it brings in."

Robert was right, and I wanted to tell him so. "Tourism means making sure you don't spend money on changing a thing."

He weighed my comment for possible irony, and finding none, cast it gently aside. Everyone had a story. "*Look at this—'Monopoly' money!*" "*What are you people trying to prove by speakin' French all the time, huh?*" The guide's view of the tourist, the most unflattering angle of the least lovely people, raised to a principle of history. An empire of perverts guided by a colony of pimps. "I had another one today," said Michou, who was really wound up, "who only wanted to see churches. I asked if they were Catholics. '*No, we just want our children to see where you people threw away your money.*'"

"Typical," sneered Robert.

"They were Jews, then," said another, boldened by all the *Kristalnacht* rhetoric, meaning perhaps they were Protestants, or Americans, and I finally broke in. I didn't care what Michou thought, and I hoped that Kiki wouldn't mind. "Look, this is sick!" I cited examples from civil rights in the States. Love your oppressor; white Americans and English Canadians were festering with guilt—work on *that*. Have faith in a moral structure behind the iniquities, don't build on ugliness and become a perversion of everything you hate. What's your real problem? Being shat upon . . . or not having anyone under you to catch it? I stopped short of asking Linda's question: when do the ovens go up? They seemed to listen, at least those at my end of the table. But no one took it up, their own wounds were open and flowing and my little Band-Aid was quickly washed away—by memories and excuses reaching back not just to the afternoon but over a lifetime, parents' helplessness, historical abuse. Then Kiki, who'd seemed more amused than pained by it all, suddenly tensed and started a story. The others were talking, except Robert, and I made it a point to listen. She spoke into the din: voice soft, memory private. "When I was in high school, I went to Toronto for a month on exchange. I started talking to an old couple on the train and they asked me where I lived. I said '*Quebec City*,' in my best English, and their eyebrows shot up. You know what they asked next? '*How do you like living with the natives?*' All very sweet and they never knew—"

"They never thought!" Robert cut in.

What had begun as political and familiar from my days on the fringes of CORE had become something new, the single whine of resentment: nothing ever forgotten, every cell of the race—or were we just a tribe—feeling the pain for every other. It was a temptation I had to fight, not to feel part of an aggrieved minority with five million brothers and sisters all set to avenge the past. Like Linda in Israel, at least for a summer.

I still wasn't sleepy at two o'clock—though getting numb in the brain and bottom—when the tables started emptying and the help from the kitchen came out to sit with us. We were the head table, the group that stayed after the doors were locked. We were waiting for someone else.

At two-fifteen, after the lights were turned down, he rapped once. Robert jumped up to let him in. He was short, young and stooped, with ovoid glasses like Leon Trotsky's perched on his nose. He wore a black cape which glistened from the rain; his frail neck pitched his head far forward, under a burden of tightly curled hair. The small beard was straggly, confined to a stringy wedge in the middle of his chin. Despite the props, the impression was of a priest, and though I met him another time that summer looking much different, he remained to me a priest.

His fingers trembled as he rolled a Gauloise, fingers stained a chain-smoker's orange. Enough of his sentences started with "*En France vous savez . . .*" to remind us all that he had attended the lectures of all the great thinkers, had been accepted by cells of Algerians then active in Paris, and had absorbed all shades of opinion from the Left Bank journals before their adulteration in Québec or New York. Coffee was brought. Quivering with purpose, he began to speak.

He singled out a boy from the kitchen in stained white apron and rolled-up sleeves. "What is your name?"

"You know my name." The boy was smiling.

"Answer to point. What is your name?" The boy stopped smiling.

"Raoul."

"Given name, Raoul. Surname?"

"Binette."

"Very good, Raoul Binette. Now, time for our English lesson. What is Binette in English? This is very important. *Who knows what Binette is in English?*" He looked at me over the rims of his foggy glasses. "How about you?"

"A rake of sorts."

"*Say it please in English.*"

Foolish straight-man, I said it in English. He seemed mildly astonished at my accent. He had the rapid delivery of a master interrogator, pointing a shaking, orange finger and demanding respect. "A rake of a very special sort, wouldn't you say? It is a manure-spreader, is it not? Might we not say a *shit-spreader?* So you are *Raoul Shit-Spreader;* kindly do not forget it. And you? I know your name is Lucille. But Lucille what? Say it please in English: *I am Lucille Warm Bread.* Ah, what a cozy, comfortable race of bakers and shit-spreaders. And you? *Oakgrove? Raspberry? Miss Flame. Miss* (no, I can't take this one!), *Miss Liberty?* Who gave us such names? *Miss Pretty Heart?* Listen to me: we must see ourselves the way *they* see us. Can you imagine some banker in Westmount picking up his *Gazette* and reading that Mr. Robert Raspberry was arrested for planting a bomb in his mailbox? You, *Mr. Paradise.* And I'm not forgetting little Michou *From the Gardens.* What do you see when you look at us? I will tell you: you see a strong-backed, stupid, open-thighed race of cooks and clowns and backwoods fornicators. Our names show it. In France, you know, the first thing the people did after the Revolution was to throw away their degrading *métier* names. But we were too good to revolt. Too busy chopping wood and saying our rosaries. So it's good we kept our names. It's good to see ourselves just the way *they* see us, till we get just as sick of ourselves as they are. For within a revolution, even a stupid hopeless bourgeois revolution like ours, there are other revolutions, and they might count for something. First of all, we must not have illusions about ourselves. There is nothing noble or interesting in our history. We're just a bunch of drunken Indians. Marie Crawls-like-Snake. Hector Sits-in-Shit. At least those names had some individuality. How can we have pride in ourselves when we sound like characters in a nursery rhyme?

"Listen again: we of Québec are unique. We took this land, we are the people of this land, and all that shit of Church and Confederation is behind us. *Vanished. Gone. Buried.* We are one people, agreed? In France even factory workers know that uniqueness demands analysis. To understand one's uniqueness in the world is to have identity. The Americans have it. The Chinese have it. The Canadians will never have it, never. We have a chance, a very small chance. And the implications of our uniqueness demand sovereignty." He slurped two cups of cold coffee, rolled half a dozen cigarettes, joked awhile with some of the boys in a less hectoring tone. Michou introduced me. He stood behind the two girls' chairs. His hands were soft and moist. Probably some of the orange stain rubbed off on me. His name was Pierre, a *nom de guerre. Pierre Tombale:* gravestone. His cape had dried, he refused a lift and then an umbrella. It was three o'clock when he left.

"He never sleeps," Kiki said. "He hands out leaflets, he goes out to Gaspé, up to the lumber camps. He has this passion—"

"Do you?"

"For independence?" She smiled, as though the whole question of independence—or was it merely my asking it of her—was faintly absurd. "If it comes, I will accept it."

"What is Pierre's real name?" Who did he think he was—the Pepsi Pimpernel?

"No one really knows. He changes it every few weeks."

Christ. "And where is he from?"

"*They say*—people who don't like him say—that he's like you: an American. He used to be talking all the time about America.

Then he talked about Indians and they thought he was *métis*.
But he's not Indian."

"Do you like him?"

"He is very intelligent and he is honest with you."

"Except about who he is and where he's from."

"Personally, I don't care where anyone is from. And names
don't offend me. He keeps trying to demonstrate that the past is
not important, not even your personal past. Just the future. And
he tries to make sure that the future is a true future based on new
ideas. Or else it will be the historical future, won't it? That way
the future only confirms the past and makes real change impossible." The French had a way of discussing ideas; they could do
it unself-consciously, like a compulsion. Kiki's level of abstract
French was just about as high as I could follow; in my mind, I
busily translated for someone like Linda. *She says we must
choose our future. Real future or historical future.* I could see
Linda's special frown. I could hear her gentle whisper: "What
a load of crap!" And this time I would have told her, no—he's
right.

"What are you smiling about?"

"Everything."

Michou came over to say good night. I kissed her cheeks in the
approved French method, and shook her hand. She seemed
pleased enough that I was talking with Kiki, but she was an
older woman from the one who'd called on me that evening. I'd
let her down and Robert Laframboise was with her, waiting at
the door. He looked like a sea lion. I could picture him sliding
gleefully on his belly down a rain-slicked street.

Kiki came outside with me, holding a red umbrella. We were
the same height and she wouldn't let me hold it for her. We
bumped along hip-to-hip on the cracked, puddly pavement.
Every now and then I took the gutter when the sidewalk got too
narrow. I felt a strange sort of intimacy; no girl had ever held
an umbrella over me. She wore moccasins, now wet as a chamois-
cloth. My own feet ached with cold just from looking at hers.
What is the proper etiquette, I wondered: is she here because
she likes me, because I'm a helpless stranger, because she lost
a bet? All the lines I tried out seemed flat and contrived ("Look,

I don't have much I can offer . . ." "What about your poor wet feet? Why don't you dry them up in the room . . ."), yet without my leading her we were climbing the Alley of the Drunkards up to the Vaillancourts'. *Out with something!* She expects it. Things have changed in the past ten years, no more fathers and priests and gun-toting brothers. Even little Michou was out all night with that slimy Robert. Or was Kiki spoken for, perhaps by the Pimpernel himself, now waiting for her under his soaking cap-of-curls in some dingy working-class room? We were at the last intersection.

"I hope I'll see you again," I said. It was the best I could do: tongue-tied freshman in a foreign language. Considering it was three-fifteen in the morning under an umbrella on a deserted corner, stunningly absurd. *Christ.*

"You know your way now, isn't it? I will say good night here and get a taxi from the Château. I know the boys down there, so they will look after me." I stared at her a good ten seconds. Words wouldn't come, neither French nor English. She took my fingers and gave them a little tug. "Good night."

She tipped her umbrella and a flood of water washed my face. She didn't look as if she needed help, but something in the way she'd asserted her independence made me want to call after her. But she was running, faster than I ever could, and the wind was loud. I was dripping from my nose and fingertips by the time I got inside. Twenty-four hours ago, I'd just gotten up to pack.

We came in for a spell of good Québec summer weather: cool, cloudless days of ubiquitous sun, warm air, and fresh breezes. The nights were cold: wool sweater and hands-in-pocket weather with more, and brighter, stars than I'd ever seen. I would stay out till long past midnight; the bars were closed, the last tourist had left the *terrasse* behind the Château, and slowly the lights across the river blinked off. The heavens seemed three-dimensional; of course it had been right to tell stories about the stars— their patterns were obviously prearranged. Out on the river there'd be ships, slow-moving constellations, no closer, it seemed, than the belt of Orion. I passed whole days without a word to anyone except a waitress, a postal clerk, a groceryman who'd sell me milk and a bag of oranges. My own voice surprised me. Inwardly, I'd debate with Linda and, with a lover's special privilege, try to project myself into Selma-through-her-eyes, but all I saw were other lovers, jeering whites, squalor. During the abbreviated night and long morning of sleep, I dreamed again those near-waking visions. Debating only with myself, I won intricate arguments with Linda, Robert, Nick, Pierre Tombale, John F. Kennedy. I won so many that I never knew for sure if I'd spoken them, dreamed them, or written them in letters. I felt I was the only person in Québec who understood every nuance of every word, walking benevolently and anonymously among students and tourists, hearing all and saying nothing. I was such a giant the earth itself seemed to curve underfoot.

Even if there'd been anyone to talk to, I would not have made much sense. I would have asked simple, drunk-sounding questions. Is every human life a universe in itself, like the stars? The million small choices made in a day, and the ten thousand people we meet in a lifetime and the ten million faces we see, each with its own ten thousand people and ten million faces and untold millions of small daily choices—is each life a universe of random potentiality? Then surely we must impose no puny limits on its own self-renewing energy. We must drift. Or is our life merely a design, an imposition upon a nullity, like Orion in the skies? Is it knowable, a mystical pinwheel issuing from a convergent core and spinning into nothingness? If so, surely we must conserve, define, and not venture forth. Ruthless self-knowledge, monasticism. Be an *éplucheur*. I felt at times capable of either, but of nothing in between. I'd read my Wolfe and Dreiser, and for the first time I let myself think that Wolfe had won the argument after all: flow, drift! Screw necessity! I saw nothing to contain me, least of all the false alternatives of school or service (*all parts of my historic future, you see, Linda?*). What did citizenship really mean? That was something the workers needed, or the tourists, but not a man who walked through walls.

I was aware those few weeks, as I never have been since, of the random plenitude of life. That merely by walking to my breakfast down one alley instead of another, I would become, in some vastly complicated way, and in some remotely future time, a different person. The greatest pleasure in life was knowing that the next day, the next town, the next job, was a separate creation. Life itself was a self-creating voyage through a still-infant universe. So much variety implied benignity. Peace Corps, graduate school, languages, travel, foreign women, a profession, wife, children, the public moments that even then were building —they were not just slices of a seventy-year slab of salami—they were simultaneous events and simultaneous Hector-Pierres in an expanding universe. I, or the harmony that called itself "I," simply intersected those moments and passed through those shells of being on my way to something larger and final. They say Wolfe is a young man's writer, a boy's writer, but I was a man who'd never felt young and free a day in his life, and who'd interpreted life as stern obligation and fleeting opportunity extended once and then withdrawn. I'd never felt that boundlessness of mainline America, and it took two weeks in July alone in Québec to show me what I'd been missing.

From that first day at "Elsie's," I'd never been separated more than three days from Linda, and somehow I'd always suspected that she'd be a lousy letter-writer and that I'd be a good one. I was right. The first two weeks in Québec I wrote a letter a day; she never answered. This was punishing to the Nick and Pete side of my ego. Why hadn't I said, "Reckon I'll be movin' on, ma'm," and been done with it? "It shore was nice." I felt I'd thrown her into a bear pit, a lone Northern girl among Negro radicals in racist Alabama. I imagined the sex life of white Alabama to be crudely Arabian—comely young women, white and black, dispatched to the barracks, abused to unconsciousness, and then discarded. And for a white woman living with Negroes, something worse.

From Linda's silence, and from hours of morbid self-inspection ("*Ne t'épluches toi pas,*" Michou cautioned after an uneasy dinner at Uncle Achille's), I began to fear that somehow our sex roles had gotten reversed. I'd come fresh from a wife-beating culture; it wasn't easy to admit that for all my early friendship with Nick and Pete, I wasn't like them at all. Living alone and talking to no one, and looking back over an underpopulated and ungratifying sexual battlefield where Hooker Lessard had been more a pitfall than a prize (and hadn't I lost her to Duane Lafleur?) and then to Harvard where my confidence had been so shattered by early contact with Radcliffe girls that the best I could do was compete with the sailors in Scollay Square, I saw that I was still a sexual adolescent. In *making love,* that cool euphemism I'd heard first at Harvard, I was still a virgin. Then Linda. And with Linda I'd hardly been masterful. Wasn't she the one who ran the risks, who'd seen the world, who held convictions, who put her life on the line? She'd even been trained in a bit of fancy commando stuff in Israel and had lost her virginity to a hulking artillery commander under a gun emplacement somewhere on the Syrian border. (He'd showed her the tattoo the Germans had given him on his wrist. She was fifteen, fresh from Los Angeles. Then she'd found out he was an El Al mechanic visiting his kids on a nearby *kibbutz.*)

Beats where I lost mine, in Denny Pelletier's summer cabin on Sunapee Lake, breaking in with Hooker and two other couples during a February thaw. That other side of me, the morbid side that Thomas Wolfe couldn't silence for more than a week or two, looked back on ten years of dismemberment. Sweet and subtle temptations like America and Harvard and Radcliffe girls, all in the faith that I would outgrow an unpromising start. But I was cut out for something more! I was a river that had been ambitiously dammed and greedily diverted once too often. Shallow and stagnant, running everywhere. I'd misinterpreted those mystical whispers from the logs in Maine; they'd simply said, *You have failed. You know nothing. You are nothing.* Peter from-the-gardens. Still no answer from Linda. I called Michou, who'd been away in Montreal, and asked about Robert (gone to Labrador to work on the dam), and Kiki (just working—had I called her?). By the way, she said in just that offhand, significant way of things that change your life (like old "Dragnet" shows, I later thought: *Oh, lieutenant, one thing.* Yes, ma'm? *About those hold-up men*—Yes, ma'm? *Would it help if I gave you the license number?* Yes, ma'm, that might help.): some of the Laval kids were taking off for a camping trip in the Laurentians. Would I like to come along?

Start straight north of Québec, on the way to Lac Saint-Jean, and within an hour you're in the highest reaches of the Laurentians. They're not mountains even by New Hampshire standards, but they're more than rolling hills, and the timber is dense. The population is thinner, the rivers cleaner and swifter, than anything further south. When it's cool in Québec, it can be cold in the Laurentians; I remember fishing with my father in the early summer and dropping trout into a bank of snow. Frost can occur just about any time.

Kiki and Michou picked me up in a brand new Renault. Tents were strapped to the roof and the floor in the rear where I sat was littered with sleeping bags, windbreakers, an ice chest, and a Coleman stove. All close-out items from the camping section of Achille Desjardins et Fils.

They said the others would already be up there. Within half an hour we were out of the suburbs and into the bleak villages where toothless grandfathers sat on porches, under their blankets, and a few toddlers played in the street with rusty tricycles and broken wagons. Nothing poorer, meaner, outside of Appalachia; only the churches gleamed with their fresh gray paint and metal roofs (*"I want to see where you people wasted all your money . . ."*). Quebec City was only fifteen miles away—the bluffs and the Château were still clearly visible. Two stop signs per village; we passed five settlements before entering the area of the park. Threatening clouds rolled in from the north. We closed the windows half way. Every few miles we passed a gas station, with its weathered, madly flapping sign against a backdrop of cold, green-black pines. Some of the larger rocks in front of the gas stations were painted white and inscribed: VERS. It was hard to imagine worms in that cold, rocky ground. Barefoot children in unbuttoned shirts and short pants stood out front selling wild raspberries. Blond, dirty children with permanent gooseflesh selling wild berries from rusty coffee cans, against a wall of scrawny black pines. *"Quelle scène dépourvue,"* I wanted to say, but Kiki and Michou might have misunderstood. I meant that it was in me too, as much a part of me, and them, as the miraculous grotto of Lourdes.

The campground was just outside the limits of the park on the banks of a wide pebbly stream spliced by boulders that had fallen from the far-side cliff. Three small cars were already there and two largish yellow tents were getting put up. The men in sweatshirts, hammering stakes (metal on metal in the water-loud woods), I already knew from *Le Patriote*—Binette, Paradis, and Lafrenière. There were two girls down by the water; all together, four and four. In a show of self-confidence I took our tents, poles, ax, and stakes, leaving Kiki and Michou to struggle with the ice chest. I put up two tight, solid tents (tighter than the others' by a fluke I'll always be grateful for), and Kiki threw two sleeping bags inside. The men came over and introduced themselves as though we'd never met. I was still the outsider, a blind date and a foreigner to all but Michou.

It simply wasn't an American outing. They behaved like strangers with one another. The men fished by themselves, or went to their cars to read, and the girls were content to cut up vegetables and start the stoves. No one had deep fried the chicken from the night before. No one had brought a special-recipe potato salad. No softballs, no bats. It was August but it felt like April—pleasant now that the trees deflected the wind—and we could have used a roaring fire. Girls were sent to gather wood. Earlier, someone had dug a pit. I longed to hold a hot cup of coffee in my hands.

There was nothing for me to do. I sat on a log over the water, watching Binette and then Lafrenière take to the stream in hip boots and fly rod. From their equipment, their seriousness, I knew there'd be trout for supper. But trout for all? It was like a *kibbutz* picnic, a little private, a little communal. I wanted to earn my fish, but there wasn't anything I could do. Bottles of white wine had been sunk in a basket in a deep pool of water behind my log. I was out in the woods with the best campers in North America; it was nice, for once, to be among people who knew what they were doing. *Drift*, I told myself. Quit picking on yourself. Don't try to plan tonight. Whatever, whoever comes is welcome. By morning I'll be a different person. *Flow.*

"Hector, would you help me?"

Kiki took me with her to gather wood. She wore jeans, and by now she'd put on a heavy sweater. She gave me a burlap sling for holding wood. Her hair was purple-black, gathered in braids. I followed along a narrow path. A cool, promising breeze blew from deep in the woods. My feet were numb but my face felt on fire. We could hear the others' voices from the clearing, but we couldn't make out the tents or cars. I felt suddenly that we had slipped back through time, and I heard myself saying—feeling compelled to say it by the tall, slim girl who led the way—"You're Indian, aren't you?" It made sense, she had to be. She stooped almost as she walked, snatching dry wood even where spider webs glistened with raindrops, and she merely looked back, smiling.

"It rains here every day," she said, pointing up to the tiny windows of gray light drifting over the treetops, "but hardly any of it ever touches the ground." It was spongy underfoot, but the twigs she gathered cracked as she broke them into the sling. It seemed like twilight, though the flickers of skylight had turned from gray to cloudless blue. It warmed slightly.

"Come back here."

She led me under boughs, through shrubs, and over saplings that soaked my jeans. We heard laughter, both sharp and remote, from Binette, who'd caught another one. The roar of the river was so unvarying as to be a form of quiet. Yet we were in the deep woods, in a sudden blinding intensity of green that felt moist and hot, like a greenhouse. "Isn't it beautiful here?" she asked. "It's always bright. Even when the moon is out." It was all a cushion: rocks and trees coated with moss, soft grass. She picked some mushrooms. "That's why I'm the one who gets the wood. If they picked anything here and tried to eat it they'd be dead by morning." I found some dry wood and tossed it into the sling. The obliterating green of everything—like watching my bones in the outlawed fluoroscopes of my childhood shoestores—seemed to detach me from my body, my need to act. I was in the very socket of fertility and my eyes took in more than they ever had before: caterpillar tracks on the leaves, the edges of ferns, the mushroom gills, the stark, laddered termination of a long white scar on Kiki's leg that I quickly decided I didn't want to know about.

"It is beautiful, thank you."

She smiled and undid her braids, shook her hair out, blacker than the nighttime sky. She put her kerchief down and spread the mushrooms in a little half circle.

"Come on, closer."

We could hear them pounding stakes; I could even sense it through the ground, a split second before the sound. She stretched on her side, elbow propped to hold her head, hand disappearing in the flow of black hair. I sat like a professor, legs crossed in front of me, afraid to move. I wanted to talk, but any question I could ask would take us back too far. We were going to be lovers even before I knew her full name. I edged a little closer, near her elbow. I don't know how long I sat like that; each second seemed an eternity, yet only an instant before I'd been sitting on a log over the river. I plucked a mosquito from the air and crushed it deftly on my pants leg. Trivial ego-building.

She giggled, almost as though she were watching something in the woods that I couldn't see. I craned my neck. A foreign horn honked, way out in the clearing. "How very observant you are, Hector. I'm practically wearing feathers today and you ask me if I'm Indian."

"I thought I was being *very* sharp."

"Having some Indian blood is the new *chic*." She put her hands on my shoulders. The professor in me collapsed. "Hands here, come on."

"I *know*," I said, reaching for the buttons, fingers expecting cool soft flesh. "No, you don't know," she said, helping with the buttons. My fingertips felt a kind of cold, stiffened plastic, and then I saw a jackfrosting of old burn scars, a dense white foliage. I kept my fingers on it. "Don't ask," she said. "You don't want to know." She guided my fingers over her body, determined that I should see the worst. Her eyes never left my face; I wanted only to look into hers.

"On my leg, that was an operation when I was very little. We were out in the country then and the kids used to play on the road just like it was a yard. It *was* a yard. One day a car hit me—cars were always using those roads for races and no one ever patrolled where the Indians lived. They had to put in a piece of metal to straighten the leg and make sure it wouldn't shorten. Then I had to do exercises for years—it wouldn't do, being a limping Indian, would it? That was in Ontario. Then we moved to upstate New York for a while—we're treaty Indians so we can move anywhere in *our* nation—and that's where the fire happened. I was in the burn center in Rochester for eight months —they even wrote about me in *Time*. 'Indomitable courage of her people' or some-such. But if you look at my face and watch me walk you'd never know the damage underneath, isn't that right?"

I wanted to talk and make up for the abruptness of our beginning. But she already knew a lot, from Michou, and for the rest, she proved herself clairvoyant. "You must be having a girl friend in Boston," she said. "This trip to Québec is only a vacation for you."

I denied the very existence of Linda, but she refused to believe me.

"You act like a man who has a very settled life with a woman. You want more to get away from women than to chase them. *Coulisse!* I'm always messed up with men like that. All you really care about is finding where you fit in and everything else you treat as a distraction. I could see that night how you hate politics—"

"Just certain politicians."

"Don't think because they are my friends that I believe everything they say. I think they are very innocent, and innocent people can be very dangerous for people like me."

"I knew an innocent girl once," I said.

"I think you must still be knowing her," she said, this time laughing.

"You can't tell innocent people anything."

She was dressing. I closed my eyes and stretched out beside

her, and even the seepage through my shirt seemed warm and somehow green. I could feel her breathing on the hairs of my arm. I heard myself talking, and tried to stop. "There were so many things in my background that made no sense to her." *Christ,* I thought, *shut up.* She seemed to know Linda as though they'd been introduced. I told a story instead, something I'd once tried to get through to Linda as a tale of thwarted splendor, but she'd gotten up and drifted away, even before I finished. During the Depression, my father had hitchhiked from Québec to Guadalajara, speaking nothing but French all the way. He'd made his way through New England towns where English was barely understood, through the Belgian community in Charleroi where he'd even landed a job, then drifted through the river communities where Cajuns and peddlers had settled, then on down to Louisiana and east Texas and into Mexico where Maximilian had left behind some mission schools. My father told it to me one day over beers in a bar in Manchester, as though he were giving me my inheritance. One of my uncles, the one who'd gone to California, had taken the easy northern route across Ontario and the prairies, then down the west coast lumber trails, without missing a single French *messe* along the way. All America is riddled like Swiss cheese, with pockets of French. The *ancien régime,* refusing to die. My father's story had seemed slightly noble that day in Manchester; in the retelling, it seemed only quixotic. As a tale of cultural persistence, it didn't amount to much. No wonder it hadn't impressed a Jew. We seemed like pathetic inheritors.

Kiki listened with interest, perhaps indulgence. She smiled but her eyes were closed. She seemed to understand that my story had been serious, at least to me. "I can still do it," she said. "I could cut through the States as though it didn't exist. I could take you to Guadalajara or even farther. The Indians are still there, just like they always were."

"The French conk out after Manchester."

"They've killed all the tribes," she said. "Sometimes I dream of them. Sometimes I dream of going all the way to Bolivia or someplace without having to say a word. We don't have to speak."

I'd never met a bigger dreamer than I was. It was a little frightening. I'd stayed close to realists, always.

She held up one finger, "*Shh*—they know we've gone away."

I listened closely to the shouts I'd been ignoring. "*Kikihector? Hectorkiki?*" It was Michou, calling as though she expected no answer. I hoped Kiki wouldn't mind the publicity.

"This place wasn't real, was it?" I didn't know if I actually said it, or only thought it with a special vividness. *I'm dreaming all this. I will wake up on my squeaking bed under the picture of the miraculous grotto and I will be depressed for days.* I kicked the grass and didn't wake up. *It's true. I am lying in the woods with an Indian girl. Me.*

"It's very real, I assure you. And I'm very real." She gave my arm a vicious pinch.

Before it got too dark, and before our clothes became irretrievably wet, we left. Naked, we'd been warmer. Truth was mystical, now I knew.

From still deep in the woods we could hear new voices and see new cars. A jamboree of tents had been put up, and cars were scattered all over the clearing like at a country auction. We passed other wood-gatherers, heading for the woods. I left the shadows, blinking as though I'd been at an early show and had stumbled out in a glaring afternoon. There were a dozen tents now, some flying the Québec flag. The pit had been filled with charcoal, wood, and cardboard boxes, and a wooden scaffold erected to hold a spit. So many cars, so many tents, so many happy people came as a blow to the kind of mood I was in. I'd just won a girl in the woods, something unique in my history, and I wanted all nature to hush with respect. But this was a giant weenie roast, and I didn't have that kind of composure. Never would. I wanted to take her somewhere upriver where we'd camp inches from a mountain stream, reaching out through the netting with a tin cup for the morning's coffee water.

She was a step or two ahead of me as we reached the clearing, and I held out my hand so we could walk the last fifty yards together. But she turned when I called her name, and she looked at me as though I were a stranger who'd chased her through the

woods and had nearly caught her. "Kiki!" I called, and sent her
my most innocent glance. She kept on running to the others,
just as she had that rainy night in Québec, not looking back and
dropping her woodsling near Michou's car. She hugged the
first three boys she saw, kissing each on the cheeks while I
slogged far behind in soggy shoes, picking up her wood and
emptying it into the pit. Out in the stream Binette and Lafrenière had been joined by a dozen others. They'd have to be
geniuses with a fly rod to catch a thing.

In the next several hours I passed through all the moods I'd
ever known. In minutes I'd gone from the almost holy woods to
the midway of a carnival. I was dispossessed. A girl was combing
her hair on my solitary log of an hour before. How dare Kiki
know so many people? ("*The boys down there are friends of
mine.*") I even remembered the Hemingway stories, the anec-
dotes of my father's fishing-buddies about Indian whores. I remembered all the high school tough-guy talk, Helen's fall to
"Hooker" over a summer vacation; the semiprofessionals on Scollay Square who offered a screw or a night of love, depending on
the bar and price; all those nice pieces and fine pies and boxes
and cunts and beaver; the "Gee, but it's great after eating your
date, brushing your teeth with a comb" sung by Nick in a greasy
high school baritone that disgusted the preppies on our floor—
and I hated the perversity of my memory, for I knew that I had
truly *made love* and that for the first time in my life the phrase
had seemed appropriate and not a trembling WASPy euphemism.
What the hell had I done? She acted afraid of me, disgusted
by me. She was as good as a mile away, laughing with a bunch
of older, lower class, bowling-alley types. I found some cardboard and threw it on the fire. She was their mascot. But she
didn't care for them, she'd just finished telling me that in the
woods.

Every time I looked back to the stream, one of the boys was
unhooking a trout. Very well, they were geniuses. Everyone else
was a genius and if I'd always been the smartest person in Pinardville High, it was only because I'd been associating with stupid people. At Harvard, and then maybe for the rest of my life,
I'd learned what I really was in the company that counted: high

average. In love affairs, a zero. It seemed that Kiki was looking straight at me without even a smile of recognition, and I could hear Michou laughing behind me in the dark with ill-disguised "Hectors" sprinkling her conversation. When your lover of the past half hour deserts you for a pack of older men in leather jackets—taxi drivers by the look of them—you know something about her or about yourself that is worse than a nightmare.

I wanted to get away. I had to walk past them to reach the logging road that had taken us in. With luck I'd get to the main highway before dark. *Scène dépourvue:* Harvard boy by the roadside without his can of raspberries, begging a ride. I wondered if I'd been deliberately set up, part of some enormously complicated humiliation planned by Robert and forced on Kiki to prove her loyalty. I didn't want to get caught in the woods at night. Wolves. Mosquitoes. Iroquois.

"Hector—don't leave!" Kiki's voice was high, almost singing. "Why are you going that way? It's all muddy that way." I tried to look nonchalant; what if these were her gun-toting tribal brothers? "Come meet my friends." She waved me over; the men looked bored. Her voice was high, tense. "This is Mario, Butch, and Leo. My friend Hector. These boys all drive taxis."

The boys were in their middle thirties. Mario was toothless, Butch had done some prize fighting after too many years of hockey. Leo was Indian. Kiki was taller than any of them. Mario spoke first, exposing bare, discolored gums. "Not tonight we don't drive taxis. Let them walk, eh?" Laughing, he had that demented look of the toothless, nose and chin growing together. And she preferred them to me! What in the name of God could I have done?

"Take a beer," he said, pointing to an ice chest surrounded by three pup tents. Innocent generosity, insistence? *Take a beer, boy, and shut up.* The cans were piled high on slabs of ice. Suddenly I wanted one.

"No thanks," I said.

Mario plucked out three cans and passed them around. "You know, my friend," he said, reaching a familiar arm around Kiki's waist, "this girl here, she's a good girl. A real good girl."

And we don't want none of you city boys comin' up here and hurtin' her, understand?

I assured him I appreciated her. They offered her beer and space in their tents, which she seemed to consider before turning them down.

Four farm boys in a pickup truck brought out a half-cooked pig on a spit, then fixed it to the scaffold, over the pit. I asked her if she'd like to walk over by the fire. She considered that too before turning me down. I walked back to the fire. A crowd cheered the roasting pig. People were milling about their cars and tents and a few were standing near the pickup truck joking with the farm boys. Flames were licking the sides of the pig. Others were throwing wood on the fire and from the woods more couples were returning with ceremonial branches fit for burning. "It'll be ready by ten o'clock," they were saying. It was now about five-thirty, very bright and ripe with mosquitoes away from the fire, whenever the wind died down. There didn't seem to be anyone else, unattached, at the whole damn carnival.

Isn't there a giant mural somewhere by one of the Flemish masters, of a boar-roast at a kind of country fair, with pigs being slaughtered in a far corner, chickens being plucked and a few headless ones being chased by those imbecilic children of the Flemish school, while in the bushes a maid or two struggles with her petticoats and lines of men pull at their codpieces in expectation? A priest is somewhere in the center blessing the pig, now glistening in its own flaming juices. In the foreground a few old-timers smoke themselves to sleep while in a farmhouse across the distant lake, thieves make off with goblets, linen, and choice livestock after murdering the watchman and raping his wife and daughter. You wonder which of these satisfied gentlemen smoking his long clay pipe will row across the lake to the scene of such desolation. We roasted a pig that night. I wandered all over the canvas. I couldn't place my feelings. Everyone knew each other: students and farmers, taxi drivers and lumbermen, wives and kids, even some grandparents.

As the temperature dropped I spent more time by the fire, hands out to warm them and to protect my face. I took a few

turns rotating the pig. The whole gathering had become un-
focused. The principle of organization, if any, escaped me. The
pig roasters at the main pit seemed distinct from the profes-
sionally fine guitarists (singing "Mon Pays," a song so beautiful it
justified everything done in its name) and singers around the
smaller, private fires who were roasting corn and trout in aluminum foil. Some tents were lit from inside by kerosene lanterns
that cast huge bizarre shadows on the orange canvas. There
were people who had brought no tents, just air mattresses and
puffy sleeping bags guaranteed to thirty below. I'd known gatherings a little like this in Manchester—parish picnics—except that
no one with the slightest education had ever been among us.
And I'd been to Harvard parties, but even the outsiders at those
large gatherings had vague, usually severed, academic connec-
tions. I'd never seen college kids mix so easily. Abstractly, I knew
that something remarkable was being demonstrated. But I was
more excluded than ever.

I felt that I was part of some manipulated but unfathomable
plot clear only from an immense comic distance, wherein I was
the lone lover looking for his recently-lost beloved. But I was frozen in mood and movement. Some subtle critic of the future
would have to spot her: "Note, the artist has provided clues:
the same grass stains on the pants of this dazed young man
near the roasting pig"—a clear symbol—"and on this tall young
lady standing awkwardly with the gang of motorcyclists . . ."
And what would follow? The slow roasting of the young lover
over the coals according to some Iroquois rite, administered by
ruffians in leather jackets, now stripped to their bear-tooth neck-
laces and breechclouts? "The artist does not commit himself, it
is random, the tension is too loose." My moods had been un-
stable ever since I left Boston, alternating between exhilaration
and despair, but never had they spun so quickly as they did in
those long mosquito-plagued hours of dusk. I ate some fish from
a paper plate and twisted off a bit of pig-crackling before it
charred, but I was watching Kiki for a sign that she remembered
me. And to think I'd felt like a god! I was a god only when I
stuck to myself; all that self-esteem, all that plenitude of experience meant nothing once I got inside another life. I couldn't

answer the simplest question of my native culture: where do you
go, what do you do, after making love?

"Hector, wasn't it?" I remembered the voice but not the face:
a self-inflicted haircut, a round young face that twitched and
fluttered, a coarse blue unbuttoned workshirt over a heavy
gray sweater. Tiny glasses tight against his face, creasing his
cheeks. "Don't remember, eh?" I admitted I didn't. "Remember
my new name?"

"Ah—*Comrade Gravestone*," I said in English. Pierre Tombale,
the Pepsi Pimpernel. He clapped me on the back as though he
were proud of my powers. He was supposed to be in the lumber-
camps, converting the *bûcherons*.

"Not now," he said. "I got a job last week with none other than
the temporary government of Québec. I'm a chauffeur in the
ministers' car pool—drive a different servant of the people home
from his mistress every night, or help carry him out of the Liberal
Club—"

"Know your enemies, Pierre."

"Or convert them, right? They like to hire students over the
summer *so they can get in touch with youthful opinion*," he
explained, breaking into perfect, solid, Indiana English. It was
as though he had thrown his voice, and his body had become a
dummy for an unseen manipulator. "So what could be better?
I'm the voice of Free Québec right in the center of government.
It's me that nationalized Hydro. Right now I'm working on timber
and mines, which might take some time. Plus I give lessons in
good French to all those imbeciles going to Paris on official visits."

"A good life."

"I prefer to think of it as the humble origins of a future leader."
Then again in English. *"Hey—only kidding, man, don't look at me
like that, O.K.?* I'm actually a very modest, hard-working ex-
ploited proletarian who used to drive a taxi and happened to
have a chauffeur's license and a friend down at Manpower and
I'm damned grateful even for a job like this, O.K.?" He
twisted off a large chunk of crackling, sending a shower of
fat-drops flaring on the coals. His voice dropped to a whisper,
back to the earnest, intense French of the coffee house. "You
came with her, right?"

I felt suddenly evasive. I must have done something terribly wrong. A contract was out on poor Pierre Desjardins. "And Michou," I reminded.

"Of course. Your cousin Michou. Everyone's cousin Michou."

"My real cousin." We stripped off more chunks of ham and gorged on the steaming, juicy meat. I acted as if I was enjoying it.

"You know Kiki well, is it not?" The interrogatory tone.

"Yes and no." An honest answer; I didn't even know her last name. I looked around quickly and couldn't spot her.

"I was talking to her not ten minutes ago. I promised her I would talk to you." It wasn't easy for him either. He was looking at his scuffed hiker's boots, then he poked in the coals with a branch. He was political; personalities were a distraction. I was preparing my denials.

"I think you are a serious man, as I am a serious man. You are going back to the States, is it not? Your life is not here, am I not right?"

"I haven't decided."

"Answer to point. Very strongly probably, is it not?"

"O.K., let's say you're right. What if I am going back?" *Tonight,* I thought, *first bus.*

"Then why in the name of God have you left her like this?" His eyes were enormous. "Why won't you see her now?" He held the stick in front of him, like a sword. He shook it at me. "What I am saying is this: don't be a typical American and think you can get away with it." He looked suddenly fierce in the dark, near the fire, cheeks hollowed, glasses smoldering. He broke into English, a trifle low and hurried, and with it his expression changed, as though one or the other Pierre Tombale was just a pose and I was the only person he could afford to be honest with. *"She's not a dog, right? It's not like you're making a sacrifice, right? It's for her good that I'm saying this. Not everyone here really cares about Kiki. Take her back with you. She's had a shit life and things aren't going to get any better . . ."*

A group of five or six came to tear off their strips of crackling and then to slice some ham. They carried a wine bottle and it was passed from lip to lip and then to me.

"She's been used enough already," he finished in French, and most of the group nodded, thinking perhaps of other "she's": *la patrie, la verité.*

She read my purpose before I was halfway there. She broke away from the men in leather jackets and we were both crying by the time we embraced. I tried to remind myself we'd only been separated six or seven hours, but it didn't work; it was as though I'd been away six or seven years in a decimating war and she'd been waiting for me, telegram in hand, under the apple tree . . . We went straight to the icy tent and we were still awake when the raccoons came to carry away the remains of the evening.

"I've waited so long for you," she said later, under the joined-together sleeping bags. "Michou has talked about you for years. You've always been a hero to her. I expected you to come some day with a girl friend, or maybe to find one as soon as you got here . . . it's not hard for an American like you . . . I was sure you had a girl back in your room that night of the rain, and I got so mad I wanted to hit you with my umbrella—remember?"

"I—" I started to confess, then thought better.

"What's a girl like me supposed to do, not that I might not have done it? Then I made up my mind to go ahead and do it anyway."

"I'm glad you did."

"Shh. You don't know what I did. Terrible things, I did. I used to walk under your window very, very late at night, and I'd see that your light was off, so I'd sneak up to your room and let myself in—and you weren't there! How could that be? You had to be out with somebody and that's when I'd really hate myself, and you . . ."

"Kiki, if you only knew—"

"Shh. I told myself you were even worse than I thought. Why should I go looking for trouble, don't I have enough? He's even two-timing that girl in Boston—"

"I told you, there isn't any girl in Boston."

"Shh. Now that I'm here, I'll tell you everything. Even if you throw me out, I'll tell you everything. Her name is Linda, isn't it?"

"*My God!*"

"I ought to know—you left your letters to her out on the table and the streetlights are very strong. I don't know how Linda felt, but let me tell you those letters were the only thing that kept *me* going. I could tell that you were very afraid for her in that place, and that you were very lonely in Québec—unless you were lying to her, and I couldn't believe you would lie—"

"I could lie, Kiki, believe me," I said, trying to preserve a shred of dignity.

"Shh. All these weeks I have been very busy piecing together this boy who called himself Pierre in those letters to a girl called Linda in a place called, what—Harmony House?"

Secretly flattered, I whispered, "You little schemer—"

"—in Alabama. Piecing him together from all those things he wrote and from one evening in a coffee house and from all those talks with Michou—you used to write long letters to her when you first went to Harvard, do you remember?—and she used to show me those letters and tell me you were the only one who'd made good . . ."

I'd forgotten about those letters; my God, no gesture in the universe is truly empty. And I'd shown Michou's answering letters to Nick and Pete and built her up as a real piece for both their benefits, but mainly for mine.

"Anyway, I told myself it's good he writes like this to his Linda, it means he's a serious man, he doesn't forget people. He is here to answer a question that another man wouldn't even ask . . . Your Linda, she doesn't understand what you are doing, you know. I can tell from the way you keep trying to explain it to her. I even hope you work it out, because she's a much better person for you than I am—"

"You're being provocative. No man likes what's good for him."

She held tightly to my neck; our faces were burning in the near-freezing tent. Our second love-making had been violent, obliterating, it was as though we were trying to pass through each other's body. With Linda, sex had been light and topical; we joked, played roles—conversations begun would be only briefly interrupted, then immediately concluded. It was like ballroom dancing from a forties' musical. But twice with Kiki it was all percussion and amplification, a seizure.

An hour passed. I thought she'd fallen asleep, but when I turned to face her she answered, "Yes?"

"Kiki—why did you run away this afternoon?"

"I—I panicked. I thought I would lose you if I tried too hard. If you really wanted me, you would come and get me."

"*That?* Nothing else? You're not afraid to break in and read my mail but you suddenly *panicked* coming out of the woods?"

"They are not the same thing. I think it is easier explaining why I was in your room. If you had caught me there I would have said, 'I am here because you didn't call me.' But back there, today, you didn't tell me, I didn't know how you felt about me. Please, Hector—"

I could feel her body shaking; she'd started to cry. I couldn't even hold her, in that pitch-black tangle of sleeping bags. "*Please, Kiki, please.*" I had to speak in English. "That's why you sent what's-his-name, to find out?"

"I had to know."

"But Kiki, *so did I!* You don't know what I went through out there. The only thing I never considered was that you were trying to protect me. I thought maybe one of us was crazy. Me."

"I'm not sure I'm not."

"And I'm not sure of you or me or that crazy guy you sent. I'm not sure of anything. I thought I was the very picture of good health. I came here only to get my bearings. I didn't intend to get involved. Now I find it's not a choice between you and Linda or between Québec and the States. It's between parts of myself."

"No, you are not parts," she said with sudden fury. "You are whole."

"Kiki—can I ask something personal? Very personal?"

She didn't answer, but I could feel the warmth of her cheek, and feel her shallow breathing on my face. "What is this Pierre Tombale to you?"

"Call him Jerry. A boy I knew."

"And stayed with?"

"Yes. I stayed with him. I have stayed with many boys, Hector."

"I don't care," I said. It was a lie. Even Linda's two earlier lovers had caused me agonies in the night.

"I thought he would give me strength."

"Why does he want you to leave Québec?"

"For my happiness."

"And because you knew him when he first came from the States?"

"He said I make him uncomfortable. He said he would have to work alone. And he does."

"You were his historical future," I said.

"Maybe. But now I am yours."

I felt a sudden pity for the boy, Jerry, and the man Pierre Tombale. And then I felt it for myself; perhaps not pity, more fear. She could love a man so devotedly it could scare him out of his wits. I wasn't used to being loved like that, especially not by Linda. It was comfortable, being loved by Linda. This was an agony. I wanted to say, *You speak to me out of a depth of love that I didn't know existed; I'm scared to death by you,* but it sounded foolish in English and I couldn't phrase it in French. She spoke to an unused part of me. If I wanted to stay here, I would have to start all over again.

"Actually," she said, very quietly and with surprising authority for a voice slow with sleep, "you belong here. You have to overstate everything the same way we do, and still you're not quite convinced. The important thing is that you didn't go to that Harmony House, and so that means that you don't care about the Negroes. I mean you are not committed to them, like your Linda. But you came to Québec—*back* to Québec. That means you have a passion to know what you are."

From one of the other tents, I heard laughter. The raccoons were as noisy and indifferent as garbagemen. I could only feel the heat of Kiki's face, but I could sense her open eyes. I may have waited half an hour before I spoke; it may have been only thirty seconds. In such blackness, time itself disappears.

"You simplify," I said.

No answer. Even breathing. I could almost hear her whispered reply. *Because I am right.* I thought of a letter I'd written to Linda the very night that I'd first met Kiki. I'd drawn a little flag of the New Québec: a plate of French fries over crossed bottles of Pepsi and Molson's beer. Bannered slogan: *ça ravigote.* Anthem: *"Fèves au Lard"* sung by a farting chorus of scratching lumberjacks. On the five-piaster note, a picture of Dr. Maurice Laframboise, inventor of over three hundred uses for stale Pepsi-Cola. Kiki must have read it. That was before I'd gone camping in the Laurentians. That was even before I'd heard students singing *"Mon Pays, ce n'est pas un pays, c'est l'hiver . . ."* and been riveted by it. I didn't know what I felt anymore.

"Maybe I'll go on that March to Washington," I said, a little louder. I hadn't thought of it before, but suddenly it seemed the noble thing to do. Why? To please Linda? I hoped Kiki was asleep and wouldn't ask.

Her voice seemed smaller and further away, but that was an illusion. She was closer, her lips were inches away. "Come with us, Hector. We'll be driving down."

The ways in which we fool ourselves: I know by now that nothing was real to me that summer. Maybe there are phases in our lives—whole years when we catch the world a little naked, in sudden beauty or sudden horror. I'd thought that coming to Harvard had been it—the break, the growing up—but I was wrong. I had carried Pinardville with me all the way through Harvard; I'd ended up in a house on Bank Street that was as close as any house available to my parents' first American house on Dover Street in Manchester; and among all the dozens of Harvard boys I'd met, it was my first two friends I'd gone back to at the end. Harvard had been a confirmation. And Québec, which I'd chosen simply because it was the smallest most comfortable thing I carried, turned out to be a world I'd never seen and couldn't master. New perceptions eating into old ones, lasting for a minute, days, or maybe months. Like our first impressions of a person, of a city: immediate revulsion growing to love. Before long we know the comfort of being able to give agreed-upon names to the strangest forms. But I'd never lived two months in that state of naked suspension; it was like a permanent imbalance.

I was sailing on ice. I felt nothing underfoot. I was a pair of eyes behind a gray curtain, and the gray curtain that refused to take on shape was Pierre Desjardins who barely remembered a place called Harvard. The grittiness of Bank Street was over. North of Skowhegan I'd entered a world of purer forms, wide screen and living color. Life in Québec seemed to be a chain of *non sequiturs*. It didn't matter what I did or said, invariably it turned out right. Alternatives arranged themselves around my whims—if one day I mentioned staying on in Québec, scholarships to Laval were suddenly offered. Michou put my name on all the government mailings: a *bourse* for Québec students to study in France; French-African studies. Kiki would show up in my room at night—not every night, she seemed to know exactly when—sometimes with a bottle of wine. Lying with her in a darkened room, sipping wine: parts of the dream were coming true.

Michou took me one day to her professor, an East European who lived in an overheated farmhouse with cats and a worshipful wife, who brought him warm milk and a silk scarf for answering the door. "The drafts on his throat," she explained. She never used his name; she treated his stout little body like a scholarly shrine. I recognized the house and the smooth white walls with pastel graphics and political posters, the good sturdy Québec farm furniture, from my first-night's dream. This is where the party will take place, Linda will somehow find her way up here, speaking French. It must have been eighty-five degrees inside. I retreated behind the gray curtain and listened to him long enough, silently enough, to be offered a research fellowship at Laval while pursuing a doctorate under him. "I can tell he is a man apart," he said to his wife, who brought me hot lemon water for my throat and bowels, "a man we must attract." His name was Imre Meierhoff; I made a note to look him up. So this is what Homecoming is like, I thought: being better trained than anyone else, having the right instincts—where my ignorant silence would be taken by a European scholar as a dignified reproach (*"Eh, what's that, my young friend? I can tell you do not quite agree. Perhaps you are right. Perhaps I should reconsider . . .").*

I was walking with Kiki the next day, on the way (finally) to where she lived. It was a late-August Sunday afternoon, hot by anyone's standards. We took a bus; perhaps that's what dislodged the memory—a hot Québec Sunday on a bus, thinking of my new-found powers and beginning to distrust them. When I was six, my father took me to Montreal to see the First of His Kind: a Negro baseball player. The old *basseville* neighborhood had deputized my father to go down to Montreal and make his report. The papers said that this player was faster *and smarter* ("That, mister, I'll see for myself"—my father felt that baseball required greater intelligence than any other sport, and since he'd once played Class C ball for Thetford Mines, he was respected for all his baseball knowledge), and that if he got on base he was sure to score a run. I remember Jackie Robinson running wild that day—four stolen bases, including home twice—pivoting some sensational double plays and dominating every phase of the game. On the bus ride home to Québec, my father had patiently explained it all to me. Nothing was proved. Buffalo was a nothing club. The steals had been against a stupid pitcher. His four hits had been part of a sixteen-hit attack—even the pitcher had singled twice. But he had to admit that his fielding was pretty slick. He might just make it as a utility man and pinch runner, who knows? But there were plenty of fast, slick-fielding whites who needed work. Lots of Tripe-A flashes never made it to the majors ". . . because, kid, Montreal may be a championship club, but it sure as hell ain't Brooklyn, and Buffalo could have lost to Thetford Mines." And that's how I'd been feeling for two months in Québec—a Jackie Robinson in the high minors—batting a thousand and stealing at will, and perhaps I was watching myself from the stands as well, The Scout, sending reports back to the front office: "He's ready, Mr. Rickey."

I'd never been this good at Harvard. I wasn't even as smart as Nick, though less of a slob. I tried to remind myself just how stupid and insecure I'd always felt there. So, I'd been a hero to Michou. So, I'd impressed a self-important, perhaps mad little scholar named Imre Meierhoff. And I was living with a girl I'd thought to be Irish and beautiful, who was scarred and Iroquois, who would tell me nothing of her past and present, and perhaps had no future. But how was I *really* doing? I'd wanted disparate experiences, but were they really equivalent? What would research under Meierhoff at Laval *mean*, compared to a Berkeley Ph.D.?

Don't compare: flow, drift. But I couldn't help it. I'd been born to see the differences, and to measure them.

Kiki wasn't living in some foul corner of the lower city (I'd even imagined an Iroquois ghetto); when we finally visited her room we had to take two suburban buses to Sillery and then get down on a street of modest split-levels that was indistinguishable (but for the *Arrêt d'Autobus* sign, which I could see myself cherishing) from any prosperous development anywhere in the States. We turned in halfway down the block, where the name "Todd" was spelled in reflector panels on the lawn.

In the backyard, an oldish young man broiling steaks called "Hi, Kiki!" and waved us over to be introduced to him, the missus, and another couple, old friends, all sipping gin and tonic, all sprawled on chaise longues under the August sun. "Bet's off today, Kiki—they're old friends from Michigan." He reached too quickly for my hand, "Hi, Bill Todd," he said, gripping my hand but squeezing too early. "Gloria, my wife over there, and the Emersons." They raised their glasses.

"Pierre," I answered, before Kiki could label me with Hector.

Todd's French sounded like English, but he knew the words. Bill and Gloria Todd still looked like older graduate students, those who had prospered in a different career and then liquidated it in order to savor the benefits of university life. He wore corduroys, a sweater over a T-shirt, and cut-away sneakers. His face was youngish but deeply lined; gray tips to a thinning crewcut.

He looked foreign.

"Pierre will be at Laval next year," said Kiki.

"Maybe," I cautioned.

Sudden interest from Todd: "What department?"

So I'd been right, he was an academic. *Of course* I'd been right. "Sociology."

"Then you've met old Meierhoff, I take it. If not—"

"Yes."

"Brilliant, absolutely brilliant mind—"

I'd kept my answers as brief as possible, and we'd spoken in French, but Todd was looking at me the way they did in spy movies, when a disguise is about to be exposed. (*"Hans, come here a moment. I don't believe I ever congratulated you . . ."* pause *". . . on your excellent German. It must have been difficult . . ."* pause, scowl, triumphant smile *". . . for an American."*) He suspected something about me, but didn't know how to express it. The charade had become sadistic.

"You will forgive my French, but—"

"Please. *I speak English.*" (*"You see, it was not so difficult. I was educated in your country . . ."*)

"I'm sure you must. Kiki speaks excellent English too. But if I'm going to reach my students in just three more weeks, I've got to speak a lot better French than I do now, right?"

"No, no," this from Kiki.

"That's why we hired her—to get the kids ready for French school and to make sure me and the missus don't slip back. In fact she probably told you about the quarter we give her any time she hears an English word." He seemed particularly pleased with that agreement. It sounded like an importation from the business world.

"We didn't discuss it," I said. I was feeling near-sorrow for him.

"And with Kiki's help, we might just make it, eh?" He winked and nudged her elbow. "We're immigrants here, you see. We've pulled up stakes and come for good. Where did you say you studied, Pierre?"

"Harvard," Kiki quickly inserted, as though she'd been waiting.

He again looked me over. The eyes said, with a certain ancient resignation: *So.* The creases deepened into a defensive smile. *"Excellente université,"* he said, *"mais un peu* 'overrated,' *n'est-ce pas?"* He slapped a quarter into Kiki's hand, winking, then added, "I think you'll find Laval more engaged, less abstract—"

"I'm sure I will," I smiled. He turned to mind his steaks. "Have fun, kids," called Gloria Todd.

We fool ourselves. So Kiki was an *au pair* girl in her own home town, being a good, simple, uncomplicated kid to a desperate couple who'd sunk it all into gin-and-tonic and broiled sirloin emigration. Kiki's room had probably been furnished for a widowed grandmother before the Todds, and the Todds hadn't had money enough to do it over. Another form of the miraculous grotto hung over the bed. Yet the room didn't clash with her (television, something bright and youthful—that would have clashed); she was a girl who owned very little and felt no need to transform her dwellings. She used the old sewing machine as a bookshelf, but she didn't keep many books. She'd always sold her college texts back. Anything else, she gave away. She sometimes thought of being a physical therapist. Other times of being a doctor. She was not preoccupied by either choice.

"The Todds wouldn't mind if you stayed. They're very broadminded about some things."

I wondered how many others had stayed. "The house seems too sad."

"The Todds are very happy. That's all they can talk about— how happy they are." But she knew what I meant. I felt she was trying to ask me if I were happy. And if I didn't watch myself more closely, I'd say yes I was, and then I'd say yes to Laval, and soon I'd want to take Kiki out of sad little rooms and I'd end up married to her by Labor Day. I was living like a drunk, having to jerk myself upright every few minutes, *get ahold of yourself,* or else I'd drift right into that planing-mill that I feared.

"Are those the kids out there?" I asked. Chubby and blond, you couldn't imagine a French word in their mouths.

"If they're outside, it means Mrs. Todd called them out." She smiled, one of those sad little smiles that had made her seem so Irish that first rainy night. "Which means they're giving us the green light."

In that room, even a kiss was unthinkable.

"And after that the checkered flag?"

"You should hear *them* sometimes. A second childhood, she

calls it." It made me even sadder. "Wait at least till they come back inside, then we can go. I won't bring you here again."

I walked back alone, thinking of the Todds.

For the next few days her visits to my room seemed less well-timed. I'd thought before she was trying to lure me out of my room, out into the streets to some dark reality I could never explore myself (she'd been there, she'd suffered, she was immortal); things changed when I knew she'd put on a scarf and trench coat in the fussy little room, seen the kids asleep, gotten on a bus by the shopping center, transferred once, then slipped in cautiously around Monsieur Vaillancourt's frequent absences. There was something frightening about a girl like Kiki working with children: all that restless energy, humming like a defective transformer. I was in a mood to think it sinister. Linda could never do it. Penny would, if Nick ever left her. Who was Kiki, anyway? I knew nothing about her, and I never would know. What am I getting myself into? The Todds, that room, Kiki—who are these people anyway?

I wanted out, so I fooled myself some more. Drift implies something outward, not a return. Water doesn't go back to its sources, and I'd become something unnatural. Everything I'd been doing was wrong: going back home again was a funny way of exploiting the plenitude. You can't improve on your memories, you can't perfect a bad thing. Unthinking—but drifting—I'd gone back to a dead language, a ridiculous name, a girl with a mute past and no conceivable future, a job at a fifth-rate college under a man who might be simply mad. Idiot! Mindless drifting ends up as inertia, always seeking a position of rest. The *active* flow, the ever wider, deeper, further flow, was from Boston out, from Harvard out, from America and English and Linda. It was already late-August. Berkeley had assumed I'd taken their scholarship and now wanted medical forms and some kind of loyalty oath. Is the West Coast far enough? Is Berkeley good enough? *Yes,* those voices said: *Today California, tomorrow the world. Yesterday, Québec.*

There was a knock on the door. I was slow in answering, thinking it was Kiki. A key opened the door. Monsieur Vaillancourt stood in his undershirt, looking fierce. "Here," he said, holding out a telegram in his meaty paw.

SAFE REPEAT SAFE STOP WRITE SCLC ATLANTA STOP MEET WASH-
INGTON FOR MARCH AUG 28 ELEVEN OCLOCK REFLECTING POOL
LOVE LINDA

There was not much time to think: a bulky explanation post-marked "Selma" arrived the next morning. Naturally, she'd spelled Québec wrong, Vaillancourt wrong, even the street. I remembered with new fondness that it had taken her months even to learn to spell my name: she used to leave notes around the house for Pirere and Peirre.

A memo-sized piece of paper fell out. *Dear Pierre,* it said, *I've tried to write several letters and I've tried to write a formal report, but I'm just not any good at it. So you'll know what happened, I'm sending you everything that makes sense. Going to Atlanta to King's organization. Then to Washington 28 August. Could you come? Love Linda.*

The contents were in three parts: one written in pencil, a kind of diary with no one to read it; another partially typed and finished in a careful hand; the final part studded with dashes and underlinings, in three kinds of ball-point ink. On the fold of a page, leafing at random, I saw HELP! TORTURE! written in capitals three lines high.

I went back to the beginning, where the tone was that of a busy ex-lover who'd decided to stay friendly: careful descrip-tions of the beauties of Carolina, Georgia, and even Alabama. She was staying in a church in the Negro part of Selma, under-going the usual instructions from local leaders of the Negro community, and tutelage in voter registration from a federal marshal whom she suspected of giving just enough false in-formation to invalidate the forms in the event of a challenge. He kept saying, "Oh, yeah, I plumb forgot," when smart young law students from Negro colleges brought up technicalities. The white Southern accent was the ugliest thing she'd ever heard. And I'd be glad to know that she'd found an unexpected compassion for Bobby Kennedy, since he was so deeply hated by

so many hateful people. (*"My enemy's enemy is my friend."*)
She didn't blame me any more for not having gone South.

Then began the typed version. She'd been picked up by a
couple of deputies on a trumped-up charge. The shorter one
was a walleyed dwarf with a salivating, tobacco-browned chin.
Looked like he was drooling Tootsie Rolls. The other one, who
gave the orders, was as lean as a snake, with a tiny head of
thick, oily black hair parted in the middle and then combed
straight back. "I could hear the deputy (the short one) cock his
rifle and he never took it off Roger's forehead. Roger is my
partner in registration. He's from Rochester, very big and strong,
and totally nonviolent. He's nonviolent the way some people are
vegetarian or teetotalers—he stays away from things in case
they might *become* violent. I don't go along all the way with
nonviolence—as you know. They hurt Roger deeply enough to
make him leave the Movement. Then, I think, they killed him.

"I've tried to write all this down for a newspaper or something, but it happens every day—they couldn't print it anyway.
Then I thought of writing it up for Bobby Kennedy, but he
probably gets a hundred of them every day—and how much
does he really care? And if J. Edgar ever got hold of it he'd
probably use it to keep me from teaching anywhere in the
country. So who really cares? I mean who really cares what our
fellow Americans do to our own people because they're Negro—
like Roger, say. If he'd been working with some older Negro
woman they wouldn't have minded. It was my fault—really my
fault—because I liked being with Roger and I even told him
that the night before it happened. I'd even started off that
morning by putting my hair up and wearing a dress for the first
time in a month because Roger had said I looked good in a
dress—so I did it for him—not to get more voters. And I'd gone
through a kind of question and answer with myself—why do
you want to be with Roger? Is it to register more voters? *No.*
Is it to make myself look more sincere about it? *No*—they're
never going to trust you completely anyway. Are you falling in
love? Is it because he's already said he's in love with you?
(Fourth day together, Pierre; it's this charm I exercise over

the goyim, black or white—though I don't think I'm about to attract anybody new for a long time now.)

"You know I'm not the kind of person who has many doubts about things. I know I could have decided very easily what I felt about him—if he hadn't been a Negro. So there's one dirty little secret out—it's easier not to face it in Boston. Maybe I should go somewhere else—forget about Roger—don't they need me somewhere else? Mississippi, say? No—another dirty secret— I'm a coward after all and I don't want to end up like Violet Liuzzo. We'd been warned about 'provoking' local responses and that the surest way is for a Negro man (a 'buck') to be seen with a white girl *alone together in public* ('alone together in public'— that's exactly what they said!). But you know me—if I'd taken showers in the CORE office with Negro boys, then why the hell should I hide my natural feelings here—especially for their fuck-ing sensitivities? Southerners are always talking of themselves as the last of the rugged individualists, so why the hell shouldn't they respect *my* individualism? I know, I know—Alabama is a dumb place to start being subtle. Anyway, here's what I wrote until I started feeling sick about dignifying it all officially. I finally turned in something that they said was good, which probably means it'll give old J. Edgar a hard-on—if he gets them."

Deputy Southwell (he had a name plate) and an unnamed deputy arrested Roger Anderson, of Rochester, New York (a Negro), and Linda Feldman (white) of Boston, Massa-chusetts, on August 12, shortly after ten o'clock in the morning, on the stated charge of driving a defective vehicle (right-hand turn-signal allegedly was not functioning). Mr. Ander-son thanked the deputy for the warning and told him he would take the car immediately to a garage. At that moment, Deputy Southwell got out of the cruiser and ordered a body-search of Mr. Anderson, and then a complete search of the car. The other deputy encouraged a crowd to gather, saying such things as "They've got grenades stashed inside. They're running guns to Martin King." We were spat upon, etc., for an hour while Mr. Anderson removed the seats, the floor panel-ing, and all the various safety devices (flares, emergency lights) from the rear. These were described as "directional beams for signaling unauthorized aircraft." They confiscated our book of addresses and emergency numbers, all relating to our work in voter-registration—it seemed clear to Mr. Anderson and to me that the book was the object of the search.

They were not satisfied with having harassed us and with having removed our documents; they then decided to take us into custody for "non-co-operation with a duly-appointed law officer in the normal round of his duty." Mr. Anderson and I were then handcuffed and thrown roughly into the back seat of the cruiser. When Mr. Anderson attempted to point out to Deputy Southwell that members of the crowd were slashing the tires and scraping racial epithets into the paint of our car, an added charge of "attempted bribery" was added to the earlier one.

While the behavior of the officers on the street could not be considered "correct" by any standard I have come to recognize, their behavior once in the car degenerated to a savagery I had never before encountered. Deputy Southwell drove, while the other kept a sawed-off shotgun tight against Mr. Anderson's chin—so tight, I should add, that his head was forced against the back-window ledge. He said the "safety" was off and that the slightest jolt could set it off. The only conversation, naturally, was between the two deputies as they talked about potholes on the road. I am not exaggerating when I say that Deputy Southwell speeded and swerved to hit every one.

Naturally there were all the normal (by which I hope is understood *ab*normal) sexual suggestions about us. I am not a sheltered woman and I am not particularly shy about sexual references, but the sadistic fantasies of these two deputies made me physically sick. Female circumcision is the most clinical name I can give it; psychosexual pathology is the field it belongs in. They sang a little song ("Cream of c—— is so good to eat, that we have it every day . . .") that suggested clitoral excision of all white girls seen in the company of Negroes, the results to be served to the Negro prisoners.

Continual references were made in the interrogation room to my having to strip for a medical inspection, with a team of "doctors" being recruited from the local bars doing the examining. This threat, if it was one, was not carried out. They showed me a large syringe (more an enema) filled with "battery water" (I later learned this is sulphuric acid) which was to be inserted as a douche for, again, any white girl seen with a Negro. There were two chairs, a table, and a huge greasy twelve-volt storage battery with alligator clamps on the floor between the chairs. We were handcuffed to the backs of the chairs. When a screw driver touched one of the clamps a purple bolt cracked out of it. The short deputy tore Mr. Anderson's pants apart, ripping off the buttons and pulling out the fly-zipper. "Gonna put the nigger on a slow charge, Slim?" the small deputy asked. "Naw, first give him a boost to get him started, har-de-har-har," Deputy Southwell answered. The windows were open and I was screaming the whole time:

HELP! TORTURE!
"Call the Federal Marshals!!!!" and from the way they were letting me scream I could tell they weren't worried about any intervention.

The typing broke off then; the rest was written in a variety of styles and colors of ink.

"I don't know, Pierre. There's a tradition in the movies of holding out one or two extra minutes beyond what you thought you could endure, and suddenly you hear those bugles of the cavalry or the police siren or whatever—it's all a lot of bullshit, but it's the only thing you have to fall back on. I kept trying to look at the door and I swear to God I expected Bobby Kennedy himself to come smashing through. Can you feature *me* thinking *that?* I kept saying it couldn't be happening—it was a dream— I was torturing myself over all kinds of new guilts and pretty soon I'd wake up—because they just don't make people as rotten as they made those two—you can only make them up in order to punish yourself. There I was handcuffed to a chair and blubbering away—I admit it, I was crying and snuffling and begging and still screaming and so was Roger and that old kid's dodge was running through my head the whole time—*Dear God, get me out of this and I'll go to—what?—temple, church? —I'll be a good woman for the rest of my life.* I kept hoping that some crying and begging was all they wanted from us (remember the rats in Room 101 in *1984?*).

"I was clinging to the hope that those two goons were really subtle psychologists—in a way they were—and that all they wanted to do was rough us up psychologically. *That* I could take. They had Roger's pants down around his knees and he was wearing those kinds of shorts you wear—funny how you remember things like that—polka-dotted things—and the deputy had his pistol right under Roger's chin and his head thrown back over the edge of the chair so he could only see the ceiling and not what they were planning to do to him. Or leastways, not knowing *when,* which is even worse. Then they pulled his shorts down and started making all the comments appropriate to degenerate whites looking at a Negro man's manhood. I am sick of my whiteness—it'll be a blessing when we're *all* sent to the gas chambers. They started off, 'Boy, you are an insult to your race. I seen hogs on eighty-year-old-woolheads was twicet as big as *that.*' 'Jiggle it around some, Slim, I can't even get the clamp on nothin' that weeny.' And they slapped it around. They pushed my chair closer so I'd have to look— they held my head so I had no choice ('Your cunt's looking at it now,' they kept saying) and finally it started to . . . what? . . . *unfurl* maybe, and that drove them wild. 'Bring the clamps!' 'Him first or her?' They were a lot more excited by stripping him than me (they didn't even get started with me—think it's the long tradition of Southern chivalry?) except to make some witty comments about performing electric therapy to increase or maybe decrease the size of my bust. It was Roger they wanted. It was always Roger.

"Their hands were shaking and their teeth were chattering

and they started not making sense—even for them—when they spoke. I should have known that we had been safe while they were merely being obscene. They measured the distance from the battery to his crotch and from the battery to my mouth. I don't know how long we'd been there by then. I couldn't remember ever *not* being there. I vomited all over my clothes —I had the dress on, remember—and I deliberately caught it in my skirt so they wouldn't have some other kind of puking-on-duly-constituted-floor charges to bring. They got a thrill out of pushing my chair till I was practically on top of him—they took the gun off his neck but he still wouldn't open his eyes. *What can I say, Pierre*—he was the man who said he loved me—he was the man who'd dropped out of divinity school to go to Buffalo and work with the toughest kids in the ghetto and he was so successful he ended up bringing ten of them to Alabama with him and they were just about the best workers we had. He was a great, dignified man, and when they undid my cuffs and told me to touch him *there* I did it because there wasn't any other place that still seemed like Roger. I touched him, and I thought maybe *that's* what they wanted after all, so big deal, and sure enough Slim was standing over me with a camera, but that wasn't what they wanted at all.

"They threw me back like I was a lever or something and that's when they did what they'd been daring each other to do the whole morning. They *needed* me to touch him. In one sentence: *they took his penis and they wet it and they pulled it till he screamed and then they set the clamp on it.* It burned—God, Pierre, I will never forget the smell, the color of the smoke, the sound, the screams that seemed to be coming not just from my mouth and his but from every part of our bodies. He went stiff and passed out and his tongue was out and bleeding and practically cut in two. When they took the clamps off a lot of skin came with it. A lot. Even *them,* whatever they should be called, they looked frightened by what they'd talked themselves into. They started talking about a 'nigger doc' they could dump him at, but I think that was more for me to hear than for them to do. '*Just give me our car,*' I cried, 'just give me the car you stopped because you said it had a bad turn signal and carry

Roger to it and let me drive him back to Selma. Please, please.'
I touched Roger again when I saw him open his eyes, but he
didn't look at me—he snarled. He wouldn't ever be Roger again,
I remember thinking—but I was still too dumb and too shocked
to think what I should have thought. That it would be the last
time anyone would ever see him alive. We have people out
looking, but no one has heard a thing.

"What they did to me doesn't seem so serious, but I'll carry
it with me for quite a long time. The sheriff insisted on driving
me back to Selma, according to the deputies. He was out in the
cruiser. I wanted to get my own car, but they wouldn't let me
make a phone call. Fortunately the deputies didn't try to hold
my arms or anything, they just walked a step on either side and
I could see they were sick from inside. One of them opened
the back door—the sheriff didn't turn around, he just had the
police radio on and he turned it up. I sat down, but the unnamed deputy held my legs so I couldn't swing them in. He
grabbed my ankles very suddenly and then held my legs
straight out and he was saying, 'We gave your boy friend
something to think about. Now it's your turn. Slim—' and before
I could do anything to turn or kick, the fucking degenerate had
his long riot stick up over his head and brought it down three
or four times in the same place straight across both shins. I have
never been hurt like that. The pain was just a different kind of
pain than anything I'd ever felt—I don't think a bullet or a
whipping or anything could hurt like that. The sheriff turned
around then and said, 'I think you're fixing to remember your
little visit to us every cold morning and every day it rains for
the rest of your life, ma'm.'

"So that's why I had to leave. I gave a lot of reports to the
CORE lawyers and they fixed up a place for me to rest at in
Atlanta. I'm hobbling around these days like a veteran after
an amputation or something, since I'm in casts and using those
aluminum crutches that you hold in front of you a little. I've
changed—who wouldn't?—Your letters were all I had to start
building on, and that's why I hope you'll come (or should I
say go) to Washington for the March. There may be a million
people there, but you can't miss me."

I hadn't thought of the date since sometime in June; I suddenly panicked that I'd missed the March. I shouted downstairs to Monsieur Vaillancourt: "Hey, what date is it?"

He called back from his deck chair outside, where he drank Molson's and held a newspaper over his chest, "The twenty-sixth! You're paid up till Saturday."

I called the Greyhound station from his downstairs pay phone: the daily express bus had already left. There was a local around midnight, getting in around ten the next morning—or tomorrow's express, getting in around suppertime.

Her letter cut the final strings. While Robert and friends dreamed of dynamiting the Canadian National trestle bridges, derailing the Queen and freeing Québec, inventing causes and oppressors, thousands of Americans were massing in their capital to protest real oppression and show they would no longer tolerate it. Could anyone imagine going to Ottawa? Pearson or Diefenbaker—whichever it was—would he meet with the leaders the way Kennedy had? America wasn't perfect, but it was the best show on the continent, and I had nothing but disgust for my own slowness in recognizing it. There was something insidious in the simplicity of Canada. I'd been sinking into that northern inertia and had saved myself just in time. Now I had to make sure that I could never go back again. I had to seal it off.

I wrote a note to Kiki the next morning, the cruelest most premeditated act of my young life. *You're sacrificing her,* a voice said, and I thought briefly of the flames licking the sides of the pig and I thought too of the scars on Kiki's body and, God help me, I drew solace from thinking she was doomed to be sacrificed anyway. *Why blame me?* I stuck the note on the door, and walked out of Quebec, forever.

> Dear Kiki: Guess you were wrong
> about me after all. Duty calls.
> It's been fun. Take care,
>   Pierre

The noon express got me to Boston six hours later. The temperature had risen twenty degrees, and I felt, for a few hours, the foreign-looking, the funny-sounding. I checked my bag in the bus station (new resolutions: travel light, forget the past, what's gone is gone) and walked out, as free as I would ever be.

The area around the Common was like a carnival. A single row of charter buses nearly encircled the Common—everything from yellow school buses and those bullet-shaped Greyhounds of the War years that had carried the troops home to Minnesota from San Francisco and New York. (I remembered the movies— Christ, the movies of my adolescence were all that I *really* knew about America.) I stood like a fool on the sidewalk of the Common, staring at that elongated egg with the tiny windows (now belonging to a private, small-town feeder service and named for a bird), and it was as though I'd become a child again, an American child this time, a New England Yankee child watching the big buses that take important people to exciting cities.

They were all mixed, every kind of bus that had ever known bourbon bottles in paper bags, squalling infants, the sudden intimacies of cross-country travelers, had been tinkered back to service for the trip to Washington. Streamers and posters were already attached to most of them: building trades locals, steam fitters, elevator installers; CORE, NAACP, Democrat precincts; various *ad hoc* committees for freedom, jobs, dignity, justice, equality; certain high schools, colleges, and nearly every university in New England. I looked for the Newton High School bus (*"Do you remember Miss Feldman? Your Spanish teacher? She'll be glad to know you've come . . ."*), but I couldn't find it. The sidewalks were littered with tightly packed bed rolls, guitars with single names and no addresses penned on masking tape; it was a hootananny mood, a campus mood, a home-coming mood with every bus like a slaved-over float, and the students were sprawled on the grass just sleeping or singing or staring into space. The capacity for idealism, I thought again; it's in me too. Black and white, laborer and student, parent and child—we'd taken over the city. Tomorrow we'd take over the country. My only regret was that I'd played no role.

We'd be leaving at midnight. Around 11 P.M. I found a CORE bus with a couple of empty seats, though I'd offered to stand. The driver was a tiny Irishman, the kind we saw in Harvard Square only on Sunday mornings with wife and daughters both twice his size, still dressed in pink for mass (I'd be sitting in the back of the "Bick" with my pot of tea, stack of English muffins, and the Sunday *Times*). The driver was reading an early copy of Wednesday morning's paper ("HALF MILLION GATHER FOR JOBS AND FREEDOM—Boston Area Leads the Way"). I asked if I could take my seat before the bus started filling, a little afraid he'd try one last-ditch racist comment before eighty-five Negroes climbed on board. But he seemed not to care, and I took a seat three rows behind him.

Picture a set of funnels. Point their necks towards Washington, their mouths in any direction. Picture the stragglers from all over New England, the boys from Brown and the girls from Bennington, the Pembroke girls, the Williams boys, Amherst, Smith, U. of Mass., all of them hitching to Boston, each holding a shirt-cardboard crayoned BOSTON-MARCH. Picture the boys with the rusty cans of raspberries north of Québec— they are out of funnel-reach. Everything south of them is on the move. Somewhere near King's church in Atlanta another convoy had already left, with Linda aboard. She would feel every bump, my legs ached just to think of her. Big funnels and little funnels draining every city east of the Mississippi of its workers and Negroes and college youth. "See you at the Monument at ten o'clock!" I could hear kids on the sidewalk making their plans as they drifted off to their separate charters. It seemed to me the most hopeful thing in the world, to expect so fine a calibration out of such chaos. As though our will alone could bring us together—how like Linda, how like them all, to minimize distance and demography. Neither one of us had ever been to Washington; I didn't know a thing about it. Its essential flavor had always seemed Republican; lobbyists and golf courses, and the recent attempts to tart it up with Harvard professors and arty evenings had only emphasized its basic failure—as though Manchester had bought itself a *corps de ballet* and built a Bolshoi to house it. But we would change all that too.

We were off by midnight with a full, unsleeping load. Only half were Negro. The whites insisted on taking the rear, leaving me marooned in front. Dawn found us between New Haven and Bridgeport, part of a long convoy of Boston chartered buses, being passed by private cars with streamers attached to their antennas. Our bus was singing: some mournful spirituals from the whites (the etiquette of integrated travel had not yet been worked out), then "We Shall Overcome," still mournful, more in the hope that the Negroes would start songs of their own. ("Man, all I want to overcome is that terrible singing," said the one closest to me.) They didn't seem ready to cut loose, not just yet.

Before six o'clock we were over the Tappan Zee and speeding down the Palisades Parkway, where *all* the traffic seemed Washington-bound, and by six-thirty we were nearer Philly than New York (I was nearing Valley Forge, my southernmost, westest-ever). The whites had died down. One of the Negroes asked the driver his name, and he shouted back over his shoulder, in a high tenor, "Dennis." (Of course, I thought, Dennis Day. Ask for a song and we'll get "Toora Loora.") Then the Negroes started clapping, a kind of churchly, chanting clap warming up to lyrics as soon as someone supplied them. "Hey, Dennis," clap, clap, "you know any songs?" clap, clap, clap. *Why pick on Dennis,* I thought. I'd never heard a question from a Negro; I couldn't tell an honest question from a prelude to something else. Dennis answered, obligingly enough, "All I know is a lot of old ones." (*"Gee, Mr. Benny, sing in front of all these people?"*) "Like what kinda songs you know, Dennis?" clap, clap. "Old organizing songs mostly. My old man was in the Union." "Like sing 'em, man," clap, clap; but the driver only looked back this time through the rearview mirror. "See me in Washington"—he tapped the crest on his Greyhound cap—"singin' ain't in the rules."

We were definitely out of my territory, even below Mason-Dixon by seven-thirty when we stopped for breakfast and a piss-call in a place that must have figured in some Civil War battle. Some buses from our group and from a dozen others were already in the parking lot; we were out shaking hands like allied soldiers who've just linked up. Rows of men reached from around the back of the building and all along the side, a multiracial watering crew, while an equally long female line cut straight through the restaurant and out the front steps—like a Sunday double-header, like intermission in the Boston Garden, democratic urinals, everyone talking, everyone pissing on each other's shoes. What would half a million people under an August sun in Washington use? They'd make short work of the reflecting pools. The Potomac? Storm the White House and use the executive john? What better sign of health than going to the capital and laying friendly siege to the President's house? He was with us anyway: the transistors in the back seats had announced he'd be meeting with the March leaders early in the morning to offer his blessings and caution against extremism. A few old men in the Senate were all that stood between chaos and historic legislation—don't alienate them now. As we got back on the bus, one of the whites said to one of the Negroes, "There was actually *grits* on the menu! If we'd had time, I would've ordered it just to drop it on the floor." He wore a "PASS THE BILL" button. His friend's said "I WAS THERE."

And so we were South, around Baltimore and down a carpeted expressway the final few miles to Washington. Nothing now but the lines of cars and buses—an indecipherable code of tiny dots and longer dashes—twenty-five miles of vehicles in bunting barely moving. It was nearly ten o'clock. Somehow I'd never believed that people lived in Washington, but soon we were passing the Maryland suburbs where local cars had driven down from their shelters to park on the shoulders of the highways, to line the stone bridges overhead, to clog the parking lots of shopping centers, to stand and sullenly watch. Inside our bus, the Negroes were singing:

> Oh, when we can stay—
> (Oh, when we can stay—)
> In a Holiday Inn

> (In a Holiday Inn—)
> Oh, when we can stay in a Holiday Inn;
> Oh Lord, I want to be in that number,
> When we can stay in a Holiday Inn.

Verses were supplied by anyone who shouted "Mine!" in time to pick it up. The whites were clapping in the back.

> And when I can get me—
>   (And when I can get me—)
> A Hilton Carte Blanche
>   (A Hilton Carte Blanche—) . . .

I thought briefly of the songs of Québec; if only there'd been a *"Mon Pays"* for the civil rights movement. Or perhaps the problem with Québec was that they were too aesthetic, too pretty, too conscious of form; they'd have the songs and thousands of students to strike the proper gestures, but they'd never get together the way they were doing today.

We crossed into D.C. and a cheer went up. The bus windows couldn't open, and in frustration we wanted to smash them in order to wave. All the houses were close together, nearly tenements, and every house had emptied to wave us on, to blow kisses, to show the flag. All of the inhabitants were black. It was New York Avenue on the twenty-eighth of August, 1963, but it might have been the Champs Elysées on Liberation Day. I'd always wanted to be part of a benevolent, conquering army, and this was the closest I'd ever come.

The buses were beaching like herds of whales under a perfect morning sun. It was almost eleven. Thousands of people poured through the narrow aisles between the parked buses, like the rush of ants through a mound of sugar. A city the size of Manchester was already on hand and it was still a couple of hours before the official beginning. A loud-speaker was asking, *"Is Miss Lena Horne in the group?"* As far as the eye could see, buses were still rolling in. A smiling, fat Negro woman with a "MONITOR" armband sold me an "I WAS THERE" button. There was a fairway, parted only slightly around groups of older men with "monitor" bands. "*Would Miss Lena Horne kindly report to the stage?*" I strained to catch a glimpse of Lena Horne, saw no one, then looked back towards the Monument. Not fifty feet in front of me stood Linda. She was dressed in jeans that had been split up to the knees to accommodate the walking casts that I hadn't wanted to believe. She'd lost weight; she was a tall, lanky girl in jeans and a workshirt, with her long blondish-brown hair down, and she too wore an armband, and glancing at the half-circle of older Negro men who were facing her and nodding as she spoke (she leaned on one of her crutches—the other she'd dropped, leaving herself free to point and gesture), I sensed their respect, and her power.

Way off in the distance, on the temporary stage, a medley of lesser Hollywood types was trying to entertain, but only when Joan Baez started to sing did the thousands stop talking and begin to listen. I waited for Linda to break up her meeting. I listened to Baez, a magic name for anyone who'd passed through Harvard when I had, when all the windows of Harvard Yard had been open and all you could hear was ". . . *and in her right hand, silver daggers . . .*" So now the Harvard style and taste were going out to labor unions, to Negroes, to all those gray-haired veterans of peace and integration movements. I'd been there from the beginning, this time.

When I looked again, Linda was standing alone, listening to Joan Baez.

We had an argument in the first five minutes. We embraced but didn't kiss, and then we began the long march from Washington Monument to Lincoln Memorial, where all the speeches were to be given. One of the monitors offered to drive her in a VIP golf cart, but she turned him down. She walked as quickly as she ever had; the casts made her a little taller than me.

We were out on Constitution Avenue walking fifty abreast under banners, silenced by chants and gospels and a few more digs at Holiday Inn, Colonel Sanders, and Aunt Jemima, and every one was loose and happy, singing or not. Then I looked off to the side under the trees and saw a gray-haired, middle-aged Negro in a business suit, surrounded by kids with auto-graph books. I fell out of step, Linda called, "What is it?" and the marchers behind swirled around me without a break in step.

"Linda, my God, it's Jackie Robinson."

"Robeson?"

"Robinson."

"Which one?"

"There."

Marchers behind me, following my finger, also stopped. *"Hey, Jack!"*

"What does he do?"

My God: *Linda, please.* "He doesn't *do,* he *is.* He was the first Negro baseball—"

"Oh my God, not a jock!"

But for a moment, a hundred thousand people had van-ished, and he and I were under a tree in a park. His hair wasn't white and his neck wasn't humped, and I wasn't six years old with my father nor was I twenty-one but feeling forty-five, either. There wasn't a woman on crutches pulling at my elbow. There was a question I wanted to ask. There must have been a question I wanted to ask. Then we were marching again, Linda was scowling, and I made up my mind: to hell with Jackie Robinson and all that nostalgic crap. If he wants to bust his hump for the Republican Party, let him. But not on my emotional time.

It was star time at the Lincoln Monument. Baez again, Ralph Bunche, Dick Gregory, some of the actors taking a turn on the podium the way heavyweight challengers do before a title bout. Linda had been standing for seven straight hours; she leaned on me, but still she needed rest. We began to walk away to find some grass and shade about the time Mahalia Jackson began to sing, and we walked back along Constitution Avenue, under the trees this time, listening to bits and snatches of the official speeches from loud-speakers hung in the trees. We turned onto a fairway where grass grew in patches and hundreds of marchers had spread blankets and picnic hampers. A few college boys in cutoff jeans and baseball caps tossed

Frisbees over the heads of black and white picnickers, eating together. Then we finally sat.

"*Let us not wallow in the valley of despair . . .*" The rhetoric was oppressive, a little embarrassing. It was a Southern voice, but Negro. We closed our eyes and listened. "*Now I say to you today my friends—*"

"Who's that?"

"Damned if I know."

"Could it be King?" I asked.

"At his worst, it could be."

"*Even though we face the difficulties of today and tomorrow, I still have a dream—*"

"Yes, it's King," she said.

"*It is a dream deeply rooted in the American dream. It is a dream that one day this nation will rise up and live out the true meaning of its creed—*"

I began to listen; I too had been dreaming. Some students walked behind us: "Hey, is there television at the motel?" asked one. "I can't wait to see what they do with *this*. Man, we're sitting on *history!*" They carried Frisbees.

"*I have a dream that one day on the red hills of Georgia—*"

"Pretty weird, isn't it?" Linda said.

"Why?"

"We pulled it off, that's all. This is the first time in American history that *the people* actually pulled something off. I feel sort of empty so I guess it means—we won."

"*I have a dream that one day even the state of Mississippi, a state sweltering with the people's injustice—*"

"Did they . . . you know . . . find him?"

"Roger?"

I'd been afraid to ask, but I knew I'd have to.

She answered calmly. "He's alive. I'd rather not discuss Roger."

"*I have a dream that my four little children will one day live in a nation—*"

"Come on, Pierre, I have to walk. I can't stand up and I can't lie down, I can only walk. And King gets a little thick after a while."

"This is our hope. This is the faith I go back to the South with—with this faith . . ." We were walking again, out of loud-speaker range. I could call Linda beautiful now. I wanted to share her victory, I wanted to share King's hope, as unworthy of them both as I knew I was.

"What's next, Linda?"

"Rest. Rest for months and months. No teaching, no school, nowhere to go. Free at last, thank God." She gave me a crutch to carry, then held my hand. "Like you."

People had been waiting for King's speech and now they were packing their hampers and very slowly drifting away. It would take hours, but the peak had been reached.

"I'm not that free any more," I said. "I'm going to take that scholarship to Berkeley. I tried to drift, but I'm not the type."

"A lot of the Selma people were from Berkeley—"

"—I'm not finished. It's a generous scholarship. What I'm saying is, two people can live on it."

"Dear boy, two people *always* live on a Berkeley scholarship."

"Rest on *my* time, Linda. I don't want to lose you again. In Berkeley things will be different."

"I think so too."

I caught a familiar sight out of the corner of my eye: a purple flag waving from a tree limb. The Québec flag. A cheap card-table had been set up under the tree and a poster "For a Free Québec" taped to the edge, the way a child might advertise "Kool-Aid 2¢ a Glass." On the table lay petition sheets with a few dozen signatures, stacks of pamphlets, and empty Coke bottles crawling with flies. I could hear the Pimpernel's Ameri-can voice somewhere nearby. Lafrenière and a group of others stood around a garishly-painted VW van. One girl looked tall and dark-haired from behind; beside her stood a *gamine*. Linda hadn't noticed. I steered her out of the way.

"What exactly are you proposing?"

"I am proposing that you tell your father that the Frog became a Prince Charming."

"We had a marriage on the bus coming up, if that's what you're thinking."

That was it, exactly. I hadn't thought once of marriage on the long trip down. I hadn't thought of it when I saw her, but it was the answer to every question I'd been trying to ask in Québec and earlier. I didn't need permission from Pierre Tombale. I didn't have any questions, man-to-man, for Jackie Robinson. Suddenly it was all in my power; in marriage the harmony would be restored. I raised objections, only to sweep them away —wasn't there *any*thing about her that I didn't like? Nothing in myself that was still unresolved? Nothing. It was the right move, the inevitable move.

"I, Pierre-Hector Desjardins of Quebec City, Pinardville, Cambridge, and points south and west am proposing marriage to Miss Linda Feldman of Boston, Washington, Los Angeles, and points on three continents."

"I've already warned you—I don't speak French."

"I'll never speak it again."

"I can't spell your last name—"

"A piffle. I'll change it to Gardner."

"Linda *Desjardins?* It would kill my mother."

"That is no reason in itself to say yes."

"We'd be outcasts."

"Never again."

"You've given it careful thought?" She was trying to ask her father's questions. We were almost back to the Washington Monument, past the booths of Muslims and Nazis, Ban-the-Bombers and Palestinians. Cars in the parking lots were starting to move.

"I've been thinking of nothing else," I said.

"It's crazy, isn't it? Just hold me tight, I need to lean on something." We walked that crazy way, as though we were tied together, all the way to the buses. Finding the strength from somewhere, I even carried her up the steps. Somewhere near Philadelphia she agreed to become my wife.

AT THE LAKE

All those lakes up north with unsavory names—Lac Têtard, Lac Bibitte, Lac Sangsue (who would buy a cabin to share with tadpoles, biting flies, and leeches?)—take their names from a surveyor's map and not from their pests. Long ribbony Sangsue stretches out at the flanks of two steep ridges six miles long and a quarter mile wide. When I bought the property on Lac Bibitte, Serge explained to me, "Sure, *bibitte* means bug. But look at the lake, round like a ball on top and shaped like an egg down here. It's not Lac des Bibittes, you know . . ." Têtard, on the other side of Mont Tremblant, has a triangular head and a broad branching river that drains its tail like larval legs. Anyway, the names might discourage some people. Closer to the city the developers have been at work and the homely generic names have gone through their initial manorial transformations: Lac des Mulets, Lac Quenouille, and Lac des Castors into Lac Gagnon, Lac Ouellette, and Lac Sauvé; thence into their death agonies as "Lac Paradis: 45-minutes-on-4-lane-open-all-year fully winterized landscaped-in-your-choice-of trees-ranch-ettes-from $10,000." I have the diminishing satisfaction that a place is worth twice as much after three years of unimprovement and decided deterioration.

There are families on the lake who've blasted crannies into the soaring granite cliffs a hundred feet above the water: Germans who thread their way like mountain goats balancing a weekend's beer on their heads, who dive like Acapulco professionals from a board on their porch into its unsounded depth below. I have watched them in summers past from the wide porch of our cabin on the low, marshy shore across the way—fat men of fifty in bikini briefs walking to the board, their laughter and joking clear, if foreign, from a mile away. Beer can in hand, laughter clapping over the water, he raises his arms in a diving motion but releases his empty can instead and sends it spiraling to the water. Then he crumples from the board—it's serious and competent he is—straightening in time and cutting the water like a missile.

We used to go up for the middle of every week from early July when the black flies died until the end of September when autumn was well advanced. I'm an academic and like the blessed commuter who lives in the city and drives to a suburban job, I found myself always moving against the crowds. We abandoned the lake on weekends to the waterskiers and speedboaters, when gasoline generators and long horn blasts waked us from the dream of a northern retreat. I preferred Wednesdays on the lake. August Wednesdays when it might be eighty-five degrees in the city and a bone-warming seventy at the lake after a swim, when the sun burned with a rare intensity through the clear, polished air. Erika and I would lie on towels on the dock, dangling our fingers for bluegills to nibble, peering down the pilings to the sandy bottom where the sluggish mountain carp sifted through the mosses clinging to the wood.

I spent those summers envying the Europeans and a few Canadians who've blasted the granite and erected the A-frame bunkers on girders sunk in into the bare rockface (their twin flag-standards flying down at dock level, Red, Black, and Gold of the *Bundesrepublik*, and the adopted Maple Leaf), and I envied Serge, who hadn't missed a weekend at the cabin in fifteen years. Every weekend he has added cubits to his lands, his sewage, his dockery, his cabin, his soul; whereas I—a younger man more aware a thousand times of ravages, impurity, and decay—have found the battle, or challenge, overwhelming. I ask myself what did I really want: electric blankets, pavement, a stove and fridge? And I say no, of course not; I wanted my son to grow up with nature. Skier, swimmer, fisherman, even hunter; I wanted him to grow up unflawed. I wanted the lake accessible yet remote, I wanted my cabin rustic but livable, I wanted a granite resolve to do on my marshy shore what old Germans had done on their cliffs; yet I wanted never to lose my immemorial torpor, my hours of dozing on a creaky dock peering at carp through the widening cracks. I wanted the end of black flies but no spraying, no lancing the swamps fed by fifteen feet of winter snows—relief from modest unfulfillments, exemption from levies I couldn't pay.

I was suckered into buying the place. Serge had advertised it in an English paper, and I'd called him at his hardware store in Lachute, gotten complicated directions, and then headed off one Sunday morning for the Laurentians, up past St-Jovite into Mont Tremblant Park. It was high summer, cool in the mountains (I drove with the window halfway up), the air was clear and the colors pure, as though I'd just awakened from a nap. The leaves were waxen, not yet dusty. The gravel road branched twice, snaked its way around the rim of Lac Sangsue, then sent off a single trail that rose steeply through an uncleared forest, like a logging road. I peered about for *gros gibier* prancing by the ravine at the edge of the trail. In the first mile there were two cabins, both of tarpaper studded with tin foil. I climbed one last long grade then came suddenly on the lake. There was an extensive marina and dozens of cars were parked over a sandy clearing. Most were foreign and expensive: Mercedes-Benzes, Renault 3000s, Volvos. I drove a VW van and had been feeling, until that moment, properly rustic and prepared. By prearrangement, I sent out three long *ooo-gahs* on the VW horn, and from far across the basin of the egg-shaped lake, a tall bearded man in tan shorts swung his arms over his head then got into his boat and speeded my way.

I said I was suckered. In the keel of the aluminum boat lay two large trout, and propped in the bow were two trolling rods with Daredevil spoons. Serge was about forty-five with stiff black hair and a well-trimmed beard, mostly gray over the chin. "Just caught them twenty minutes ago—c'mon, you like to fish?"

We sped to his cabin and had a beer. There were two large rooms, one for cooking and eating with floor to ceiling windows looking out on the lake, and an elevated unwindowed room with a high-beamed ceiling containing a wood-burning fireplace, bunk beds covered with animal skins, a guncase, and some mounted trophies. On the dining table I saw a freshly cut loaf of the round white bread they sell by the roadsides up north, a pot of still warm coffee, and Henri Troyat's *Tolstoi* in Livre de Poche. I'd always wanted to believe that somewhere not too far from where I would settle, *quincailliers* read the classics and fished (and academics worked with their hands and fell asleep sore and exhausted), that nature preserved as well as provided. That there was, in a part of the world I aspired to buy, a different heartbeat from the one that was dwarfing my manhood. Serge gutted the trout, fried the *filets* in garlic and butter, and I swabbed my plate with dabs of fresh bread, as I would after snails in a good French restaurant. We discussed manly things: dressing venison, tracking deer, baking corn and potatoes. I felt like a Boy Scout. We got back in the boat and Serge hauled up the minnow trap he kept at the end of his dock. He dumped a few minnows into a coffee can, threw out a tadpole that had slithered in and had already sucked the flesh from two minnows' bones, and then extracted a smallish fish that was three or four times longer than a minnow, and sleeker than a sunfish. *Trout*, I thought: *trout already! Lousy with trout! I'll buy!*

"Ah, just what we need."

"A trout," I said knowingly. Cannibalistic brutes.

"No, it's what you say in English?" He snapped its neck and laid it out in his hand. His hand was long, thick, pink-palmed, with old cuts etched in grease. "Carp, no?"

I almost laughed. Carp, *here?* In this lovely lake? We were circling out beyond his dock, heading at high speed down the middle of a blue mountain lake. Water gurgled under my feet. *Carp are garbage fish.* Where I grew up we used to hunt carp with bows and arrows where the sewer pipes emptied into the river. If the water was clear enough, and the smell not too bad, we could see them below the surface. And where it was really bad we used to shoot at their fat black humps above the water line. Twenty-pound garbage bags. Suckers, we called them. Sewer carp. If we caught one, no torture was undeserved. We cut them, burned them, stuck them, kicked them. Then we nailed them head-down to a tree. Sometimes they'd still be flopping the next morning. I wanted to save my son from that kind of nature.

"Mountain carp," he said. "Keeps the lake clean. In Bibitte you got only carp, bluegill, and trout. You get your perch in here or your *doré,* and—pfft—there goes your trout. They eat the little trout—see? And trout most of all goes for *this.*" He took my line, the heavy spoon and striped spinner, and then cut it off. He threaded catgut through the dead carp, through the mouth and out the anus, then reattached the cluster of hooks so they nestled at his tail.

"Lethal," I said.

He winked. On his own spinner he simply attached a longish plastic ribbon, white on one side, with spots. We were under the high bluffs where Germans waved down. "Your place is just across," he said. "That little cabin with the yellow door." That was the first time I saw it. "We'll go ashore after we catch your supper." I was hooked.

There was still time that first summer, it being early July when we bought it, for a lot of indoor camping in the cabin. There was, by communal agreement, no electricity. The cabin had been a fishing camp with a wood-burning stove, an icebox, a pair of iron bunk-frames and rusty springs with giant sodden mattresses that wouldn't burn, and a two-drawered dresser with a blistered top. We brought new things with us on every visit; a two-burner Coleman stove and a cold chest with twenty-five pounds of ice inside. We learned to live on cans of soft drinks, steaks and fruit, cereal and powdered milk, and at night after the baby fell asleep, cups of instant coffee on the porch. We bought sleeping bags, a card table, a chemical toilet, lawn chairs, and a pump. I threw away the springs and iron frames. I bought hoes, shovels, trowels, scythes and rakes; fishing rods, snorkels, grass seed, and paint. Drapes, incinerator, and asphalt tiles. An aluminum boat like Serge's, decidedly no motor. I liked to hear the water bubbling under me as I rowed. Each small repair revealed the bigger ones I couldn't yet handle. But that's why I bought the cabin, to gain skills, to become more competent. One summer I would devote to the dock; another to indoor plumbing. Eventually we would build on higher ground, where Serge had already sunk a foundation. That first August I scythed half an acre of virgin grass, picked a dozen quarts of delicious wild raspberries, dug out the little marshes, and lined the cutoffs with rock. Built a retaining wall. I dug out a substantial base for the incinerator, then built a fence around it from the iron poles and rusty springs of the old bunk beds, to keep the racoons away at night.

After a month it was possible to sit under the naphtha lamp reading Painter's *Proust* at ten in the evening and step out onto the porch with a hot cup of coffee into a blackness primevally bright, stars spread like grains of sugar on a deep purple velvet. If I'd ever felt pride in something I'd done, and in a decision I'd made, it was this. Erika would come out too, sensing I'd left the cabin. If the mosquitoes had not been out, we could have shed our clothes and picked our way cautiously to the dock; we could have sat on the granite boulders and dangled our feet in black water in the dead of night when it seems less cold than daytime. I moved the baby out, bundled up safely, to let him sleep as we talked. But we stood instead on the porch wrapped only in the sounds of water slapping the aluminum boat, wind disturbing the trees, the sharp mosquito whines, and miles away, tunneled over water and through the mountain ridges, the logging trucks changing gears just outside St-Jovite. That was the peak of my satisfaction.

On the first and last visits, in a summer, I would go alone. Too much work to do, no time for swimming and guarding a two-year-old from the rickety dock and water. I had come to see myself mirrored in my property; each summer I would try frantically to keep pace with nature, even to gain a little. We could live three days comfortably without help or supplies, and we could come and go with little more than a full, or empty, ice chest. We were still years away from Serge's standard, and more years away from my private dream of a hand-assembled cedar chalet (F.O.B. Vancouver, $5,600), but at least we'd never lust for such German comforts as battery-powered television, twin 25-h.p. outboards, and kennels full of yapping lapdogs. I could see how sensible summers could stabilize a winter's excess and suggest humbler ambitions than the manipulation of knowledge.

I went up alone on a Sunday in late September. Few cars were there: Serge's Renault of course, and the Germans' Mercedes. Serge and the Europeans got along, especially in the winter when they staged snowmobile races on the lake. I rowed to the cabin, proud of my summer calluses, the tan, the rightness of owning something and trying to keep it the way it had always been. I beached the boat and pulled it under the porch, turned it over, then chained the prow to one of the pilings. First thing next summer, I told myself, clear out the scrap wood. Reinforce the steps. Paint the porch. I leaned the oars against the cabin, and unlocked the front door. At first I didn't believe what I saw. I sagged against the door and covered my eyes.

A large rock lay in the middle of the sleeping-room floor. The back-window drapes fluttered. Glass crunched and scraped underfoot. The sheets and blankets were chewed to fluffiness. Maybe some dishes were missing, I couldn't tell. My fishing rod still hung above the bed. Thank God, we'd taken home the sleeping bags the week before. The boxes of sugar and cereals were chewed open and littered everywhere. Raccoons, mice; the whole north woods had tramped through the cabin, except that 'coons don't throw rocks. I sat at my card table where the naphtha lamp lay leaking on its side. Hoping almost to hurt myself, I pounded the table. I'd never been invaded, never been stolen from before.

Later, of course, I swept up. After a long time I threw away

the rock. The back window had always been shutterless. I had
no yardstick to measure the frame; replacing glass would require
a *vitrier* paid by the hour, driven in from St-Jovite and rowed
to the cabin, sometime next spring in the middle of an academic
week. I had only an ax and the old blistered dresser, antique
or not. I knocked it down into planks in half a dozen blows. I
nailed the drawer-bottoms to the sidings; they covered the hole
but it looked like hell. Then I went on with my chores, letting
water out of the pump, sealing the chimney flues, storing the
oars, latching the other shutters, stripping down the beds, and
burning the remains of sheets and blankets and rodent dung with
all the splintered wood and cereal boxes. Erika would not have
to know.

In the winter I have to think of other things: I dare not believe
that Serge still drives to St-Jovite and parks his car for the
weekend, then snowmobiles the rest of the way over back trails
(chasing wolves, he told me once, finding a deer carcass steaming in a snowbank and circling out from it till he finds the pack);
that the snow on the lake is as hard as concrete from the Ski-
Doo rallies and the racket must be louder than a dozen sawmills
at peak production. Our winter life doesn't allow for dreaming
like that.

Spring is always an ugly season in the north; the snows melt
slowly and with maximum inconvenience. Ours is not a landscape for unassertiveness; subtleties are easily lost. The stabbing
summer green, the blood-red autumn, the pure white death of
winter—but not the timid buds, the mud, the half-snow and
week-long icy rains of spring. I begin in April to think of the
damage up north, the puddles that must have formed under the
tons of snow, the ravenous stirring-about of whatever animal
spent the winter in my sleeping bag. Ice will float on the lake till
the middle of May. Serge will take his ritual swim on the
fifteenth of April. I will be marking final papers, delaying till the
last possible Sunday the computing of my taxes. On my side of
the lake the black flies are thick till the end of June. Erika
can't take the flies, her face swells out, her eyes seal shut. Old
bites will bleed for weeks. I go up alone on the first of July.

This time, I bring a yardstick. Window putty. All my sharpened tools. My swimming trunks and snorkel. I turn the boat over and haul it into the sun. Cautiously, I open the cabin. It is precisely as I left it: no famished bears, wolverines, caches of dynamite, mutilated corpses, no terrorists playing cards. Just the trapped coolness of winter inside a gloomy little camp with the shutters sealed, on a bright summer Monday in the mid-seventies. I wanted to call out to Erika, as though she were with me— as though I had confided all my fears—"*It's safe. We made it through another winter. I'll go out and catch our lunch!*" And I'll say it next week, after I fix the window.

As the vision of liquor lures the drunkard off the wagon, so the lake called me on a hot summer day. I measured the window frame and lifted out the shards of glass, primed the pump, and repaired the broken lamp. I pumped up the Coleman stove and I put water on for coffee. The cabin had warmed up; I changed into my swimming trunks and dug out my snorkel.

As always the water stunned for a moment, one of those expanded moments I'd embraced as the essence of all I wanted from a place in the woods. Pain, astonishment, and a swoon of well-being.

I paddled about for a timeless afternoon, snorkeling halfway across the lake, where only my hands flashed white and puckered in my vision, then back along the shore near the dock, watching the bottom with its placid carp and bluegills rising to nibble my fingers. The deep exaggerated breathing through the snorkel was the sound of summers on Lac Bibitte. It was my own breath universalized; it was my collective body that drifted over the underwater swarms of tadpoles that rose from the mossy branches. *Cities of tadpoles!* I knew only that my back was burning, that the coffee water had boiled, and that I was ready for coffee on the dock and sun on my face and belly before locking up and heading back home.

What finally happened to me that day is still happening. I remember pulling myself out of the water, drying myself with the towel I'd left on the dock. I felt myself restored. I was going to fish a bit, then maybe measure the loose planks on the dock. I went back inside where the valiant Coleman had boiled a large pan of water, and I stood barefoot on the asphalt tile aware of slivers of glass still about, but feeling too strong too care. Feeling reckless, swimsuit dripping heavily—*plop, plop*—almost thickly, on the floor. I spooned in the coffee, poured the water, snapped off the burner. My back was already registering the heat.

I must have turned about then, coffee in hand, taken a step or two toward the door. Barefoot, I felt something in the puddle of water at my feet. Water was still rolling down my legs. Thinking only of broken glass, I then glanced down at my feet.

In the puddle that had formed as I was making my coffee, three long brown leeches were rolling and twisting, one attached to the side of my foot and the other ones half on the tiles, slithering away. Another *plop* and a fourth dropped from my trunks, onto my foot, and into the wetness. I dropped the coffee, perhaps I deliberately poured it over my feet—I don't remember. I don't remember much of the next few minutes except that I screamed, ran, clawed at my trunks and pulled them off. And I could see the leeches, though I tried not to look, hanging from my waist like a cartridge belt. I swatted and they dropped in various corners of the cabin. I heard them dropping and I heard myself screaming, and I was also somewhere outside the man with leeches, screaming; I watched, I pitied, I screamed and cried.

Even later, when I was dressed and searching the cabin for the dark, shriveled worms, scooping them up with a coffee spoon and dropping them in the flames of a roaring fire in the stove, my body was shaking with rage and disillusionment. I watched the man with the blistered back sit in his wretched little cabin, burning leeches. After an hour, losing interest, I turned away. I haven't been back since.

HE RAISES ME UP

The lone satisfaction is recognizing the comedy. Not that it is funny, being stranded at two in the morning on a deserted cloverleaf in the dead of winter. It is the situation. New car, three hundred miles over the warranty, of course. Two in the morning on a night I'd not worn boots or cap or even gloves. Erika in her party coat and unlined gloves. The cloverleaf desolate as only cold concrete under mercury lamps can be. Merciless quiet. And a car that even I know to be ruined, though freshly waxed that afternoon. First speck of rust, proudly Brillo-ed out. Even with the hood down I can smell the inner damage, the ozone, the thermal clatter, the fusion of once-moving parts.

Comic because of the way I'm dressed, the five dollars (baby-sitting money) in my pocket, the faith I'd placed in advertising, the simplicity of my dream of merely getting home in a well-groomed car after a *paella* dinner with Haitian friends; like the great comic heroes of the silent films, a simple man oddly dressed with a modest aim of, say, crossing a street. Wind blows his bowler, his skimmer, into what—a woman's purse? Fresh concrete? A baby carriage? Guileless but guilty, before he crosses that street a city will learn to cringe. Some enormous frailty will be exposed: technology, wealth, politics, marriage, whatever organizing idiocy that binds us all together will come flying apart, for the moment. Not funny for the clown, of course; his features remain dead-pan, as grim as mine wondering if I should try to start the engine one last time, for heat.

A mile or two down the road a yellow light, the oil indicator, had flashed on. I'd thought it was odd, being low on oil so suddenly. No reason for it, I'd had it changed a thousand miles before, checked at least twice a week. All very proper. Nevertheless, a twenty-four-hour garage had loomed ahead and I drove in to add the oil. It took two quarts and the engine even then was smoking. But I know nothing of motors; neither did the boy who added the oil and checked the stick. I'd driven off, the yellow light didn't object. Two miles later we climbed a bridge and the light went on again. No shoulders, no turning back. I drove on and we landed here at the foot of the bridge, just off a cloverleaf where no one turns.

Cars are an apt measurement of the inner man. Blessed are the carless. Like dwellers in high-rises, their every need at hand, never required to answer an unmonitored door, to touch a shovel, to call a heating company. Never to mow, to paint, to polish, never to fret over plumbing and roof. Radiantly helpless. Fortunate too are the tinkerers, grown men driving around with tool chests in their trunks, those grease-stained knuckles, those teen-age tattoos under the business suits. Rapturously self-reliant. And for the rest of us there comes a moment when we prowl the vacant city in a cashmere coat, doubling back over a deserted bridge where any witness would take you for a potential suicide. Flagging at cars that spray your shoes with a gray pasty slime. *Clown,* you tell yourself. If necessary there's still that garage where you added oil. But your wife is in the car and the garage is still out of sight. Somehow, you feel, the night is all but empty. *All but.* One car, one driver, has seen you. Saw your motor smoking. Saw you leave. Saw your wife in her cocktail dress, bundling the expensive coat tighter around the throat. As you crest on the bridge and start down the far side, he turns on his lights and cruises silently to her, off the cloverleaf where no one turns. By the time you panic and run the half-mile back, red lights recede in the distance. Your wife, unmurdered, lies asleep across the seat. She asks you to stay, now that you're back.

This is the car I had looked after the best. Little noises, little inconveniences, immediately repaired. This is my second car. The first one got us through our student days, my first two jobs, over two kids, our moves across country. It picked up dents that we didn't fix, it ran for weeks low on oil, the floors in the back where I'd never sat or put my feet in seven years had never been cleaned. Grocery slips, trading stamps, newspapers and candy wrappings, shreds of paper diapers, bottom thirds of ice cream cones and the meatless stubs of hot dog buns. When I scraped it clean and hosed it out the day before trading it in (it was a van with eighty thousand miles) I even found some student papers from my first teaching job. It was an indictment of the way we were living, of what we'd become, and I vowed I'd never let it happen again. And since that day seven months ago, I have been meticulous.

Perhaps when your time has come, all the care is superficial. That old indestructible graduate school Volkswagen was my youth, belonging to the years when they paid for my promise, when I carried no insurance, and the government returned more to me than I ever paid in. When teachers said "Read this" and "Write that" and the freshmen I taught so indifferently thought I was a god.

Speaking of God, He sends a tow truck off the bridge. I can sense the throbbing yellow light and hear the far-off clunk of chains from a good mile away, and he turns off the bridge a hundred yards from us. I flag him down from the middle of the road, and though he has another couple in the cab (far older than us, a stunned woman of fifty and her embarrassed husband) and a sleek new domestic sedan on his tow (I've lost the knack of identifying the American cars, even the low-priced three are huge these days), he promises to return to me in about an hour. "Can you start it?" he asks and I tell him I'm afraid to. "How's the oil?" And I admit that the oil is gone.

"Your motor's jammed."

"Serious?"
"Finished."

Seven blissful months I have maintained my posture. Posture in the universe. An oiled, greased, rustless, spotless, vacuumed, silent car. Some exercises for the muscle tone, a diet to bring down my weight. A visit to the dentist for the first time in years, and a settling of the old dental scores that I knew were mounting against me. I'd been aware for over a year that my mouth was botched and those pulpy bitches were all but doomed. And the dentist, like a priest, had confirmed it all.

"What did he say?"
"He said the motor's jammed."
"Is that serious?"
"He said it's finished."
This satisfies her. She still trusts.
"Wake me when he comes back," she says.

Even on that first day when I came in for the professional brushing and X rays, he'd poked around a bit with a pick, lifting out food, chipping at holes, testing the pavement over the nerves. He's a whistler, my dentist, soft aimless tunes as he drills, as he packs, as he strangles the urge to lecture me, burrowing deeper to pull a nerve. "You were dying, you know," he says. Tiny reservoirs of abscess have been draining through the pulp and out the gums, rivulets of poison inching up the nerve canal into the sinus cavity. "Ah, yes," he says, turning his back, whistling a bit, "thinking about your mouth has ruined my day." A day of special urgency last week, when two canals had to be packed and all my fillings removed. "It's not just your hygiene, which is bad enough . . . it's your bite.

"How old are you?"
"Thirty-one."
He whistles. "Unless I change your bite, you won't have a tooth in your head five years from today. I'll change the biting surface of every tooth. We'll immobilize your jaw for a day or two, till it loses muscle-memory. You'll need to learn to bite again. Like a child . . ."

Like the victim of some terrible brain damage.
Stroke.

His car, his teeth. Inescapable indices of the inner man. Not
his wife, not his children, not his work—I used to think these
things before I was thirty-one. How can she sleep in this burned-
out car? How can she be so trusting? How do my children call
me daddy—seven years old and he hasn't seen through me yet.
The dentist will cost me a thousand dollars—I gambled and lost.
Five dollars is all I have for a tow, a taxi, and seven hours of
baby-sitting. I acknowledge my own defects; no thirty-year war-
ranties yet on the market. And that is the lesson of thirty-one
years.

But *this*, this smoking engine, this jammed motor, I will fight.
Though I'm three hundred miles over the warranty, my heart is
pure and ready to fight. In a cold seizure I see the world com-
posed of symbol, an underlying metaphysics concretely mani-
fest. There is maintenance, for which we are responsible; and
the yellow lights, for which we are not. This car has suffered a
stroke, a heart attack, in the prime of life, the blowing of a cere-
bral gasket. Cut down while jogging, aneurysm in the organic
garden.

I sense the return of the amber lights, long before they cross
the bridge. He pulls off in front, jockeys back at full speed, and
skids to a stop inches from my bumper. Erika wakes, clutches
my arm before realizing where she is. The bad dream is only
starting.

He hooks us up, a grim little Lou Costello, coatless, in overalls. I go out to talk. Penetrating moisture of 4 A.M.; I'd been dry
but frozen inside the car, and now I'm shivering.

"O.K., where to?"

"Can you fix it at your place?"

"Buddy—it's jammed. Nobody can fix it."

"Then dump it at the dealer's."

"Twenty-five dollars."

"Take a check?"

"Nope."

"Shell? Gulf?"

"Nope."

He takes his hand off the winch. Whistles a little tune, bends down to loosen the hooks.

"Look—I don't have twenty-five on me. When I went out tonight I didn't *expect*—"

"Look, buddy. I just turned down three other guys out on the expressway. I don't *need* to take no checks."

"But I've got identification. All you need. Look, I could fly to Europe. Tonight. I can stay in a hotel. I can eat anywhere. All I need is a tow—"

"You got one of those bank cards?"

"Yes!" I nearly cry out with gratitude. "Yes, yes."

He takes it, stamps it in the cab of his truck, "MAX'S SPORTING GOODS," and writes in underneath, "Camping equipment, twenty-five dollars." No winks, no significant gestures, no more whistling. He hits the switch to tighten the chains. Somewhere deep in the exchange, lies an issue. An important one on a summer night perhaps, about the rights of a victim and consumer. About the arrogance of providers, the frailty of identity. The man is a free-lancer, his truck bears no names. A gypsy? Max moonlighting? How many gypsy tow trucks ply the city streets, the bridges and deserted cloverleafs, night after night making hundreds of dollars between midnight and dawn, when, like bats, they disappear?

"That your wife?"

He stops the winch and the chains give an eerie shudder. "Better get her out."

"What if we stay in the car?"

He shrugs. "Not safe."

"What else?"

"Illegal."

"We'll stay with the car."

Erika wakes as I slip in beside her. Through the windshield we see the icy rods of arc lamp, the diffuse brown urban night. The chain rumbles taut, gathered like a spire at the pulley wheel, taller even than the saurian light-standards. The steering wheel jerks sharply as we follow the curve of the cloverleaf, back to the city. How peaceful is this surrender, stretched out on the front seat, feet up, head against the cool, moist window, holding Erika in both arms, swaying in the metal sling of my broken car.

AMONG THE DEAD

In a certain season (the late winter) and in certain areas (those fringes between the city core and the river that makes it an island) Montreal is the ugliest city in the world. Despite its reputation, its tourist bureaus, most of the island of Montreal will break your heart. Most of us live with broken hearts, thumping little fists constricting our throats. In this, Montreal is truly the Paris of North America. The same bleakness, the same *bidonvilles* stretching for miles beyond the city walls. Our dream had always been salvation and *bonheur*, even knowing that we'd ingested the worst of both worlds: the suspicions and ignorance of the *petit commerçant*, with the arrogant sprawl of America. Therefore, the Québec compromise, cropping up everywhere as *le bongoûtisme québecois*. Drive up the *Grands Boulevards* of Montreal: Viau, Pie-Neuf, Lajeunesse, Décarie—it's like a walk through those Parisian jungles filled with stalls, rat-faced children, and orange-haired women in hagglers' smocks. The difference is space: in Montreal you're in your car and you can drive for miles and the *bongoûtisme* is unrelenting. In the easy targets like Monsieur Muffler and Poulet Frit à la Kentucky, in all those self-appointed *rois des bas prix*, the Gaz, the Chars Usagées, the

famous Chien-Chaud Steamé, to the beauty shops where graying heads get the standard Pontiac-Laurentian maroon rinse.
Once you climb the containing mountain, or drive east around
its flank, you've left the old and beautiful Montreal for good. Following Viau or Pie-Neuf north, you come inevitably to the river,
and those vain rows of summer cabins perched over water
thicker than most canned soups. You pass miles of flat-roofed
duplexes, even where land is cheap and space no problem, a
style forgivable only if it were public housing. It is not. Crossing
the waters you leave Montreal, arriving on another island—Ile
Jésus, consolidated now as the City of Laval—and if you turn directly east off the new Pont-Viau, you come to an old village
called St-Vincent-de-Paul (a few abandoned stone houses whose
padlocked doors stand five feet off the highway's edge), the true
village now a *cantonnement* of gas stations, laundromats, show-
rooms, and loan offices. And then on the fringes of the village
the road suddenly widens, the cheap buildings disappear (federal funds leave immediate traces), and a giant billboard stands
off to the left, near the high stone walls and turrets:

1. Pénitencier St. Vincent de Paul
2. Annexe Industrielle
3. Ferme Annexe
4. Unité Spéciale de Correction
5. Institution Leclerc

And there, I turn in.

Because I am a journalist and I want to reach people directly,
I volunteered to lead discussions at the prison. Because I work
on a liberal paper and I supposedly know more than I can
print, and because the prisoners read all the papers but lack the
background, my weekly presence was thought to be rehabilitat-
ing. Down the road from the village, well beyond the main prison
and the two annexes, the Unité Spéciale stands behind a remote
tower, in a field of bulldozed snow. Monsieur Paré, the cultural
co-ordinator, escorts me through three walls of sliding bars. The
thirteen men in bleached blue shirts and brown chino pants pass

through a metal-detector and into the classroom. They lock us in. The roof of the classroom is wire mesh; a guard with a shotgun paces the catwalk overhead. This is maximum security. It is a form of perpetual solitary confinement.

Only in the classroom is there relief from *bongoûtisme*. Suave muttonchops and collar-length hair grace the guards' dull broken faces. A subwarden sits resplendent in his pumpkin shirt, silver tie, and bottle-green suit. The suit of the cultural co-ordinator shimmers like a garbage sack, over a shrimp-pink tie and merthiolate shirt. Yet their faces are tight, and gray with distraction.

Three months ago, when I started coming out, I asked for the dossiers of the men in my class. A reporter's prerogative, to hope that facts will match suspicion. They do not. The men have killed for money and sport, in anger and fear, by accident and design. Two Indians killed a fisherman, then cut him up for bait. Others specialized in executions: lightning raids on east-end taverns in front of witnesses who turned away. One child-rapist, kept here for his own protection. Others made the front pages: FATHER OF SIX KILLED IN ROBBERY. HOLD-UP AT ROYAL BANK: GUARD SHOT. All but the child-rapist would have admitted as much. It's the only thing they're proud of.

We are locked in the room for three hours; the guard stands over us, his rifle's shadow, like a cold draft from an unheated cellar, lies flat across the wall. We are each other's hostage, despite the guard and the row of buttons on the wall behind me, despite the rotunda just outside the door where another guard keeps us covered. This is a new society: the ultimate in authority, but recognizable in convention and etiquette, nuance and taboo, madness, and waste. It is a society based totally in the present—the future has been legislated out and the past is irrelevant. "We're the most dangerous men in Canada—DO WE LOOK IT?" "That button's in case we rush you—DO YOU THINK WE WILL?" No—you don't look like criminals, only like prisoners. Lining them up, who could pick the rapist from the hit-man? Or the journalist? No—they don't act like killers, they're courteous and respectful. Sometimes lucid, sometimes mad with theory and self-instruction. Yet they *could* rush me. They can kill. They don't feel guilt. In some profound way, they cannot be reached. It is a society based on a single premise satisfactory to all: that from nine months before they were born until three days after they die, they will have passed an abbreviated life without ever having been wanted by a single soul. They never had a childhood, nor did they ever grow up.

We are talking today of strikes, or trying to. Not wholly a Montreal phenomenon, but raised here to a kind of perfection. In the past two years we've been struck by nearly everybody, from policemen to garbage collectors, prison guards to air controllers. The prevalence of strikes and the militancy of unions, along with the total absence of control and theory, is a striking example of political *bongoûtisme*, a kind of rampant self-expressionism that quickly becomes a caricature. The prisoners, in one sense, are revolutionaries. WHAT REVOLUTION EVER GOT STARTED THAT DIDN'T FIRST EMPTY THE PRISONS? Who has a greater stake in social change? On the other hand, they've never had much use for working men. They never were on the labor market, they always had buyers for the services they offered; for a man willing to make the effort, Montreal is an embarrassment of riches. Working men are the incarnations of hated fathers, brothers, and prison guards. They were always too smart to follow their fathers into a pension of eighty a month, a beer on the gallery when you're too old and sick to enjoy it. Too smart for that Yvon Deschamps world of *"un bon bosse et un jobbe stedy."* The dreams of the prisoners are more transcendent: a new planet, a new liberated man. These men, who pride themselves on their realism, their shrewdness, their nihilism, bloom like flower-children at the mention of Ouspensky, Gurdieff, Transcendental Meditation—any form of mysticism that teaches the world is illusion and the imprisoned self can be known, developed, and set free. Half the time, even if the guard above us were listening, he wouldn't understand a word. The rest of the time, he might be tempted to start blasting away.

I know their dreams. I too was raised in those flat duplexes. My night light was a ten-watt bulb in the lower ventricle of a plastic *sacrecoeur*. Even as I speak to them of minimum wages and equitable distribution, I see myself a Jesuit instructing the

Iroquois. I dream my immolation. For too long our mandate to survive on this continent was derived from what the Iroquois had done to our fathers' confessors. Here we are, the favored and educated sons of *bongoûtisme,* free of so many old tyrannies— Confederation, America, France, God, the bad old politics, the ignorance—yet the struggle still burns within us. Within me. Socialism appeals to my conservative instincts. Independence, because my heart is broken like everyone else's.

Monsieur Paré escorts me back through the three sliding gates, praising my patience and good-citizenship. Just think, an important man like me, doing it free. The men, they don't appreciate it enough. On the bench in the lobby sits a wife waiting to enter the visiting room. She's in ski-slacks and a fuzzy pink sweater she nervously pulls as she waits. Her hair is chopped straight, tinted the requisite maroon; she looks like a stray from a women's wrestling team, or perhaps the roller derby. Paré nods to her and asks, "How's Reggie?" then draws me aside. "You know Reggie? Held up a bank and shot a teller? A year ago? Yesterday he tells the warden he's a political prisoner. Says he did it under orders from the F.L. . . . you know? Now—look what he's got in there. Look—" and he jerks his thumb in the door's direction. "How do you like that? Keeps his wife waiting while he talks to *them.*"

Them: two emissaries from a volunteer group to aid political prisoners. Two fiery, vital, Gauloise-smoking idealists from the university. Two staggeringly beautiful, slim, animated girls dressed in proletarian sweaters and jeans, in oversized tinted glasses, glistening boots, nodding vigorously at everything Reggie says, laughing with him, believing him as he's never been believed in his life. Two twenty-year-old students from homes in Outremont where *bongoûtisme* is nipped at the borders, while Reggie's wife, the same age and looking twenty years older, sits sucking a cigarette, tapping her toes to a tune in her head.

"I tell you, my friend, if that was me deciding who was political and who wasn't in this damn prison, I'd stick him in solitary so fast he couldn't even say F . . . L . . . you know?"

That vacant, sullen lump on the bench, shaped by a valiant brassière and forceful stitching, drops her cigarette and reaches for another. She was as young and slender as those girls inside, three years ago.

"It's his right, my friend," I say to Paré. That *Créditiste* face, those swirling sideburns. "Who's to say, any more?"

I know those girls. I have been the husband of Madeleine Lacroix, and if those girls knew that, they'd drop poor Reggie before any of them could mouth those three sacred, forbidden initials. Back in university, she was Midou Tremblay, taking a certificate in physical therapy. I was in political science, even then leaning to journalism. We married and she worked five years in a hospital where she got her second education, in politics, and it was more than her background had prepared her for.

"I'm only treating symptoms!" she cried out one night. She'd been tossing about, breathing loudly, in a way to attract sympathy but repel attention.

"Of course. You're a therapist," I said, which was just the answer she was waiting for.

"No! All of us are treating symptoms. I'm interested in the causes. The real causes. The colonial causes."

She was then twenty-six, sitting up nude in bed. She'd determined suddenly to become a leader, to make herself charismatic. She dressed, then announced, "Your paper disgusts me." She never came back.

It's not a bad paper. It does know more than it dares to print; feels more than it cares to make public. It also has a Paris bureau, and I took it. Three years I stayed in Paris, thinking that what I wrote home somehow mattered, when all that it made me was an easy ironist. I was in Paris while Montreal burned. When I came back, a woman named Madeleine Lacroix was the head of a hospital-workers local, still as slim as any student, her glasses as wide and tinted, her sweaters just as flattering. If, as a therapist, she commanded the lame to walk, they would have no choice. On every level she is the complete radical, living a dream of liberation that no prisoner could envision. Only a husband could.

It is always terrifying to meet a truly hard woman—not hard in the old sense of crude, and not in the new sense of competent and committed—hard like a cinder is hard, as though the fires of transfiguration had already passed through her and what we are seeing is not a person but the brilliant, essential residue. It is a political quality; the politician's cunning likeness to a human being is the most striking thing about him. It torments me that I once loved her, knew her so deeply, watched her slow maturing with pride instead of wonder. As I drive these streets of the North End, she is still beside me and I am still filling her full of startling insider's facts, and she is still stammering, "But isn't that against the law? Won't they get in trouble?" Even now, driving back down Viau in the pale winter twilight, I want to reach for her hand (how well I know the pattern of veins on her delicate hands: they were always truck-driver thick under the Outremont flesh); I want to catch glimpses of her profile and assure myself that only a sensitive eye—mine—could perceive the beauty that would slowly emerge. It has. It torments me that I was taken in, that I failed to see, that she could change, that *anything* could change so drastically. Not even prisoners change so utterly. Watching her on television with the other political leaders, I wonder if she still behaves the same after sex, if her fingers still bleed in the winter, if she still worries about her thighs. Do her parents still not talk to each other?

Everywhere on the streets I see Madeleine Lacroixs. By the hundreds. Except, perhaps, here on Viau between the river and the Métropolitaine, still the heart of *sacrecoeur* country. Here between the worlds of my dead mother and my ex-wife, where it's almost comic if you can keep your balance. The snow removers have been on strike, and the plowed-up banks are ten feet high on the shoulders of the road. Narrow chasms have been cut through the snow in front of stores; tiny depressions gnawed through the banks where buses let off reluctant passengers. From some remote perspective, in the depth of winter, the whole city must seem a maze of constricted ruts, like the trails worn through tall grass by herds of buffalo on their way to water. You see, Midou? We're a resistant race, when not transfiguring.

Waiting at the red light with me is a snow-removal truck, one of the fleet of rusting hulks with an unreadable name scrawled on the door and an extra six feet of planking attached to the

driver's side above the bed, to break the force of the thrown
snow, when the crews are working. The young driver stares
down at me, forcing a nod. His smashed-in door is wired shut.
Long before the light changes, he roars from the intersection,
forcing me to cut back in behind him.

What possible cargo is he carrying? From what, to whom?
Window frames with shattered panes, slabs of asphalt sheeting,
splintered boards and broken cinder blocks, rusted rolls of wire
mesh, and tons of bundled paper, tearing away in a spume of
dust. It is as though he is carting the remnants of a dozen
chicken-coops. The truck seems a low, brute force of nature,
bearing its debris down a potholed boulevard as I helplessly follow, working the windshield washer to keep it all in sight.

I know suddenly that I'm in danger. As though I'd been
speeding up steadily, unconsciously, on a sheet of ice, simply because it was smooth and the tires were quiet. I have faith enough
in omens to know too late that the truck is a pirate on the streets,
out purely to cut and damage. I'm already pulling back, looking
for a break in the walls of snow to turn off, when half a cinder
block bursts loose from the mounds above me and I helplessly
slide in position to receive it. It burrows across the hood like a
meteorite, bounces once indecisively, hanging in front of the
windshield as I swerve, then skids harmlessly off the fender into
the gutter snow. By the time I straighten out, the truck's red
lights have already receded. Other cars have taken my place, in
cautious pursuit, rushing to embrace the city.